BLIND RIVER SEVEN

BLIND RIVER

7

T. R. LUNA

BLIND RIVER SEVEN

T. R. LUNA

ZIMBELL HOUSE
PUBLISHING
UNION LAKE, MICHIGAN

For permission requests, write to the publisher
"Attention: Permissions Coordinator"
Zimbell House Publishing
PO Box 1172
Union Lake, Michigan 48387
mail to: info@zimbellhousepublishing.com

© 2020 T. R. Luna

Published in the United States by Zimbell House Publishing
http://www.ZimbellHousePublishing.com
All Rights Reserved

Hardcover ISBN: 978-1-64390-106-0
Trade Paper ISBN: 978-1-64390-107-7
.mobi ISBN: 979-1-64390-108-4
ePub ISBN: 978-1-64390-109-1
Large Print ISBN: 978-1-64390-110-7
Library of Congress Control Number: 2019915719

First Edition: March 2020
10 9 8 7 6 5 4 3 2 1

ZIMBELL HOUSE PUBLISHING
UNION LAKE

DEDICATION

This book is dedicated to those of us that grew up in Las Vegas and believe that we grew up in a "normal" environment. It is also dedicated to my fellow alumni of Chaparral High School, especially those Cowboys that have ridden into the sunset too soon. Lastly, this book is dedicated to the fifty-eight souls that left us on October 1, 2017, and those that were physically, emotionally, or psychologically wounded by the tragic event of that day. Stay VEGAS STRONG!

THE SHUFFLE

The old man was zip tied arms to arms and legs to legs, onto one of the captain's chairs from the dining room table, sitting in the middle of the family room. Facing him was his wife, staring at him from about four feet away with stark terror in her eyes. She, too, was zip tied onto an identical chair in the same fashion, but she was also gagged with a rag in her mouth and gray duct tape slapped onto her face to hold it securely in place.

The elderly woman was dressed in pink and white silk pajamas with a matching robe, but the arms of the pajamas and robe had been rolled up to expose the flesh, and her pajama bottoms had been slit up the outside of each leg, thus exposing her legs to her upper thighs. The zip ties on her ankles were starting to cut into her paper-thin skin causing her ankles to bleed.

"What do you want?" the old man demanded. "I will give you whatever you want, but you must leave us alone!" He used as commanding a tone as he could muster, but there was a slight waver in the timbre of his voice that betrayed the real terror that now clutched at his core.

"We'll get to what I want in due time," the malevolent Voice said. "For right now, I just want you to focus on your wife. You need to understand deep in your bones that you are not in control, old man, and any deviation from my commands will result in harsh consequences."

"This is not necessary. I will comply with your requests." The old man was now pleading, all trace of bravado having vanished.

"Yes. I know you will. Now we begin the demonstration."

A large man moved behind the old man's wife. He leaned in close to her right ear and whispered. Then with an easy, smooth motion, he swiped his right hand up the old woman's right leg with his index finger extended starting just above her knee and ending at mid-thigh. The old woman immediately and violently arched her back as blood began to spill over the outside of her leg. The large man then turned over his hand exposing an Exacto knife. He grinned as the old man howled in anguish. Then he slashed another cut parallel to the first one.

"Stop! Stop! What do you want?" the old man shouted.

"I want your wife to bleed, and she's cooperating nicely," the Voice behind him said calmly. "Oh, and I want the location of your safe and the combination to it."

"Yes, yes, yes, I will give it to you. Just, please, leave my wife alone!"

"Cut her again!" the Voice shouted. "He loves to talk, but I haven't heard what I want to hear, yet!" With the old man wailing, the large man took the Exacto knife in his left hand and made two slashes on her left leg just like the previous ones on her right leg. "AM I GETTING THROUGH TO YOU?" roared the Voice.

"Yes! Yes! In the master bedroom, there is a desk. Behind the desk is a panel. Slide the desk to the left and swing open the panel. The combination is 37 to the right, 17 to the left, 23 to the right, and 7 to the left. Now, please! Stop hurting my wife!"

A third man had been writing down the information, and the man with the Voice turned to him and said, "Go check it out." The old man heard heavy steps on the hardwood floor going to the master bedroom. Then he heard the desk sliding on the rails that had been installed to make it easy for the old man and his wife to move the desk.

In about three minutes, the third man reappeared with a big grin on his face. "Paydirt," he said as he held aloft an exquisite necklace. Handing the necklace to the man with the Voice, the third man grabbed a duffle bag and headed back into the bedroom.

"There. You have all of our valuables. Now, please leave us be," the old man said with a shake of his head. Blood was dripping on the floor from the seat of his wife's chair and she had passed out from shock. When he tried to turn his head to face the voice, he was immediately struck in the left ear with a fist, and a searing pain jolted through his ear, down his spinal cord, and all the way to his toes. His head swam as he fought the pain and disorientation from the blow.

"You forgot who's in control here, didn't you? I'm afraid you'll need another lesson." Turning to the large man next to him, the man with the Voice nodded, and the old woman was cut once on the inside of each arm from elbow to wrist. Blood was now seeping from both her arms and her legs, but she didn't notice as her head remained slumped on her chest.

The old man was sobbing uncontrollably now and moaning, "Please leave us. Please leave us. Please leave us."

Without warning the Voice was suddenly an inch away from the old man's right ear. "I believe your wife is dying, but she'll probably last longer than you, old man," the Voice whispered.

The old man's eyes widened as he felt the cold steel of a butcher knife touch his neck just below his left ear. The knife remained motionless for what seemed like a lifetime, and it felt to the old man that it was growing colder by the second.

He sniffed a quick wisp of air in through his nose and smelled the copper tang of the blood flowing from his wife and pooling under her chair. The smell became a sharp metallic taste in his mouth, as he realized that the knife was now resting below his right ear and no longer seemed cold. His white dress shirt was wet, warm, and sticking to his chest, which surprised him. He hadn't remembered spilling anything on himself.

It occurred to the old man that he hadn't heard the Voice say anything for a while, so he attempted to ask the Voice if he would spare his wife from any further torture, but only a gurgling sound emanated from beneath his chin. The old man puzzled over the strange sound he was making and the strange place from where it came. Then he couldn't see his wife anymore, as the darkness enveloped him.

Life is dealt cold and raw
So you'd best be on your guard
Or soon your ragged soul will cry
For the turn of a friendly card
Because the sum of your guile
And the cast of your talents
Fall prey to the dealer
When there are lives in the balance

—Deus Autem Libido
(Of God's Whimsy)

THE HOLE CARDS

I

Jonathan James "Jack" Diamante. Diamond Jack. The Jack of Diamonds. Around Las Vegas Jack had a lot of nicknames. Some of them were more colorful than others and definitely couldn't be repeated around children.

Jack was a poker player by trade. He'd been making a living playing poker for about ten years; he also augmented his poker playing with activities that were considerably shadier than that which your typical office worker would tend to undertake. Nothing outright belligerent, mind you. Just clinging to the fringe of the shadows. Stepping in, stepping out. A little dirty, a little clean. Kind of like Vegas itself.

For instance, Jack couriered packages from one place to the next and was paid anywhere from $1,000 to $5,000—when UPS would've done it for less than $200. However, UPS has inspectors, and too many hands touch the same package. Jack asked few questions and was reliable, for the most part.

The man employing Jack for these deliveries had been his best friend in the world, Jesse Brizetta. Jesse had a 10,000 square foot home in Spanish Trail, a posh country club neighborhood in the Las Vegas valley known as the place where sports and entertainment celebrities hid behind guarded gates. Jack had a $500 a month studio apartment not far from the Strip, so when Jesse called, Jack showed up at Spanish Trail. He came so often, that the security guards at the gate just waved him through.

When Jack came to his house, Jesse knew that anything Jack might see or hear stayed with Jack. Jack knew how to keep private things private; this was a fact he proved on many occasions. One time at Jesse's house, Jack saw about $500,000 stashed in a closet. It was bound up with shrink wrap in neat little bundles like it had just come from the cleaners. Who knows? Maybe it had. Jack didn't peep a word of it to anyone.

You see, Jack and Jesse went way back. They both grew up in Las Vegas and met when they were thirteen. Jack's family had moved to Vegas from Colorado when Jack was only two years old, and Jesse's family had moved to town from New Mexico when Jesse was ten. Both boys came from Hispanic backgrounds, but while Jesse had dark curly hair and dark brown eyes, Jack's hair was blonde and eyes hazel, owing to his roots reaching back to the Northwestern coast of Spain. Both had a raw-boned toughness to them and were athletically built.

They both came from good, upright families. Their fathers worked hard in trades while their mothers worked at whatever jobs their limited education would accommodate, so neither family had much money. The neighborhoods where they grew up were on the low end of lower-middle-class, but neither family lived on "the wrong side of the tracks." The wrong side of the tracks in the Las Vegas valley at that time meant living in North Las Vegas or Henderson —which was nicknamed Hooterville. They went to the same junior and senior high schools together.

They had a lot of classes together. They played baseball together. They also got into a lot of trouble together. The parents tried to raise the boys right, but sometimes the boys just went left anyway.

It was petty stuff, usually. Just typical teenage boy pranks. It was the 1970's, and there was still a relative innocence to teenage life. Take junior high school, for instance. While waiting for school to start one day, Jack and Jesse sidled over to the car belonging to the principal, Mr. Grabatch. They looked around to see if the coast was clear and then they proceeded to let all of the air out of the tires. This turned his fire engine red Cadillac Eldorado into a lowrider. Then they used their fingers to write "Jefe Grabass" on the driver's door in the dust conveniently left behind by a recent Las Vegas sand storm. What they didn't realize was that one of the school janitors had spied them and reported them to the principal. That got them suspended for a week.

Jesse was always the instigator, but Jack was a willing sidekick. In fact, where you saw one, you usually saw the other. When they played baseball together, Jack was at second base and Jesse at shortstop. They were the best double play combo in the valley. They ate together, drank together, and partied together. In fact, they even lost their virginity together with the same girl – Julie McKenna.

Jack and Jesse had discovered the best make-out location among the sand dunes that littered the valley floor around Las Vegas before the building booms hit and swallowed up most of the desert. The sand dunes created a natural cove on dry land that was protected from prying eyes on all four sides. The only way into this libidinous playpen was through a mesquite shrouded dirt path guarded by a large road sign that Jack had discovered nearby and propped up. The sign had been abandoned by a road construction crew, and it said, "MEN AND EQUIPMENT AT WORK."

This particular soiree had been planned for a week. After one of their baseball games, Julie had let Jack and Jesse know in no uncertain terms that she was interested in having carnal knowledge with both of them. Julie was only about five-foot-three, but her hair made her look about three inches taller. She had light brown fluffy curls that fell to her eyes and down to her shoulders, and she usually styled it up and out like a helmet of whorls, all delicate and soft. Her face was Barbie-like with cute, delicate features. She was a cheerleader and ran track, so her body was lean and slightly muscular. Her athletic build boasted curves that were hard and sharp giving her an underlying primal sexiness. Lastly, she had deep brown eyes with luxuriously long lashes and an infectious smile which she flashed at every boy she saw. It wasn't so much that she was an overt flirt; she just liked boys—a lot.

Jack's father had seen her once at one of Jack's summer baseball games, and he described her as, "nothing but a couple of bones and a hank of hair," but, of course, what he really didn't approve of was her reputation. When the weather was warm, as it is most of the time in Vegas, she rarely wore anything but short shorts that must have been painted on and tank tops with no bra. To the teenage boys always ogling her, she was considered to be raw sex on jet roller skates.

It was summertime in Vegas with warm dry nights, so Jack, Jesse, and Julie had decided that this rendezvous should take place al fresco. They used Jack's beat up white Chevy pick-up to transport the three of them out to fantasy land and act as a mobile boudoir. They had thrown a mattress into the back, bought two six-packs of Budweiser, and planted Julie between Jack and Jesse on the bench seat. Julie was wearing cutoff jean shorts that were so short that the front pockets hung down farther than the jean material. She had strategically placed one leg on each side of the stick shift, so Jack took every opportunity to run his hand up her leg every time he shifted gears, and he could go a long way up her leg before he encountered any material to impede his explorations. By the time they got to their destination, they were all sufficiently loose and lively.

The moon was full that night and lit up the desert floor with a pale amber glow. The whole nocturnal scene appeared to have been cast in sepia, and the dry desert air echoed with the cry of heat agitated crickets. The cacophony ricocheted around the hidden sand dune grotto, but it was soon vanquished by the throaty rumble of Jack's truck as they pulled in and came to a stop in the soft, sugar-like sand.

The beer and hormones had long since erased any inhibitions, so it wasn't long before all of their clothes were scattered in the truck bed. At seventeen, Julie was slightly older and the veteran of the trio, so she took the lead, but Jack and Jesse soon picked up the rhythm. However, it was definitely not a sweet, romantic interlude. In fact, it was more like a giddy wrestling match between three howler monkeys, but a good time was had by all. It was a night to remember, especially for Jack and Jesse.

After several hours of initiation into manhood with Julie, Jack and Jesse decided it was time to head back to civilization. On the way out, Jesse insisted that they stop at the entrance. There he jumped out of the truck, and with a flourish fueled by his newly acquired status as a sterling specimen of masculinity and the steady consumption of adult beverages, he christened the construction sign the "Gate to Paradise" by smashing it with a half-empty beer bottle. To the three teenage hedonists, it was known as such ever since and remained an inside joke.

Occasionally, Julie would drop a hint to Jack or Jesse that she wanted some virile male companionship by asking one or the other of them if they could show her the Gate to Paradise. Or whenever Jack or Jesse were asked by anybody what they were going to do that night or weekend, if there was a female involved, the cryptic response was always, "I'll probably be beyond the Gate to Paradise." If they happened to be together at the time, they would look at each other, grin, and intone enthusiastically, "Men and equipment at work!"

All of this foolishness carried on pretty much uninterrupted until Jesse's 18th birthday the following summer. He and Jack had purchased a case of beer and decided to head up to Lone Mountain in Jesse's car to celebrate. Lone Mountain was just that—a lone sentinel on the valley floor off Tonopah Highway on the way to Mount Charleston. It was a popular party place with kids at the time. If you didn't bring your own, you could usually score beer, weed, or something stronger, as well. It was also isolated, so the cops usually didn't hassle the kids too often.

Jack and Jesse sometimes met friends out at Lone Mountain, but tonight it was just the three of them: Jack, Jesse, and the cooler of beer. They had propped themselves up on the trunk of Jesse's faded green Dodge Dart looking back at the city, and they proceeded to get drunk while waiting for the stroke of midnight to proclaim that Jesse was an adult. The summer night was warm, the beer was ice cold, and the clear Vegas night sky was full of stars. Reclining back against the rear window, they talked about girls, baseball, girls, their senior year coming up, girls, cars, and, of course, girls. With over half of the case of beer consumed, the conversation then turned strangely philosophical.

In his most serious tone, Jack asked, "Jesse, in your humble opinion, do you consider sex to be a sport or a hobby?"

Without cracking even a hint of a smile, Jesse said, "Hmm. That's a very deep question, Jack. It's one that deserves the utmost consideration. I would have to say that I consider it neither a sport nor a hobby. In fact, in my humble opinion, I believe that sex is a tragedy."

Jack bit the bait hard and wailed, "A tragedy? That's impossible! How can you consider sex to be a tragedy?"

With a dour look on his face, Jesse said, "It's quite simple, actually. In my humble opinion, it is truly a profound tragedy that I don't have sex more often!"

Jack had just taken a gulp of beer which then shot out his nose and mouth as he burst into laughter. Jesse looked at him and grinned with his eyelids drooping slightly as Jack continued to laugh and wipe beer off of his face and shirt. Jack was laughing so hard that he finally rolled off the car onto his hands and knees on the dry desert sand. Sounding like a hyena, Jack then rolled onto his back as he continued to howl with laughter.

Jesse crawled over to the spot where Jack had disappeared over the side of the car and peered over the edge at his friend. As Jack's laughter began to subside, Jesse asked with a straight face, "Jack? Don't you think it's a tragedy that I don't have sex more often?" Jack was silent for about two seconds as he stared in disbelief at Jesse. Then he doubled over in side-splitting laughter, again. It was almost five minutes before he could stand up. Jesse just rolled back over to the cooler and opened up another beer.

By about two in the morning, the two of them had finished most of the case, so they traded the rest of the beer with a guy and his girlfriend for a couple of rumpled looking joints. As Jack and Jesse smoked one of them, they heard two coyotes start to howl at each other, so the two boys began to howl with the coyotes. That prompted the coyotes to sing out even more, and Jack and Jesse followed suit. It soon became a contest as to whether man or beast could howl the loudest.

Eventually, both the coyotes and the boys lost interest, so Jesse put the second joint in the glove box for, as he put it, a happy birthday toke later. They watered the tumbleweeds one last time and then drove back towards town with Jack riding shotgun. On the way home, they drove through a Jack-In-The-Box to satisfy some marijuana-fueled munchies. They always considered Jack-In-The-Box—they called it Gag-In-The-Bag—the best cure for the munchies, because it was greasy, cheap, and open twenty-four hours.

As Jesse pulled out of the drive-thru and onto Decatur Boulevard, he looked into the sack in an attempt to pull out one of the greasiest tacos known to mankind. What he didn't do was notice the beige station wagon barreling towards the driver's side of his car. Half a second of screeching tires later, the station wagon careened into the Dart and Jesse. Jack whiplashed sideways in his seat, and his head struck the gearshift opening a large gash over his left eye.

Several seconds after the two cars came to rest, Jack was dizzy and had blood streaming down his face. He could smell the acrid odor of burned rubber and antifreeze as it boiled over and spilled onto the hot asphalt. Jack looked over and saw Jesse pinned inside the car. It was like the left side of the car had wrapped its teeth around Jesse and was trying to take a bite out of him. Jesse was semi-conscious and moaning. His left arm, left leg, and three ribs had been broken.

Jack yanked on Jesse's right arm in an effort to free him. Jesse's eyes snapped open, and he filled the dry, dusty air with a hail of obscenities ending with, "Shit! Shit! Shit! Shit! Shit!"

"Jesse! We gotta get you outta here, man!" Jack pleaded.

"Stop yankin' on my arm, you mongoloid dumbass! I ain't goin' nowhere. I'm stuck as shit, and I hurt all over! I'm just gonna wait here for the ambulance. They'll get me out."

"Shit, Jesse, the cops will be here before the ambulance, and we're drunk as shit!"

"Screw them," was all he said before he closed his eyes and passed out. Screw them, indeed.

Jesse had always flaunted his disdain for police officers and had gotten used to his juvenile status being his get-out-of-jail-free card. Unfortunately, his beer-soaked, weed blazed, accident concussed mind forgot that he was a newly minted adult and his days of chalking it up to being a kid were now over.

Jack heard sirens from a long way off. His head hurt, and when he reached up to rub it, his left palm came back sticky red with blood. While he wiped his bloody hand on his jeans, he weighed his options. He could stay here with his friend, and they'd both get busted, or he could high-tail it out now. Deciding that he'd done everything that he could for Jesse and not wanting to see the inside of a drunk tank, Jack got out of the car. Still, he wanted to make sure Jesse was okay, so he went behind some bushes and waited to see what transpired.

A police cruiser, fire truck, and an ambulance all showed up at about the same time. The occupants looked like a Chinese fire drill as they piled out of the vehicles. Each, in turn, rushed over to survey the victims. The woman driving the station wagon had luckily been wearing her seat belt, but her forehead had hit the steering wheel, and she was unconscious. The paramedics quickly got her out of the car and onto a backboard. Once strapped on, they put her in the ambulance and whisked her to Southern Nevada Memorial Hospital with the sirens screaming.

Jesse, though, was another story. He was wrapped up in metal like a cast iron burrito.

They had to use the "Jaws of Life" to get him out. Several times Jesse screamed as the car body shifted around him or the paramedics tried to wrest him free of the twisted torture cage that the car had become. It was about an hour before they finally got him out of the car and into an ambulance. Meanwhile, the cops were measuring skid marks and directing early morning traffic around the wreckage.

Once he saw that Jesse had been freed from the car and taken away, Jack walked the couple miles to his house. He had blood all over his face and clothes, but no one was awake around four in the morning, so he cleaned himself up and threw his clothes away. The cut over his eye was only a little over an inch long, but it went right to the bone. Luckily, he was still mostly anesthetized by the beer and pot. He scrubbed it out with rubbing alcohol, pulled it together, fastened it with several butterfly strips, and covered it with a couple of band-aids. It didn't look pretty, but he figured it would do. His parents didn't really ask about it much the next day. It wasn't the first time he'd opened up his head, and they figured it wouldn't be the last.

When Jack went to the hospital to see Jesse the following afternoon, he almost dreaded seeing his friend. He felt guilty for leaving him in the car, but there was little that he could've done. Still, you didn't leave a friend strung out like that in Jack's world. It grated on him, and he hoped that there would be some way that he could make it up to him.

When Jack walked into Jesse's hospital room, it smelled sharply of betadine and ammonia. The room was stark white on white with chrome everywhere, cold linoleum floors, and filled with buttons, beeping lights, and tubes. It didn't seem like a pleasant place to be. Jack *really* felt like a heel when he saw Jesse with multiple casts and bandaged up everywhere, but Jesse was in good spirits. "Hey, Bud," Jesse said dreamily. "What're you doin' here?"

"I came to see you, Jesse. Damn! They've got you wrapped up like a mummy! You hurtin'?"

"Not right now, man. They gave me some really good drugs a little while ago. Man, I wish they'd package that. I'd take a to-go box!" Jesse laughed at his own joke and then groaned, "Oooooh, I take it back. I feel like shit."

"Jesse, I'm sorry for leavin' you, man. I shoulda stayed."

"Naw, man. Nuthin' you could do. Besides, the cops woulda just grabbed you, too, the lousy bastards! They said I'm in a shitload of trouble, and they're coming for me when I get out, so I'm gonna milk this for as long as I can." Jesse then noticed the band-aids and butterfly bandages closing up the gash on Jack's head. He pointed and said, "You get that last night?"

"Yeah. I'm not quite sure how. I don't remember too much about the wreck. I just remember getting home and having dried blood all over my face and clothes. It took a little while, but I finally got it to stay closed. It's nothing compared to you, though."

"Don't let the cops see you in here with that. They were asking me if I had somebody else in the car, and I said no, but I think they talked to somebody that told them they saw someone get out of the car. They're liable to put two and two together if they see you."

Just then, a pretty young nurse came in. She was wearing tight fitting light blue scrubs, and her curly, shoulder-length brunette hair was pulled up on the sides and held back with two decorative combs that sparkled with sequins. She couldn't have been over twenty-five years old, but to Jack and Jesse, she was a sexy "older woman," and they both grinned at each other like two Cheshire Cats when they saw her. The nurse noticed the attention, but she maintained her air of professionalism and told Jack he'd have to leave. "Mr. Brizetta, you need to wrap up your giggle time with your friend. I need to change your bandages and clean you up."

"Ooo, cool! Sponge bath time!" Jesse said. "Say, nurse, hows about you give me some more pain meds, and I'll show you the Gate to Paradise."

Jack started snickering, and they both said, "Men and equipment at work!"

2

When Jesse got out of the hospital, the cops greeted him with handcuffs. His blood alcohol level had been tested at the hospital and came back way over the limit at a well lubricated .18. The cops had also found the second joint in the glove box of Jesse's car, so they charged him with DUI, possession of a controlled substance, and a host of other charges. All of this violated an earlier probation deal. In what seemed like no time at all, Jesse was tried and convicted.

At Jesse's sentencing, his public defender made a token plea for leniency, but Judge Jeffrey Oarn was having none of it. Judge Oarn had a reputation as a hard-liner, and Jesse had a steady stream of juvenile offenses, so now that he was an adult, Judge Oarn decided to teach him a lesson.

"Mr. Brizetta," Judge Oarn said gruffly, "your lawyer, Mr. Tidwell, has stated that you deserve to be given another chance to prove to this court that you can change your ways and become a valuable member of decent society. However, I remain unconvinced that you possess the slightest inclination towards amending your behavior. In fact, despite numerous opportunities to do so, you have shown a pattern of progressively more egregious offenses ending this time with serious bodily injuries to someone that, but for the grace of God, could have died. Therefore, I hereby sentence you to four years in prison at the Southern Nevada Correctional Center. Perhaps there you will learn some things about yourself and your fellow man that will convince you that you are headed down the wrong road before you wind up killing yourself or someone else." With a loud crack of his gavel, Judge Oarn arose and left the bench.

Jack was in the courtroom listening to everything. He was hoping that Jesse would get off without any jail time. He actually sat on the pew-like bench with his fingers and toes crossed in a vain effort to will the judge to let Jesse go with a slap on the wrist, but when he heard the word "prison," Jack hung his head. His body flushed cold, and he physically hurt for his friend, but he couldn't look up. He was so glad that he hadn't been caught, and he was ashamed of himself for that little bit of joy. He dared not look Jesse in the eye for fear that Jesse would confirm Jack's shame.

Jesse stood stoically and never blinked as Judge Oarn meted out his sentence. Then the bailiff grabbed his arm and marched him out of the courtroom. As he reached the side door, Jesse turned back for one last look at his childhood friend, but all he saw was the top of Jack's head.

The Southern Nevada Correctional Center is located in Jean, Nevada, about halfway between Las Vegas and the California state line. It's only about a thirty-five-minute drive from Vegas, but Jack never visited him. He just couldn't bring himself to do it. He felt guilty about that, too, but he had his own life's story to write. He was finishing up his senior year, baseball season was on, and he had met a girl. More accurately, he had been smitten by a girl.

Her name was Melinda Sue Brayson. She had transferred into Highchap High School from San Diego, California for her senior year, and Jack had two classes with her. Melinda was five-foot five inches tall with slender legs and a lithe, curvaceous build. She had a pert little nose with just a smattering of freckles and beautiful long blonde hair that hung to her waist. Adorning her angelic face was a pair of liquid, pale blue eyes that twinkled whenever she smiled, and she smiled often. She had a California tan that made her blonde hair, blonde eyebrows, and beautiful white teeth look positively lustrous. She was sun-kissed, fresh-faced, and looked every bit the part of a vivacious California beach babe.

For Jack, it was love at first sight, but Melinda kept putting him off whenever he asked her out. All through the fall, she wouldn't go out on a date with him, so Jack made every effort to sit by her in class, at the football games, at each assembly, you name it. Jack couldn't get enough of her. She always seemed to smell like honeysuckle, and Jack would snap to attention and look for her whenever that scent feathered his nose.

Melinda, on the other hand, tried to stay aloof. It wasn't that she disliked Jack. Far from it. She loved his rugged good looks and wavy, blonde hair that curled slightly around his ears. His six-foot lean, but muscular, frame was striking, and he moved as graceful and powerful as a panther. The purplish/pink scar above his left eye reminded her of a pirate, and it gave him a rakish presence that sparked a pleasant urge in her whenever he winked at her in class, which he seemed to do every chance possible. He had a mischievous grin that always hinted of equal parts boyish charm and unspoken thoughts of monkey business. He seemed so sure of himself and always made her laugh. And his eyes. His hazel eyes would change from blue to gold to green and seemed to reach into her soul making her feel safe and vulnerable at the same time.

Melinda would steal glances at him when she thought he wasn't looking. One time in History class she was staring at him from the side when he suddenly turned and looked right into her eyes. Then he smirked like he knew he'd caught her and liked it. She felt herself flush all over and quickly looked back at the teacher. Her body tingled naughtily, but she didn't dare look back at him, because she knew he'd be looking at her, and one more look into those beguiling eyes of his at that moment would have irrevocably melted her resolve.

You see, Melinda was conflicted. Her mother was seventeen when Melinda was born.

Melinda's father never married her mother, and all Melinda ever heard as far as she could remember was how boys/men would always try to take advantage of her. Her mother never came out and said that the male population was "bad." You just couldn't trust any of them, so you never gave them anything of value, like your heart.

Melinda knew all of this—or at least she thought she knew. She had also heard the high school stories/myths/ legends about Jack and Jesse and their escapades with Julie McKenna and many other willing girls, but dear Lord, did her heart ever flutter whenever Jack sat down next to her, when he smiled at her, and especially when he said her name. The sound of "Melinda" coming out of Jack's mouth was sweet music to her ears. She made up excuses to make sure there was a seat open next to her hoping Jack would find her and sit with her. She even heard from one of her girlfriends that Jack had remarked how much he loved the smell of honeysuckle, so she had searched every fragrance counter in the Boulevard Mall until she found one that had honeysuckle. After that, she never went a day without wearing it.

All of this is why she always declined whenever he asked her out on a date. It wasn't that her mom would have had a blithering fit if she went out with him—which she would have—and it wasn't Jack's less than stellar reputation. It was that Melinda knew that if she gave in, she would fall hard for Jack. Her refusals were her last line of defense.

However, Jack didn't give up. By Christmas, they were dating, and by New Year's Eve, they were steady. They basically spent the last half of their senior year in each other's arms.

They made plans together. Near the end of the school year, Jack was offered a baseball scholarship to play at the University of Nevada, Las Vegas. Melinda was going to go to Clark County Community College to get a degree in nursing. They would both graduate and start a life together. It all seemed to fit nice and neat, but fate is rarely neat and sometimes not very nice.

Early in July, the evening was as hot and dry as a brick oven. Jack was playing an American Legion baseball game. Melinda always came to his games, and when Jack came up to bat in the first inning, he looked for her in the stands. He could recognize her a mile away. She usually wore short shorts and a halter top, and her long blonde hair always caught the sunshine or moonlight. To Jack, she radiated everything that was good about life, and he beamed every time he saw her. When he looked this time, however, he didn't see her. It puzzled him because she had said that she would be at the game after running a few errands.

About the sixth inning, Jack saw her climb into the stands, but from a distance, she looked tired. She didn't seem like the usual vibrant Melinda. She was dressed in blue jean cutoffs and a plain white t-shirt. Her hair was pulled back in a ponytail, and her bangs hung into her eyes. He figured maybe the heat was getting to her, but he was glad to see her.

As soon as the game was over, Jack grabbed his gear and sauntered over to Melinda. He'd stroked three hits, stole two bases, and scored the winning run, so he was expecting a hero's welcome and a big kiss from Melinda. Instead, her face was as long as the light towers at the baseball field.

"Melinda, what's wrong?" Jack queried her.

Melinda looked around at all of the familiar people climbing out of the stands and said, "We need to talk, but not here. Can we go someplace? Someplace a little more private?"

"Sure. Are you okay?"

"I'll tell you when we get where we're going."

Jack didn't understand the cryptic answer. Either she was alright or she wasn't. Why couldn't she just tell him?

They walked together away from the baseball field. It was about eight-thirty in the evening, and the sun was starting to set. It was a typical desert sunset with magnificent oranges, yellows, reds, and pinks splashed across the sky like someone had flung gallon cans of Day-Glo paint against a pale blue wall. There was a dry summer breeze blowing that cooled anything wet and parched anything dry. It was a breathtaking Vegas evening, but Jack could only think about Melinda and the fact that she barely held his hand as they walked.

When they reached a big cottonwood tree, Jack dropped his equipment bag next to it. He took the baseball cap off his sweaty head, ran his fingers through his curly, wet hair several times, and sat down. He had infield dirt all over his uniform, and it was caked on his face with dried sweat streaks melted through it. Melinda sat down facing him. She crossed her legs Indian-style and hung her head. Her long flaxen ponytail hung down by her face and settled in her lap.

After a few long moments, Melinda let out a big sigh, looked up into Jack's eyes, threw her ponytail around her shoulder onto her back, and said, "In answer to your question, I'm alright, but I'm not. I've missed my period two months in a row, so my mom took me to the doctor today. I'm pregnant, Jack." Melinda let the last sentence hang in the air for about five seconds before she elaborated.

"When the doctor told us the news, my mom freaked. First, she was pissed at me. Then she was pissed at you. Then she was pissed at both of us. Then she was pissed at God. I'm surprised that she wasn't pissed at the doctor. I was crying and didn't really hear half of what she was saying, but the gist of it was that I let her down, I let myself down, you betrayed me, and why in the hell would God let this happen? Anyway, we talked, and I'm definitely having the baby. Mom said she'd help me out. I'm going to ask my boss if I can go full-time at work so I can save up some money before the baby is born."

Melinda continued, "It's not your fault. I mean it is, but I don't hold you responsible. I knew better, but now I'm pregnant. Anyway, I think we should stop seeing each other. I've got to work as much as I can, and you're going be starting at UNLV in a couple of months. There's no point in trying to hang on for that little bit of time. It's better to just make a clean break now." When she was finished, Melinda sighed and hung her head, again.

Jack was dumbfounded. His throat was dry, and his tongue felt like it was made of lead.

All he could do was stammer out, "Melinda, you can't."

Melinda's head jerked up, and with anger in her tear-filled eyes, she shouted, "I can, Jack, and I am! I'm having this baby! My mother didn't throw me away when she got pregnant, and I am *not* going to do that to *my* baby! I'm *not* getting an abortion, and that's final! End of story! Do you understand?" She emphasized her last statement by pointing her finger at Jack and jabbing it in his chest.

Jack looked at her with a pained expression and said, "Yes, I understand, but you don't understand. What I mean is you can't cut me out. I love you, Melinda, and I love our baby. *Our* baby. Yours and mine. *We* made this baby, and

I'm not giving either of you up. I'm not sure how I'm going to do it this instant, but I'm going to take care of both of you. I don't care what it takes. I want to marry you, Melinda. I want to be with you forever!"

"You're not making sense, Jack. You start classes soon, and between baseball and school, you won't have time to work. You can't take care of us. You'll be too busy taking care of yourself."

"I'm not going to classes, and I won't be playing baseball."

"What do you mean, Jack? You've got the scholarship to UNLV. Baseball is your dream. You love playing, and you're great at it. You're going to UNLV," Melinda said with exasperation in her voice.

Jack shook his head and said, "I gave up my scholarship. I did it just now, and I do love baseball, but I love you and the baby way more. I said I want to marry you, Melinda. I want to marry you *now*. This very instant. I don't want to wait. If you say yes, I'll hang up my cleats tonight. I'll get a fulltime job, and I'll support us. You'll see. Say yes, Melinda. Say yes!"

"Jack, you can't be serious," Melinda said, but there was hope in her eyes.

"I'm dead serious. I'm as serious as a heart attack! Marry me, Melinda. Make me the happiest guy on earth!"

Melinda shook her head and said, "Jack, what you're talking about is forever. There's no fooling around. This is *epic*, Jack, and there's no wiggle room for mischief. If I say yes, I'm pledging my whole heart to you and the life of our child. Do you understand? Can you make that same commitment?"

Jack got on his hands and knees. He lowered his head, kissed each of Melinda's sandaled feet, and laid his forehead on her legs where they crossed. He clenched his eyes shut and whispered, "I know exactly what I'm doing and what it means. Please, Melinda, just say yes."

Melinda looked down at him. She started stroking his head and arranging the scattered curls of his hair. She visualized the scar above his left eye. She knew how he had gotten it, and it warned her that Jack would always be a rascal. Tears were streaming down her face, and she looked up into the heavens. She had pictured this moment in her dreams quite differently, but she knew what she would say. She always knew what she would say to Jack. She slowly closed her eyes, and with a sigh, she said, "Yes."

Jack's head bolted up. "Yes? You mean it?" Melinda lowered her head and looked at him through tear-blurred eyes. She slowly nodded her head yes. "Woo hoo!" Jack shouted.

Then he sprang on her and pinned her to the ground on her back. He started kissing her all over her face, neck, and ears. Melinda started laughing, and the more he kissed her, the louder she laughed.

Finally, she said, "Jack! Stop! You're as dirty as Pigpen, and you stink to high heaven. Besides, I'm a mother now, and I can't be roughhousing anymore!"

Jack stopped and looked at her. Then he cocked his head slightly up and to the side while looking up, pausing for a moment, like he was considering it. "Like hell!" he said, and he started kissing her even faster.

Melinda shrieked with surprise and joy. She wrapped her legs around Jack's back and locked her ankles. She clasped her arms around his neck with an enormous grin on her face and let him continue to kiss her. She didn't know how they were going to make it, but she knew they would. She, Jack, and the baby were going to be a family.

3

The next morning Jack called the American Legion baseball coach and quit. Then he called the head coach at UNLV, Skip Dalli, and told him he wouldn't be going there after all. Coach Dalli tried to talk him into honoring his letter-of-intent, but Jack's mind was set.

Before the day was through, Jack wanted to have a full-time job lined up. He had worked construction as a laborer during the summers for extra money, but he decided he needed to learn a trade. Jack knew that the father of the catcher on his American Legion team, Charlie Bellville, was a locksmith, so he called the son, Cary, and asked if his dad was hiring. Cary said he thought his dad might be looking for somebody, so Jack got the phone number and called him. He made an appointment to go see him later that day.

Charlie Bellville was a black man about six-feet, two-inches tall with broad shoulders and an even broader smile. He was only forty-five years old, but his hair was completely white, and his hairline was starting to creep away from his face. Jack saw Charlie working on the inner mechanism of a lockset with tiny tools as he walked into the workshop that was located in the back of the building. Charlie's hands were large with long fingers, but they were very meticulous and precise, and Jack marveled at the intricate adjustments he made with such large hands.

The workshop was pristine and well lit. There was no dirt or trash on the floor or benches. Everything was in its place, and Jack could tell from the condition of the workshop that Charlie took great pride in his work and his business. Every tool had a niche, and it seemed like there were hundreds of tools. The organization and order was impressive, and Jack felt a yearning to be a part of it.

Charlie ignored Jack's presence for about five minutes as he continued to work. He knew Jack was there, but he decided to test Jack's patience. When Jack remained quiet, Charlie eventually looked up from his project. "How ya doin', Jack? That was a great game you played yesterday. You looked like Ricky Henderson himself stealing those bases! I got to catch most of the game before I had to leave to go on a call-out. So, what can I do for you?"

"Thanks, Mr. Bellville. I'm here looking for a job. Cary said that you might be hiring."

"Well, I am looking for someone, and it could be someone with no experience that I could train, but I need someone that can work fulltime. And that would include possibly nights and weekends. I don't see how you'd have time with playing baseball."

"I'm looking for fulltime work, Mr. Bellville. I quit the team so that I could work."

Charlie looked shocked and asked, "What? Why did you do that? I thought you had a scholarship all lined up. What about baseball?"

"I gave it up, Mr. Bellville."

"But why, Jack? You're so talented, and I know you love the game."

"I do, but I love someone else even more, and now I'm going to be a father. I asked her to marry me, and she said yes, so I want to learn a trade that I can use to support my family."

Charlie hung his head for a moment and then looked up at Jack. "My, my, my. I had no idea. The team's gonna miss you, Jack, but I understand. I made a similar decision when I was seventeen. I was a baseball player in high school, too. A pretty good one, but my dad died about six months before I graduated from high school. I had my mom and two younger sisters to think about, so I gave up playing when the high school season ended. I didn't have any skills other than hitting a fastball, so I enlisted in the Army and sent my mom part of my paycheck every month. I stayed in for six years until my sisters were out of high school.

The Army taught me to be a locksmith, so when I got out, I found work and eventually started my own business. It wasn't an easy thing for a teenager to do, but sometimes life doesn't wait for you to grow up before it demands that you become a man. It sounds like life is calling for you to grow up. Are you ready to answer? Are you committed?"

"I am, Mr. Bellville. I've already talked to Coach Dalli at UNLV and told him I wouldn't be taking the scholarship. I really need to get going as soon as possible. I'd like to work for you if that's possible."

"Alright, Jack. I'll start you out at five dollars an hour, and we'll see how it goes. If you pick up the skills and work hard, I'll raise you up to ten dollars an hour so you can start to really earn a living. There's four things that I require. You've got to be dependable, you've got to be honest, you've got to follow my instructions, and you've got to call me Charlie," he said with a smile.

Charlie stuck out his hand, and Jack shook it with a big smile. "You've got a deal, Mr. Bellville! I mean, Charlie. You won't regret it!"

"Fine, Jack. You start next Monday at eight o'clock. By the way, congratulations on the new baby and on getting engaged!"

"Thanks, Charlie. I'll see you Monday morning at eight!"

4

Jack and Melinda got married in August, and they rented a small efficiency apartment. They furnished it sparingly, and the furniture they acquired was from the local Goodwill store. The window treatments were temporary corrugated paper blinds that became permanent, and their china and silverware were all made of plastic. It was all rather spartan, but they both worked hard, saved what little money they could, and they loved being together.

Jack learned the locksmith trade quickly. Charlie never had to worry about him being on time or giving a full day's work. In fact, many times Charlie would come into the shop to see Jack already working on the bench trying to figure out some new lock configuration. Jack even fashioned some new tools that were more effective at picking locks, resetting combinations on safes, or repairing broken locksets. He got the reputation as being able to open any lock, no matter how mangled or complex, in under a minute. Charlie was impressed with his dedication and ingenuity.

In no time at all, Charlie had promoted Jack to fulltime status as his assistant rather than as an apprentice. With Jack's added capability and expertise, Charlie was able to take on bigger, more lucrative accounts. Jack began to go out on calls by himself and was soon making fifteen dollars per hour. That allowed Melinda to quit her job as a waitress five weeks before the baby was born.

Lisa Ann Diamante was born on February 14th–Valentine's Day. She was six pounds ten ounces of innocence and spunk with curly blonde hair, sparkling blue eyes, and a cherub's face. She was constantly observing everything and everyone around her. Lisa rarely cried, and she was the most precious thing Jack had ever seen.

Jack had been a highly coordinated athlete, and he routinely installed and repaired very delicate machinery, but he felt like his hands were made of concrete when the nurse handed him his newborn daughter to hold. Lisa seemed so breakable! It also seemed so natural to cradle her in his arms.

Melinda took to motherhood like she'd been doing it all of her life. The first time she nursed Lisa she beamed at Jack and started to cry. Watching Melinda cry as Lisa suckled made Jack tear up, because he just knew that he could not love anyone or anything more than he loved Melinda and Lisa. He vowed that very day that he would do everything in his power to keep these two women safe and happy.

Lisa was the living, breathing expression of Jack's and Melinda's love for each other. They often referred to her as their Valentine baby to the point that she got the nickname of Val. As she grew up and eventually went to school, everyone else called her Lisa, but Jack and Melinda always called her Val.

Jack and Melinda made the decision that Melinda would stay home to raise Lisa rather than going back to work. To do this, Jack took every opportunity to work overtime and work any type of project. Within a couple of years, he knew the locksmith business inside and out. No job was too dicey or provocative. He was providing for his wife and little girl, so he would do whatever it took.

Las Vegas has had a culture of live and let live and anything goes as long as nobody gets hurt. Since its inception, for instance, Las Vegans have always accepted the mantra that the less the government knows, the better. With a major portion of its workers relying on cash tips for 90% of their income, a huge cash economy grew up in Vegas that burgeoned with the intent of concealing income from the IRS. A majority of customers paid for goods—and especially services—with cash, and cash transactions always stayed off the books.

It was in this atmosphere of wink-wink and look the other way that Jack got the reputation as someone that could be discrete. If a hotel manager needed to get into a room locked from the inside without alerting the occupants, he asked for Jack. If a philandering husband needed to get back into his house after his angry wife had changed the locks—which Jack might've changed—he asked for Jack. If a local politician needed to get an incriminating video out of the hands of his favorite prostitute, he asked for Jack.

Jack saw many things on the other side of the door—drugs, money, bodies, you name it. Some of the bodies were dead, some were alive, and some were very *much* alive. Many times, Jack walked in on people in the throes of passion. Two or three people, and sometimes many, many more, would look up at him—or down from a chandelier, once—in shock and surprise. Sometimes it looked like a three-ring debauchery circus, but Jack never peeped a word of it to anyone.

Jack soon learned that the stickier the mess, the fatter the fee that he could charge. It was simply a matter of supply and demand. He never shorted Charlie if he charged extra, even if it was a cash deal, but Charlie didn't always approve of the motivation behind a customer's request or the methods required to fulfill it. Jack didn't care as long as they paid, because he was supporting his family. One day things came to a head between Jack and Charlie.

Charlie was on call this particular night when he got a message from the answering service to call Lauren Burtell at the Par A Dice Inn Motel on Fremont Street. The Par A Dice was an old Las Vegas mainstay that was originally built in the 1950's. It had two levels of rooms open to the motor court, and it was bejeweled with two giant dice swiveling on a spindle above the office. It was located at the convergence of three major thoroughfares: Fremont Street, Charleston Boulevard, and Eastern Avenue. Once a nice motor lodge that catered to traveling families, it was now part of the seedy end of Fremont Street.

Lauren Burtell was the live-in owner of the Par A Dice, and was as tough as a steel-toed boot. Burtell was a forty-five-year-old, chain-smoking, petite brunette with big brown eyes. Her hair was cut in a loose shag hairstyle that fell in curls to her shoulders and always looked like she had just gotten out of bed. In addition, her makeup was always a touch too heavy, and she always wore clothes that hugged her a squeeze too tight, especially given her pride and joy set of, as she put it, store-bought boobs. She looked unkempt somehow, even though it was obvious that she put time and effort into her appearance.

All in all, however, she wasn't a complete disaster as far as her looks. She appeared as though she could've been someone that shined up nice if she just knew how. That is until she smiled. Lauren Burtell had what was referred to as summer teeth: summer here, summer there. Her teeth crossed over each other and stuck out at odd angles. When she smiled, you automatically thought of a picket fence that was in dire need of repair.

She loved Jack Daniels whiskey and was never far from an open bottle. The whiskey always helped to loosen her tongue, which was already as loose as a five-dollar whore's reputation. When she unleashed a salvo of expletives at anyone or anything, the paint on the walls would curl up and peel off. Lifer Marine sergeants would shudder when assaulted by her colorful interpretation of the baser levels of the English language. One look at her, combined with a modest sample of her vituperation of anyone or anything, and you just knew that universally she had been there, done that, and thrown up on the t-shirt!

Charlie hated working with her, but she had been a loyal, prompt-paying, long-time customer, so he put up with her on most occasions. This night, however, Burtell wanted Charlie to come over and break into one of the rooms and help evict a tenant that had broken a key off in his door. She had noticed a foul smell coming from the room and assumed that either someone was dead in the room or a herd of wet goats had taken up residence there. Either way, she wanted the tenant out and the mess cleaned up with no police involvement. Some of her best tenants were hookers that paid well to use the motel to turn tricks. The girls rented the rooms by the month, but they had their "dates" rent their room for the night with Burtell. That way Burtell got paid to look the other way and neither Burtell nor her benefactors wanted any representatives of the Las Vegas Metropolitan Police Department snooping around.

Charlie turned Burtell down flat. He wanted nothing to do with her predicament, so Burtell called Jack directly. Jack had done some work like this for Burtell before, unbeknownst to Charlie, and she had his number on speed dial. Burtell told Jack that Charlie had turned her down, so he knew that Charlie wouldn't care for Jack going behind his back. Charlie had told Jack that all extracurricular activity for Burtell had to cease after they got their heads handed to them by Metro when one of the jobs had gone south. However, Burtell offered Jack $500 to do the job plus an extra $100 tip for Jack. Figuring that he had her over a barrel, he insisted on getting $800 for about twenty minutes of travel time and five minutes of work plus the $100 tip. When she consented, Jack came over. It was a decision that would change Jack's life in more ways than one.

When Jack pulled up to the Par A Dice office, Burtell was standing outside to greet him.

She walked up to the company van while Jack rolled down the window. Tonight, she was wearing jeans and a too small bright pink tank top with spaghetti straps that said, "Size Matters" in white across the chest. The shirt was stretched so tight that Jack could almost hear an audible squeal coming from the thin cotton fabric. He grinned and said, "Hey, Lauren, doesn't the city have an ordinance prohibiting excessive cruelty to articles of clothing?"

Burtell got a puzzled look on her face. Then she looked down at her shirt and had a smirk on her face when she looked back up. "You're a funny man, Jack. Admit it. You're just jealous, because this shirt is on my tits, and that's where your hands want to be, you leering son-of-a-bitch."

Jack started laughing, and Burtell gave him a full toothy smile. "Lauren, you think the world of those monstrosities, don't you?"

"You're damn right, I do! These are my babies!" she said grinning as she palmed and hefted them with both hands.

"Lauren, you haven't looked in the mirror lately. Those aren't babies anymore. Take it from me. They're fully grown."

Burtell gave Jack a proud, toothy smile and winked, "Damn right they are, and they're for mature audiences only."

"Then why are we having such an immature conversation about them?" Jack said shaking his head.

Burtell burst out laughing and said, "Shit, Jack, you say the damnedest things! I think that's why I like you so much. You keep me thinking. If you weren't married to that princess, I'd jump your bones right here in public! By the way, how's that sweet little daughter of yours doing?"

"She's doing great. She just started first grade."

"You should bring her down here sometime. Hell, I'll babysit her, so you and your princess can have the night to yourselves. Then me and the girls will show her the ropes around here."

"Damn, Lauren! She's not even seven years old, yet!"

"A girl's gotta learn sometime what makes the world go 'round."

"Yeah, well I think she can wait another fifteen or twenty years before she learns that!"

"You sound like you've already got her fitted for a goddamned chastity belt!"

"Now that's a great idea! Why didn't I think of that! Thanks for the advice, Lauren!"

"Yeah, right, you son-of-a-bitch. Get your ass over to room 212. I need that door open, pronto."

"I'm on it."

Jack drove the van over to the staircase nearest to room 212 laughing the whole way. As crude and obstinate as he knew that Burtell could be, he always had fun bantering with her, and she always treated Jack with respect, in her own way.

By the time Burtell walked all the way up the stairs and to the room, Jack had finished getting the broken key out and was ready to open the door. When he did, the security chain stopped him from fully opening it, but the pungent stench of death and excrement tumbled out the door anyway. Jack grabbed another of his homemade tools out of the toolbox, quickly unlatched the chain, and swung the door completely open. Jack could see the now-dead occupant sitting in a chair beside the nightstand next to the bed with a needle still stuck in his left arm. He had evidently died of an overdose. The lamp on the nightstand was on, and the implements of his addiction were scattered beneath the light. Nothing else appeared to be out of place. Jack covered his nose and mouth with a rag as he looked in the door. Burtell never flinched, but she filled the open sky with the foulest obscenities imaginable.

When the fusillade of vulgarity began to subside, Burtell handed Jack $900 and told him to scoot. She had someone coming to remove the body any minute and didn't want Jack exposed to him. It was all supposed to be very quick and very under the table, and she didn't want any complications from the participants.

Once Jack had loaded up the van, he left with a wave out the window, and Burtell waved back. Ten seconds later, another man dressed in dark blue coveralls came up to her from behind and said in a low voice about three inches from her left ear, "How the hell are ya, Lauren? Where's the stiff?"

Burtell jumped and said, "Shit, you're quiet! Don't sneak up on me like that! The goddamn body's in 212. Get it out quick. I don't want any cops snooping around."

"Sure thing, Lauren. When I'm done, you want me to slide in and rub your back like last time?"

"No. My back doesn't need rubbing. This time you can start rubbing on my front," she said with a grin. "Just make sure you clean yourself up beforehand. The last time you smelled like a decomposing skunk carcass rolled in shit."

"You didn't seem to mind, as I recall."

"Yeah, well, you were busy rubbing, and I was busy enjoying," she said with a smile. "Now go get rid of that body."

He laughed and said, "Yes, ma'am. By the way, was that Jack Diamante I saw pulling out of here in the locksmith van?"

"Yeah, why?"

"Oh, nothing. You obviously believe that he can keep a secret. I just thought maybe I'd say hi next time."

"Jesse, you leave him alone. He's doing just fine without you. Now get to work before someone gets curious. I'm not paying you $3,000 to stand here with your thumb up your ass like some slack-jawed, shit-for-brains schmuck!"

"No need to get your panties in a twist. I was just wondering, is all. Alrighty, then. One cadaver au jus removed from the menu, and later I come back for a fur burger and a side of thighs," Jesse said with a leer.

Jesse quickly bagged the junkie's body and strapped it onto a hand truck. That allowed him to easily get it down the stairs. Opening up the rear double doors of his panel van, he slid the body and hand truck right into the back and slammed the doors shut. Before cleaning up the room, Jesse wanted to dispose of the body, so he drove it out to an abandoned mine on the way to Mesquite, Nevada. He had found the mine about two years ago, and he had used it three times previously. He just wheeled the body in and dumped it in a hole.

When he returned less than two hours later, he opened the side doors and removed some cleaning equipment. It only took him about forty-five minutes to clean up and deodorize the whole room since there hadn't been any blood on the carpet or bed. Burtell would be able to rent the room out the next night after the chemical smells had died down a bit. Most jobs like this required him to clean blood and other vile things off of walls, beds, drapes, and couches, especially with shootings. Suicides by shooting were remarkably messy. The victim/perpetrator always shot up to the ceiling or sideways to a wall. It splattered everywhere and made scraping, washing, and painting all that more difficult. He charged extra for those. He also charged extra for police shootings. When the cops put hair on the walls, as they termed it, there was always the additional residue left behind by all of the crime scene techs. Fingerprint powder, luminol, etc. left quite a mess. And, of course, he charged extra for off-the-books body removal/cleanup jobs, like this one.

Jesse was transitioning out of the crime scene cleanup business, though. He had made some decent money at it, but there were several other options that interested him. He had other irons in the fire that didn't require him to get his hands wet, although, there was a part of him that was going to miss it. There was just something about the mayhem that had occurred in those rooms that beckoned to him.

The next day when Charlie came into the shop, Jack was already there working, as usual.

Jack had placed the $800 fee he had charged Burtell on Charlie's workbench along with a completed work order for the Par A Dice Inn Motel.

"What's this, Jack?"

"I did some work on the sly for Lauren Burtell over at the Par A Dice."

"You did work for Burtell last night?"

"Yeah, it was a quick pop-a-lock on one of her rooms. She paid $800, so I wrote up a work order, even though it was already done."

Charlie looked at the money, looked at Jack working on the bench, and shook his head. "Jack, this money's yours."

"What do you mean? You get all the fees."

"What I mean is that you went off the reservation. You know I didn't want us getting involved in any more of Lauren Burtell's underhanded schemes, so when you did that job, you ceased working for me. You were working for yourself, so this fee is yours. It's been a pleasure working with you Jack, but I can't have my employees putting my business in jeopardy. I'm sorry. That's the way it's got to be."

"Charlie, I really didn't mean to cause you any trouble, and in fact, no one was the wiser. Plus, she paid $800 for a $150 job. I didn't figure you'd mind."

"Well, you figured wrong, so this is your money. Consider it a severance, and I wish you luck."

Jack got up, took the money, shook Charlie's hand, and left. By now he had his own tools, so he left everything on his bench and never looked back. Jack figured it was probably high time he went into business for himself anyway, so he took the $800 along with $2,000 he had in savings, and after seven years of working for Charlie, Jack started his own locksmith and security system business and named it Diamond Security.

Jack worked long, hard hours in order to allow Melinda to stay at home with Lisa, and his business grew. After only six months, he was making double what he had made working for Charlie. After a year, he was making five times that amount. However, he never wanted the price of being his own boss and growing the business to include a sparsity of time with Melinda and Lisa. He treasured his time at home or weekend outings with the family. He used to love holding Lisa's hand or having her ride on his shoulders as he had his arm around Melinda while they walked in the park. He would often push both of them side-by-side on the swings and cherished the giggles and laughter that would bubble up out of both of them as he pushed them higher and faster.

Once when Lisa was about eighteen months old, Jack was pushing them on the park swings. He moved around in front of Melinda and dared her to jump out of the swing into his arms. As she launched from the swing, everyone in the park could hear her shriek with a mixture of excitement and terror until she landed on Jack, and they toppled to the ground. She was kneeling on top of him with her long blonde tresses creating a silken privacy barrier that enveloped them in a world where only they existed. Melinda said, "I love you, Jack," and she deeply kissed him. Each of their tongues explored the other in a private, passionate moment that lasted about ten seconds until Lisa started crying, because Jack was no longer pushing her. They both looked up and laughed as they spied Lisa sitting there with tears on her cheeks and a big indignant pout on her face.

Nothing was really easy as they struggled to grow the business and be a family, but it was good, and Jack's link to Jesse and his wild child days continued to fade like the evening sun over Potosi Mountain. However, like the sun, it came back around and started creating shadows.

It was after 11:00 on a hot night in August. The temperature had peaked at 117 degrees that afternoon, and it was still over 100 degrees as midnight approached. Jack was tired, sweaty, and felt like he'd been trudging uphill in an oven for the past fourteen hours. He had just finished a job at one of the local "no-tell" motels, and he was really looking forward to heading home to Melinda and Lisa when he got an unusual call from his answering service.

"Hey, Jack, this is Terri. You've got a callout on a locked vehicle. Seems the owner decided to get out of the car and lock it while it was still running."

"Okay, Terri, what's the address?"

"There's no address, Jack. The guy just said he was on Annie Oakley Drive a little south of Russell."

Now there was nothing unusual about getting a call like this. People got drunk, got lost, and did stupid things at all hours of the day and night in Vegas. No, what was unusual was the location. It was where Jack knew the Gate to Paradise once stood guard over the carnal arena that he and Jesse had initiated almost ten years before.

"Are you sure there's no address, Terri?"

"No, Jack, but the guy said you couldn't miss it. He said there would be a sign by his car that says ..."

"Men and equipment at work."

"Yeah, Jack. How'd you know?"

"Unlucky guess."

THE FLOP

5

As much as Jack was sure that Jesse was waiting for him, he urgently hoped he was wrong. The old feelings of guilt surged back in, and his life with Melinda and Lisa, while not perfect, was enormously more stable since Jesse had been sent to prison. It was the old adage of addition by subtraction.

Jack knew that Jesse was due to get out about five years before, but Jack's life had changed. He was no longer the rowdy hellraiser that Jesse knew. He had a wife and child, and he was a businessman now, so he made no effort to get in touch, and he was relieved that Jesse had done the same—until now.

As Jack pulled onto Annie Oakley from Russell, the brights of his van caught the glint of chrome about a hundred yards ahead. Whatever kind of car it was, it had a lot of bling. Jack didn't remember that being Jesse's style, so a faint glimmer of hope emerged that the car belonged to some other foolish mook, instead of Jesse. As Jack pulled up beside a brand new, fire-engine red Cadillac, he noticed the construction sign was in the old familiar spot. It was a little worse for wear and tear, but it still boldly displayed their make-out mantra. To see the sign there was odd, because the Jack and Jesse love grotto was now a vacant lot flanked by two recently built homes. Jack had driven by this location many, many times during the day, and the sign had always been absent.

Jack turned the van off, but he left the headlights on. He figured if it was Jesse, there'd be no problem, but it was better to be safe than sorry. He also checked to be sure that his snub-nose .38 Smith and Wesson revolver was securely in his ankle holster. He had never actually had to fire the gun other than on the practice range, but it had come in handy several times when he needed to sober up some drunk that figured Jack looked like he needed a beating. That familiar click-clack of the hammer being pulled back had a way of making people pay attention. "Better to have it and not need it," Jack thought to himself.

As Jack got out of the van, the driver's door of the Cadillac opened and out stepped Jack's past. "Hello, Jack boy! How the hell are ya?" Same old Jesse.

"I'm fine, Jesse. How're you?"

"Well, I'm kickin' ass, smokin' grass, and got no class!" Jesse threw his head back and laughed. Same old Jesse sense of humor, too. About Jack's height, he was leaner and more muscular than Jack remembered, and he was dressed well in designer blue jeans and a skin-tight red polo shirt that matched the color of the Cadillac. Jesse's hair was still black and curly, but it was cut short compared to the fluffy long hair he had in high school. From the car to the clothes, Jack smelled money. This made him wary, although he couldn't help but grin at his old friend.

"You outta gas, too? Is that why you called me out here?"

"Oh, hell no, Jack. I just figured this would be a good place for a reunion and talk a little business. Hey, you remember that night you and I were out here with Julie McKenna? Man, was that a screaming good time or what?

No pun intended, of course." Jesse laughed, again. He always did like his own jokes best.

"How could I forget? We sure did raise a ruckus that night. Julie got pretty loud, too, if I remember correctly. Now, what's this about business?"

"We'll get to that. I just wanted to catch up a little bit first with my ol' buddy. I hear you got married, gotta kid, and gotta nice little business. That's good, that's good. Me, I got a nice little business, too. Yeah, I own a bunch of them self-serve car washes. You cannot believe the gold mines those little bastards are! Anyway, I'm makin' money hand over fist."

"I see you're driving a red Eldorado. I can't believe after what we did to Principal Grabass' car that you'd buy the same kind of car."

"Ha ha, Grabass, that son-of-a-bitch. Hey, I disliked him, but I liked his car! This one shines up real nice, doesn't it?"

"Yeah, it's a beauty, all right. It's got so much chrome I was hoping it would belong to some Hollywood starlet instead of your mangy ass," Jack said with a grin. "I see that you reinstalled the Gate to Paradise."

"Yeah, I saw it out here a couple of years back under some tumbleweeds. I couldn't imagine that Clark County would abandon such a historic landmark, so I took it home. It seemed appropriate to bring it out for the reunion. Whad'ya think? Looks nice, right?"

"Very appropriate, and I'm shocked, too, that the county didn't respect this valuable piece of nostalgia. That sign was witness to some of the most epic adventures ever seen in Las Vegas," Jack waxed with a wink. "So, I'm glad to see you're doing well. Now what sort of business you got for me? You want some security cameras on those car washes?"

"Naw, I got somethin' else in mind. You see, these little gold mines are an all-cash business, so I don't always tell Uncle Sam everything. He thinks they're just silver mines, and I'd like to keep it that way. I've got a banker in L.A. that takes care of my extra cash, if ya know what I mean. Anyway, I need someone to make a delivery of cash down to my guy in L.A., and I figure who can I trust if not my ol' buddy, Jack?"

"I'm flattered, but I've got a business to run. I don't really have time to run down to L.A."

"Oh, c'mon, Jack. You're down and back in eight hours, nine hours tops. I'll pay you for your time."

"Why don't you drive it down yourself?"

"Well, let's just say I have some other business that I gotta attend to here, and I can't leave right now. Listen, I'll pay you five hundred dollars for your expenses and twenty-five hundred dollars to make sure the delivery gets there safe and sound. That's three grand. You can't tell me you'd make that kind of money pickin' locks."

"No, you're right about that. Three thousand dollars to make a delivery of money for you? How big is it? I'm not gonna have to rent an armored truck, am I?"

"No, no it'll fit in your van or in the trunk of a car. That's why I'm giving you the five hundred dollars. That'll cover gas and rental car if you want. How 'bout it? Do your ol' buddy Jesse a favor?"

"When?"

"Day after tomorrow. My banker will be expecting it then. Just be there before five p.m., otherwise he'll be gone."

"You're telling me straight? All I have to do is deliver some money to L. A.?"

"That's it, ol' buddy. Straight up."

"All right. I'll do it. Give me the details."

And that is how Jesse weaseled his way back into Jack's life. Jack didn't really like the idea at first, but he figured it would square his conscience for abandoning Jesse, and, well, Jesse was right. Jack would *not* make anywhere near three thousand dollars in one day. Three thousand dollars was three thousand dollars, and he could use the money right then.

The next day Jack was headed down I-15 on his way to Los Angeles. He had picked up three large black satchels at Jesse's house in Spanish Trail. Jack had rented a blue Ford Taurus to make the run. He decided against using his company van. He didn't want the added wear and tear on it, and he was a little concerned about what he would be transporting if it turned out to be more than cash. He figured a Taurus would be more inconspicuous than his van. As it turned out, the satchels were just filled with cash, so Jack stashed them in the trunk and hit the road.

The trip was uneventful, but every time Jack noticed a highway patrol car, his sphincter sucked canal water. Deep down he knew that what he was doing was probably illegal, but he figured that he'd be able to get away with it this once. Three thousand dollars was enough to soothe his conscience, but that didn't mean that it soothed his nerves, and he couldn't wait to drop off the load.

When Jesse told Jack he was going to see the "banker," Jack assumed he would be delivering to a regular branch of a bank. When he pulled up to the address that Jesse had given to him, Jack was shocked to see that it was a rundown office building in a seedy part of town. He thought he had misread the address, but when he pulled up, a heavyset Hispanic man with a full mustache and a balding head opened the front door and waved him around to the back. Jack drove around the building past the graffiti-laden garbage dumpsters and pulled up to where he thought the rear entrance must be located.

When the man opened the back door, he was chewing on an unlit cigar that looked like the business end of a baseball bat. As Jack exited the Taurus and shut the car door, the man took out the cigar, shook Jack's hand, and said, "You must be Jesse's man. He said you were new, and I was afraid you wouldn't find the place."

"I must admit that I was looking for a building that looked more like a traditional bank," Jack said with a grin on his face.

"Don't let the looks fool you. There are all kinds of banks. This one is just a little more low profile than Bank of America," the man said with a laugh. "But we do plenty of business. Jesse's one of our best customers, but he's only one of many. Our customers like to stay under the radar, and so do I. You can call me Fernando," he said as he waved Jack inside.

Jack nodded to Fernando and said, "Jack." Then he retrieved the bags out of the trunk and took them over to Fernando. "Do I get any kind of a receipt or something saying that I made the delivery? No disrespect, Fernando, but I don't know you from Adam."

"No problemo. I've got Jesse on the line now telling him you made it. Here, you talk to him, Esse. He'll give you the receipt."

Jack took the phone and asked, "Jesse?"

"Yeah, Jack. Everything's cool. Good job and thanks. I'll see you back in Vegas."

With that, Jack gave the phone back to Fernando, shook his hand, and got back in the car. He got onto I-10, but it was rush hour in Los Angeles, so after struggling with traffic for a while, Jack found a nice restaurant in El Monte and cooled his heels. Since Jesse was paying, Jack ordered a big porterhouse steak with all the trimmings, a twenty-four-ounce draft, and finished it up with apple pie ala mode.

Jack felt pretty good about his adventure. After expenses, he was going to clear almost $2,700 for one day's work. And the work wasn't that tough. He headed back to Vegas and was home about ten-thirty. Melinda was still up, and when she asked him about his day, he told her about the money he had made. He didn't tell her how he made it, but it had been a good day, and they celebrated in bed that night.

Jack had told himself that it would only be that one time, but pretty soon he was making three to five deliveries a month for Jesse. It was usually to Los Angeles, but sometimes he went to Phoenix, and once he went to San Diego. They were all day trips and usually transporting money. Jack never knew how much, but it was sometimes more than a trunk-full. And Jesse always paid cash.

Jack was getting paid anywhere from $10,000 to $15,000 a month. His own security business suffered a little, but Jack was clearing more running errands for Jesse than from his business, and Jesse's cash was tax-free. Still, Diamond Security was *his* business. He had built it, and he didn't want to see it lose any steam, so he worked extra hard on what used to be his "off" days.

Jack never told Melinda where the extra money came from. As far as she knew, Diamond Security was doing double the business. It made sense because Jack was working longer hours and taking less time off. She liked the new house they had purchased and the new car that she drove now, but she missed seeing Jack in the early evening. Jack always had call-outs late at night, but he usually started the evening at home. Now it seemed that he worked straight through the evening into the night, and sometimes he wouldn't get home until four or five in the morning.

Melinda worried about him. While Jack had told her about the job that precipitated his leaving Charlie and starting Diamond Security, he didn't share much of the details about what he did now. However, Melinda wasn't totally in the dark. One of her girlfriends from high school worked as a manager at one of the hotels downtown. She had hired Jack to install surveillance equipment in a hotel room and the employee's breakroom. They had caught employees dealing drugs and performing acts of prostitution while on the job, and she had told Melinda about it at lunch. The hotel fired the employees without involving Metro, thus saving a boatload of negative publicity and red tape. In addition, Melinda knew that he had worked with the cops on a few things and also worked against them on other occasions. She never let on that she knew about some of the more dangerous or provocative work that Jack performed. She knew it was just a risky part of the business that he tried to shield from his family, because he didn't want her to worry.

She appreciated how hard he was working and all of the effort that he put into providing financially for her and Lisa, but what Jack was no longer providing was private time with Melinda. She yearned for Jack and his companionship. She *needed* time with him, and so did Lisa.

It was about this time that Lisa started to stutter. She had never stuttered in her life previously, and it concerned Jack and Melinda. They didn't really know what to do about it except to keep an eye on her. However, Melinda got more and more concerned as time went on, so she took Lisa to the pediatrician to see if there was something that could be done. The doctor's answer would change things dramatically.

When Jack got home at three-thirty in the morning, Melinda was waiting up for him sitting Indian style in the bed.

Jack looked a bit startled and said, "Hey, sweetheart, what are you doing up so early?"

"Actually, it's late Jack. I've been up all night waiting for you."

Jack's look instantly turned to concern. "What's wrong? Where's Val? Is she okay? Why didn't you call me?"

"She's in her bed sleeping, but I'm very concerned about her. I didn't call, because I knew it could wait until you got home. I took her to the doctor today to see if he could help her with her stuttering. It's gotten worse over the last two weeks, and she's not growing out of it like we had hoped."

"So, what did the doctor say? Does he know what's causing it?"

"Yes and no. He said there's nothing physically wrong with her. He also said that stuttering can be caused by physical or emotional trauma. I told him that I didn't think there had been trauma of any sort. Then he told me that it could also be caused by separation anxiety. He asked me if either of us had been away for an extended period of time. I told him we hadn't, so he said to continue to watch her and see how she does in the next couple of weeks. Jack, I was thinking, though. You have been gone. I mean, you've been here in Vegas, but you're gone from us. You're always working, Jack. Is there any way that you could get some more help or cut back? We don't need more money, Jack. We need you. I need you. Val needs you."

Jack hung his head, and tears started to form in his eyes. He looked at his hands and then at Melinda. "Oh, honey. I'm so sorry. I didn't mean to neglect you two. You and Val mean the world to me. Things have just been really busy lately. I'm trying to get it under control, though. All I want is for us to be together and be happy. I promise I'll figure out a way to make this right."

"I know you will, and I'm so proud of you. You're out there working so hard and putting in an enormous amount of time, but I need some serious Jack time, too!" Melinda said. Then she winked at him, did a half turn with her left shoulder, pulled her hair around the left side of her face until she was peeking up and down at Jack through her flaxen locks, and she blew him a kiss.

It was then that Jack noticed that Melinda was wearing a new royal blue babydoll negligee with white lace trim. Melinda crawled out of the silk sheets and comforter on her hands and knees over to Jack with a seductive grin on her face. The babydoll hugged Melinda around every curve, and Jack could imagine everything he could not see. Melinda could still light his fire with just a wink and an air kiss. If she really wanted to start him blazing, she'd take her long blonde tresses and draw them over his face, arms, or legs.

Jack grinned and said, "Is that why you waited up for me in that pretty little handkerchief you're wearing? Plus, I see you curled your hair. You don't normally do *that* before going to bed. You know what that does to me. I swear you look good enough to eat, and I'm talking in one bite! Wait a minute. Do I smell honeysuckle?"

"You better, you big lunk. I think I sprayed enough of it on me and around the room to float a battleship."

"Say no more, my lovely. Let me get a shower, and I'll see if I can figure out where that honeysuckle smell is coming from. I promise that I will leave no lingerie unopened until I have thoroughly investigated the mystery of the honeysuckle!"

Melinda got a sly look in her eye and said, "How about I get in the shower with you and wash your back?"

"You can't do that!" Jack said in mock horror. "That will wash away the honeysuckle scent. How will I ever track down the source, Madam Lusciousness?"

"Well, I guess we'll just have to play hide the honeysuckle all over again when we get out."

Jack shook his head. "But I was planning to eat you in one bite. Now I'll have to just nibble around the edges until the honeysuckle is found. That might take a loooong time," he said with raised eyebrows.

"If we're lucky," Melinda said, "it might take hours and hours. The question is, do you feel lucky?"

Jack paused for just half a moment to gather his emotions. "Melinda," he said with a catch in his throat and a smile on his face, "right now I feel like the luckiest man alive."

"Well, Mr. Lucky, in that case, I believe we're wasting time. Your back needs washing, you stinky rascal," she said with a broad smile as her big blue eyes danced all over him.

"If I'm that stinky, I believe you're gonna have to wash more than my back," Jack said with a big wink.

"Well then, last one in is a rotten egg!" Melinda squealed as she hopped off the bed while Jack swatted her playfully on her backside. Then she went running into the bathroom laughing as her waist-length blonde curls bounced behind her. Melinda couldn't wait to get in the shower and wrap her arms around Jack. She felt exhilarated to have his undivided attention. It had been a while since he had been this playful, and she had sorely missed it.

By the time that Jack had undressed and entered the bathroom, Melinda was already enjoying the sensation of the hot water streaming down her body in the shower. She beckoned to him through the fogged shower glass, and he swung the door open and climbed in. The sight of Melinda and the feel of the roiling steam made him catch his breath.

The torrid water not only cleaned their bodies, but it also cleared Jack's head. As he and Melinda embraced and explored each other's soapy, slick curves, he realized everything he had been missing lately. Here was the love of his life, and he had been neglecting her. He was ashamed and distressed, but he vowed to change the picture.

Later, as Melinda slept, Jack lay in bed listening to her steady rhythmic breathing. She seemed so serene and at peace that he pictured her as a baby, and he realized that the picture in his mind was that of Lisa. Lisa always seemed to sleep with a wry smile on her face like she knew something clever, but she wasn't going to share it with you.

Slipping out of the covers, he put on a bathrobe and walked down the hall to Lisa's bedroom. Poking his head in her doorway, he heard the air conditioning compressor bray at the night as it started up outside her bedroom window. She shivered slightly as the cool air hit a bare leg protruding from the covers. Jack gently pulled the sheet and blanket over her leg, and he watched and listened to her sleep. These were the women he loved more than anything in the world, and it was there standing in Lisa's bedroom that he made a decision. He would sell Diamond Security.

There were a couple of other security companies in town that would buy his equipment and pay him to take over his steady accounts. He figured he could clear about $100,000 all told. That way he would still run errands for Jesse, make at least $10,000 a month, and he could be home most days and evenings to be with Melinda and Lisa. There was just one problem. How was he going to explain making all of that money after he had sold his business? The answer came to him like a bullet to the brain.

Poker. Jack would learn to play poker. He could play at night, explain that he had won, and it was still an all-cash transaction. Not only that, but Vegas provided a myriad of poker rooms open 24/7. It was the perfect cover story. Vegas was full of professional and semi-professional poker players, and the tourists always brought more money to town. In addition, by playing at night, he could be with Melinda and Lisa during the day. It was the perfect plan. Now he just had to set the wheels in motion. However, before he sold his business, he had one more job to finish.

6

Jack had always wanted to get a really nice wedding ring for Melinda. When he had proposed to her, he couldn't get her a ring at all. By the time the wedding rolled around, he had saved enough to buy her a small ring with a one eighth carat diamond. The diamond was so small that it looked like something you would wipe out of your eye. Even though Melinda had never mentioned that she disliked the ring, Jack had sworn to himself that he would one day replace it with something befitting his beautiful wife.

Moscowitz Jewelers was one of Jack's biggest clients. It was a family business run by the patriarch Tobias "Toby" Moscowitz. Jack had worked with them since his days as an apprentice locksmith. Old man Moscowitz had taken a liking to him, so when Jack had mentioned that he wanted to get Melinda a really nice ring, the old man took him into the back room to see the "private stock."

When he entered the privileged enclave, Jack couldn't believe what he saw. Diamonds the size of grapes. Emeralds and rubies that were even larger. He saw every colored gemstone under the sun, and when Moscowitz turned on the light over the diamonds, Jack would have sworn each one of them was a miniature nova. Jack was agape.

"So, you like what you see?"

"Toby, this is magnificent," Jack stammered, "but I could never afford anything like this. Maybe we should just look through the case out front."

"Ah, the case out front. That is for the tourists. I would never let your Melinda wear something from the front case."

"You don't understand. The diamond ring I gave her on our wedding day is so small, that the rings in the front case make her ring look like it should have come with a gumball in the middle. She deserved something nicer, but it was all I could afford."

"Yes, yes, I know, and I understand. There is nothing wrong with that ring. There is love in that ring. There always will be, but now you want to show her that she still means the world to you, yes?"

"Yes."

"And for that, we come to the back room. This is where exclamation points are added to 'I love you'."

With that, the old man walked over to a fancy wooden cabinet. It was made of rich cherry hardwood, stood about six feet tall, and it looked like it weighed ten tons. The doors were hand carved with the nude images of Adam and Eve in the Garden of Eden. Adam was on the left door, and Eve was on the right. Eve was semi-reclined on a large pedestal while Adam was kneeling and reaching out to her with a rose. There were cherubs winging above and standing to the sides among the trees.

Toby took an old key out of the right pocket of his vest and unlocked both doors. He swung the doors open, adjusted a lamp down that was attached above the doors, and switched the light on. In the cabinet were drawers stacked one above the other from the floor to eye level.

Pulling open one of the drawers in the middle, he tilted up a lid, and inside were row upon row of beautiful diamond rings. Jack marveled at the glistening fire emanating from that drawer as the lamp shone on the rings.

"These are for your Melinda. Take a look. The center diamonds in all of these rings range from three carats to five carats with side diamonds or other stones that make each one unique. I have chosen the stones and the settings myself. Go ahead. Look. Find the ring that will set your Melinda apart from her friends," he said with a chuckle.

As Jack looked at the rings, he felt like a hungry kid in a candy store. Each ring seemed to be more beautiful than the next, but there was one that caught his eye and screamed, "Melinda!" He picked it up and turned it over and over fascinated by the way the light danced and accelerated through the diamonds.

"Ah, yes, that one. You have a keen eye, Jack. That center diamond is four carats. The two side diamonds are one carat each, and all are of the highest quality. I would sell that ring at retail for two hundred fifty thousand dollars."

"Oh, my god! I could never afford that!" Jack hurriedly tried to put the ring back in the drawer, but the old man closed his weathered hand over Jack's hand to stop him.

"I said that was retail. You do not pay retail in the back room, Jack. This is for family and good friends. For you and your Melinda, this ring is one hundred thousand dollars."

"It's beautiful. It really is, but even as good as the business is going, I still can't afford that now."

"I tell you what, Jack. In a couple of weeks, you are to put in the new security system we ordered. You have quoted me a price of about sixty thousand dollars, yes? I will give you this ring in exchange for the security system and forty thousand dollars. This you will afford, and your Melinda will know that she is a queen, yes?"

"Yes."

"Good. Then it is done. I will put this in a safe place here away from the others while it waits for your Melinda."

"Thank you, Toby."

As he was turning, a flash of light caught the corner of Jack's eye. There on a work table laid out on a black velvet display pad was a magnificent necklace the likes of which Jack had never seen before up close. It reminded him of the extraordinary necklaces worn by famous movie actresses on the red carpet that even they could not afford to own but only borrow for the evening. Huge diamonds alternated with rubies and sapphires of varying size.

Toby caught Jack gawking at the necklace. "Ah, now you see my wife's exclamation point!"

Jack realized his mouth was hanging open, and he had to grin sheepishly. "That is some exclamation point! It's beyond beautiful. I've never seen anything like it!"

"Nor will you. This necklace I had made for my wife. It is one-of-a-kind, just like my wife. We have been married forty-two years, and I still cannot believe she said 'yes' to me all those years ago. The center teardrop diamond is twenty-three carats, and the whole necklace was appraised for insurance purposes at over six million dollars. It is called the Slezy Bogov. In Russian, it is Tears of the Gods. It is here today to be cleaned. Tomorrow it will be worn by my Elena at the Wynn charity event, and then it goes back into our safe."

Jack stared at the necklace. He marveled at how the light seemed to travel from one stone to the next accelerating as it reached a crescendo at the enormous diamond in the middle and then exploding into a thousand laser beams of magnificent color. He imagined how it might look around Melinda's neck, and he entertained the thought of asking to borrow it someday, but he quickly put it out of his mind. To think of it would only torment him, and such a beautiful necklace should only be associated with happy, loving thoughts.

"It's extremely beautiful, Toby. I'm sure that Elena looks absolutely gorgeous when she wears it."

"Oh no, Jack, it is my Elena that makes the necklace look beautiful. These stones, while beautiful, are cold and hard. My Elena is alive, soft, and warm. She is life. She radiates. These merely sparkle, but every woman likes to wear some sparkle," he said with a grin as he covered the necklace.

7

Jack planned to arrive home early. He had stopped by Moscowitz Jewelers and picked up the ring for Melinda. He had reservations for dinner at the Golden Steer, Melinda's favorite restaurant, and he had arranged for a babysitter for Lisa. Lastly, he had called the answering service and told them he wouldn't be taking any service calls tonight. In fact, Jack thought, if things go as planned, he wouldn't be taking any service calls ever again.

Melinda knew they were going out to dinner, but she suspected something bigger was going on. Jack *never* arranged for the babysitter. Melinda always handled that. When Jack had called, he had simply said to get dressed up, because they were going out, and he had taken care of everything. Melinda was skeptical. She thought back to the time when Lisa was four months old. She and Jack were going to a restaurant for the first time since Lisa had been born. Melinda was still breastfeeding her, so naturally, they were taking her along. Right before they left the house, Melinda asked Jack to "grab the diaper bag." This he did, and they went to the restaurant.

While they were eating, Lisa started to get cranky, and Melinda figured it was time to change her diaper. She asked Jack for the diaper bag, and when he gave it to her, she discovered that it was empty! It had never occurred to Jack that "grab the diaper bag" meant fill it with everything before you bring it. He had just "grabbed" it. Luckily, Melinda kept a spare diaper in the glove box of the car, but after that, she always double-checked.

Knowing that Jack had arranged for the babysitter, Melinda half expected to have some biker chick with tattoos and nose rings show up at the front door. When her mom walked in, Melinda was relieved, but her curiosity went into overdrive.

Melinda's mom, Kiersten Brayson, loved spending time with her granddaughter.

Kiersten's middle name was Rose, and she had taught Lisa to call her Grandma Rose. Kiersten didn't really like the moniker of Grandma Rose, because she thought it made her sound matronly, and she was anything but that. She was only thirty-six when Lisa was born, and, although older now, she still had a great figure and the blonde good looks that Melinda inherited. Kiersten still turned heads when she walked into a room. However, when Lisa was learning to talk, she always said "keister" when she tried to say Kiersten. Jack used to crack up laughing when it happened, and Kiersten would give him a dirty look which only made Jack laugh even louder. Kiersten decided she didn't want Lisa calling her Grandma Keister for the rest of her life, so she went with her middle name.

Kiersten had babysat Lisa countless times before, but Friday night she usually went prowling Vegas with her girlfriends from work. They would hit the country bars, like Stoney's, Hogs and Heifers, or Gilley's, and dance and drink until the wee hours. One time they even coerced Melinda into going with them to see *The Thunder From Down Under*, which was a male strip show at the Luxor. Melinda figured Jack must've made some kind of spectacular deal with her to get her to give up girls-night-out. However, she wasn't about to look a gift horse in the mouth. She just counted her blessings and got ready to have a nice evening out with Jack.

Melinda decided to go all out and dress to the nines. She wore a shimmering royal blue evening dress that was bare at the back and slit up the side to mid-thigh. The dress hugged every curve of her lithe body. The blue of the dress made her blue eyes jump out, and the décolletage was designed to make everyone else's eyes jump out. The exposed curves of her bustline issued a shouted whisper of things to come for Jack. She topped off the deep blues and greens in her eye shadow with a bit of red to add some spice. She had styled her long blonde hair in big, full sweeping curls that swayed and danced every time she moved. Her bangs nestled in just below her eyebrows and softly accentuated her eyes. She thought about pulling her hair up on the sides with tendrils left hanging alongside her teardrop diamond earrings, but she decided to leave her hair down, because she knew that Jack loved her long blonde curls around her face. Lastly, she fastened a gold ankle bracelet around her right ankle and climbed aboard some six-inch royal blue pumps that put the icing on the cake.

When Jack walked in the front door, Melinda was there to greet him with a kiss. As their lips parted, Jack backed away but held her left hand high as she twirled for him. He looked at her breathlessly from head to toe and said, "Wow! You look absolutely stunning! I'm torn between taking you out or ravishing you right here in the foyer!"

"Jack, I put a lot of work into this look, so let's go out and have a good time. I want to be Melinda Diamante tonight instead of mom. I do give you permission, however, to ravish me later," she said with a wink and a wiggle of her eyebrows. "Deal," said Jack.

The Golden Steer is an old school steakhouse that has been in Las Vegas since 1958. It's located one block off the Las Vegas Strip in a building that also houses a pawn shop and a tattoo parlor. While the outside looks seedy, inside it has an old Victorian ambiance reminiscent of the Gold Rush era of San Francisco. Throughout the sixties and seventies, it was the favorite hangout of many of the entertainers that frequented Vegas like Frank Sinatra, Dean Martin, Sammy Davis Jr, and Elvis. Regular customers are always greeted with respect as Mr. and Mrs. and then led to their favorite table where their favorite libation is waiting. The restaurant is steeped in leather, mahogany, and the smell of charred oak whiskey casks. While all of Las Vegas around it continues to change, the Steer has retained the "Old Vegas" feel and level of service. It was always the personal service that made it Melinda's favorite.

As they entered the Steer, Emilio Camellini, the maître d', greeted them. "Good evening, Mr. and Mrs. Diamante. We have your table ready for you." When they reached their table, Jack palmed a hundred-dollar bill and a small velvet box to Emilio as he shook his hand. Emilio nodded and leaned into to Jack saying, "Everything is as you requested, Mr. Diamante." Jack nodded and thanked him.

The entire time that they were being seated, Melinda noticed that Jack seemed preoccupied with something. She hoped that he hadn't received a service call. It always seemed that someone locked themselves out of their house or car and waited until Jack and Melinda were going to have some intimate time together before they called. She swore that the locksmith gods always conspired against them.

Before ordering dinner, the wine steward brought over a bottle of Dom Perignon champagne. The bottle was immersed in ice in a fancy silver champagne bucket, and the exterior of the bucket was coated in a fine mist of condensation. Draped around the neck of the champagne bottle was a tiny pink ribbon, securing the gorgeous diamond ring that Jack had picked out at Moscowitz Jewelers.

"Jack! What is that?" Melinda exclaimed.

"That, my dearest Melinda, is your wedding ring."

"What do you mean, Jack? I already have a wedding ring."

"Yes, you do, and at the time, it was all I could afford, but I have always wanted to give you the ring that you deserved. Tonight, I am able to do that, and I would be honored if you would let me put it on your finger where it belongs," Jack said as he carefully lowered himself to one knee in front of Melinda while she sat in her chair.

Melinda's mouth hung open in a tiny "O" as she looked at Jack. Then she slowly closed her eyes and bowed her head, her blonde curls covering her face. Her shimmering blue dress began to shake ever so slightly. When she looked up, her sparkling azure eyes were brimming with tears. "Jack, when I married you, it wasn't for money. It also wasn't because I was pregnant. My mom raised me alone, and I could've done the same with Val. I married you because I loved you, and I *knew* you loved me. I saw how hard you worked to earn enough money to buy my ring, and I cherish it. I know the love that is behind it. I don't need a big fancy ring, as beautiful as this one is, to remind me that you love me."

"I know you don't, Melinda, and that's just one more reason why I want you to have it. I want everyone in the WORLD to know how much I love you. Please, let me put this ring on your finger. A lot of love has gone into this one, as well."

Melinda looked at the ring Jack was holding and then into Jack's eyes. What she saw was pure adoration and love. "Alright," she said, "on one condition. I'm not trading in my wedding ring. I'm simply adding to it. I'll wear them both."

"I can live with that," Jack said with a broad grin. As he slid the new wedding ring on Melinda's finger next to the original one, he looked into her eyes and smiled. Then he raised himself up and kissed her deeply.

Unbeknownst to Jack and Melinda, most of the other diners around them had been watching all of this unfold. The restaurant commotion had ceased, and it was so quiet you could've heard a pin drop. When Jack kissed Melinda, they all broke out into applause with a few cheers and whistles. Melinda looked around and turned beet red. Jack started laughing, and she punched him in the arm which made him laugh even more.

"Jack, you slimy toad! You've been acting squirrely all evening. I was afraid you had gotten a service call, and we were going to have to call tonight off."

"No, no service call. In fact, I have another little piece of news for you. Actually, it's a big piece of news. There will be no more service calls pulling us apart anymore."

"Why, Jack? What do you mean?"

"What I mean is that I'm selling Diamond Security. I'm giving up the business. I want to be a better husband to you and father to Val, and I can't do that when I'm at everyone else's beck and call."

"Oh, Jack, but you love that business. You built it from nothing."

"Yes, I do, and yes, I did, but I love the two of you much, much more. It's already done. I've sold the business, and we sign the papers on Monday. I did well in the sale. I actually got more than I had anticipated."

"But what are you going to do? What about our new house?"

"Don't worry about the house. We won't lose the house."

"Jack, I'm not worried about losing the house. I'll live in an apartment as long as the three of us are together. I just meant it seems like bad timing."

"It's alright. I have some things in the works. I don't want to share them until they become real, but we're set for quite a while just with the sale of the business. Just know that I've got it under control and that I love you."

"I love you, too, Jack, so very much!" she said as she placed both of her hands on either side of Jack's face and kissed him, again.

8

Jack took to poker like a fish to water. He'd always been good with numbers and reading people by their reactions. Once he learned the ins and outs of the game, he wanted to immerse himself into the nuances of it as a profession. And he did. With a vengeance.

Jack started out in small stakes limit games. He would take $100 and play until he had lost it all. In the beginning, it didn't take long to bust out. Eventually, though, he started to break even and finally to come out ahead. Then he progressed to no-limit games for small stakes.

Unlike the limit games that had no big swings in money won or lost, the no-limit games would swing wildly from several hundred dollars ahead to busting out in one or two hands. Jack had to learn the discipline of the game and pick his opportunities to go "all-in" much more carefully.

After a couple of months of trial by fire, Jack got his feet underneath him and started to run. He first worked the poker rooms that primarily catered to the locals, like the Orleans and downtown at Binion's, and he worked the Strip frequenting places like the Mirage, Venetian, and sometimes the Bellagio. However, his favorite haunts became Caesars Palace and downtown at the Golden Nugget. Both hotels had poker rooms with constant play and a good influx of tourists. Tourists brought new money every day into these poker rooms, and Jack was there to welcome them to Vegas.

Jack played the occasional tournament or $1/$2 no-limit Texas Holdem cash games, but his bread and butter was live $2/$5 no-limit Texas Holdem. As the name implies, the bets started out at $5, but it was not unusual at all to see thousand-dollar pots in these games, especially between 11:00 p.m. and 3:00 a.m.—or later on the weekends. Jack could easily clear two thousand to five thousand dollars a night, and he only had to play two or three nights a week. If he had something planned for the evening, he could easily find a game during the day or play a tournament on the weekend. That left plenty of time for Melinda and Lisa. He also still did the occasional delivery for Jesse, so life was good.

Melinda had her doubts at first. She always considered any type of game in a casino as "gambling," and she didn't want Jack to lose himself to the casinos. Jack assured her that this was not the case. Still, she was skeptical. After about six months, however, she began to understand what Jack had been telling her; played correctly, poker was a game of skill and not luck. Oh sure, luck was a factor in the short-run, but over time, the mathematics and probabilities won out. Then it became a matter of outplaying your opponents rather than "praying" to get a good hand.

Without a doubt, though, Melinda loved that Jack was home so much more. By necessity, he had been gone for too much of Lisa's childhood, but now he was totally involved in her life, and her stuttering had become a thing of the past. He was taking her to school, dance lessons, and even shopping. He never missed a birthday party or holiday function and never had to leave in the middle of an event as in the past when he'd get a call-out for the business. Jack had even started to go to church occasionally with Melinda and Lisa. Melinda knew that he only went because she asked him to take them, but she figured it would be good for him and the family. If he had to play poker at night into the wee hours a few times a week or take a Saturday or Sunday to play a tournament once in a while, to Melinda it was a small price to pay to have her husband and Lisa's father back, so life was good.

Lisa was growing up to be quite a winsome, precocious young lady. She had Melinda's blonde hair and blue-eyed, fashion model good looks, but she had Jack's temperament and flair for adventure. Lisa was close to becoming a teenager, and Jack knew that when she did, she would definitely be a handful. Plus, he knew that every hormone-ravaged teenage boy would be drooling over her, and he didn't want her ending up behind a "Men and Equipment At Work" sign. So what if it was a double standard. This was his little princess, and he'd be damned if she'd become the latest conquest of some pimple-faced high school would-be stud! Anyway, Jack was now around to make sure that Lisa was safe and sound, so life was good.

Then Melinda got a headache. It wasn't really a big headache as headaches go. Melinda had experienced much worse in the past, but they had all eventually subsided. This one lessened after a while, but it never really seemed to go away, and then it would come back stronger.

Melinda dealt with it and didn't say much. She was never one to complain. She just figured it was some form of migraine, so she treated it with over-the-counter medicine, and that gave her some relief.

After about six months, though, Melinda's headaches got worse. She went to the doctor, and she prescribed some Tylenol with codeine and a mild sedative to help her sleep. Melinda wasn't too keen on becoming dependent on medications to function, but it was the only way that she could continue being Melinda. She lived for Jack and Lisa, and she reveled in being able to provide a loving home environment for both of them. Lisa was getting older, and Melinda knew that one day soon her daughter would become a teenager and suddenly her friends would become the focus of her life, so she was not going to spend days in bed when she could be helping her daughter become a woman. Plus, despite all of Jack's physical and temperamental strength, Melinda knew that he relied on her to keep the home-front stable. He faced plenty of stress outside of the home without being subjected to it inside the home. She also wanted to be there for Jack as a lover. She knew that a strong and active love-life could heal a lot of wounds in a marriage, and her relationship with Jack was paramount in her life.

The new prescriptions helped considerably, so Melinda was able to maintain the status quo. She kept up with both Lisa and Jack with little or no break in her routine. She didn't even tell Jack about the headaches. Jack always fussed over her and tended to be overprotective. She figured that they were not a big concern, and she didn't want him worrying needlessly. However, the new-found relief only lasted for about six more months.

Then the gates of Hell burst open.

Melinda and Lisa were going to make dinner for the three of them. Jack was on his way back from Los Angeles, but he would be home in a couple of hours. Melinda used to wonder why Jack went to California or Arizona a couple times a month. He had explained to her that there were special poker tournaments being held that were quite lucrative. He was never gone overnight, and he always seemed to come home with several thousand dollars in winnings. What she lacked in poker knowledge she made up for it with Jack knowledge, and she trusted his commitment to his family, so she didn't press him.

Melinda and Lisa had gone to Albertson's to get the groceries necessary for dinner, but they debated on what to make. "Val, how about a nice pot roast with potatoes and carrots? We could put it in the crock pot with some onion soup mix. It would be easy and yummy, wouldn't it?"

"Mother," Lisa said, with a heavy emphasis on the last syllable and a pained look on her face. "That's soooo boring! We need something with some pizzazz!"

"Pizzazz? Since when did you start using words like pizzazz?" Melinda said with a chuckle.

"Since you started suggesting a meal of pot roast, potatoes, and carrots!"

"Okay, then what would you suggest?"

"I want Italian! How about manicotti or shells filled with cheese, grilled Italian sausage, and a big salad with some garlic bread?" Lisa purred with her hands together in a not-too-subtle prayer stance and a hopeful look on her face.

"Italian, huh? We could do Italian, but you need to help. I'm pretty tired, for some reason."

"Done! Yippee! Dad's gonna be so surprised!"

Melinda and Lisa found everything they needed and headed out to their SUV. It had been fun for Melinda to shop with Lisa and plan the dinner. She cherished these times when she and Lisa would just do girl things. It drew them closer the way Melinda had been close to her mom growing up.

Upon walking out of the store, Melinda suddenly got a screaming headache. She debated whether or not to go back into the store to get a bottle of water in order to take her pain medicine, but she decided to wait until she got home. They would be home soon enough, she thought.

On the way home, Melinda and Lisa were sitting at the traffic light on Rainbow Boulevard waiting to make a left turn onto Charleston Boulevard. They were chatting about that night's dinner and possibly going to a movie with Jack afterward. There were two left turn lanes, and Melinda was in the rightmost of the two lanes. When the light turned green, she proceeded into the intersection, but before she actually started to turn their big Lincoln Navigator to the left, Melinda suddenly lost the sight in her left eye. Everything in her line of sight to the left went black, and she felt as if the left side of her skull had become two sizes too small.

As Melinda was trying to wrap her head around her sudden blindness, there was a driver making a right turn onto Rainbow into the lane that Melinda was now about to enter, and the other driver was looking to the left for oncoming traffic instead of ahead at Melinda. The driver began to pull into the lane, but then stopped abruptly in mid-turn as he saw Melinda and realized that he was too late to make it. Panic-stricken, Melinda pulled too far to the left on the steering wheel to avoid what she thought would be a certain collision with the oncoming driver, but unable to see the car on her left that was turning with her, she struck that car on the passenger side sending it into the median.

Melinda's perception then decelerated the events into slow motion, and while she struggled to comprehend the implications of her partial blindness, she also struggled to maintain control of their lurching vehicle. As her right side vision began to tunnel down, she over-corrected to the right, and in her shock and confusion, she mistakenly slammed on the accelerator instead of the brake. Melinda and Lisa careened headlong over the sidewalk and into the steel structure supporting the traffic signals, bringing the Navigator to a violent stop. With what sounded like a shotgun blast, both airbags exploded into their faces. Groceries flew out of the second seat becoming unguided missiles hitting Melinda and Lisa from behind. A glass bottle of apple juice shattered upon striking Lisa's head, and she was rocked from consciousness.

While he was northbound on I-15 approaching Barstow, California, Jack got an urgent call from Melinda. "Jack! There's been an accident! We're in an accident! Oh my god! Aaah!" Melinda shrieked.

"Melinda! Slow down, honey. Are you okay? Is Val okay?"

"Aaah! Jack! She's not moving! Val's not moving! Oh my God! Oh my God! Oh my God!"

"Melinda! Melinda! Where are you? Are you in the Navigator?"

"Yes, we're in the Navigator! Jack! Val's not moving! What do I do, Jack? She's not moving!"

"Melinda, try to settle down a little. You're the one there. Call 911. Call 911, Melinda. I can't call them. You have to do it. C'mon, Melinda. Call 911, and then call me back. Hurry!"

After about five minutes, Melinda called Jack, again. He had been sweating bullets waiting for her call, and he was now on the other side of Barstow and driving twenty miles an hour faster. He figured if he got pulled over, he would just explain the situation to the patrolman, but if he didn't get caught, he could get there a lot sooner.

"Jack, I called 911. They're on their way. Oh, Jack, she's not moving," Melinda sobbed. "Melinda, is she breathing? Can you tell if she's breathing?"

"Yes! Yes, she is! Thank God! Oh, thank God! Jack, she's breathing! I can see her chest moving!"

"Okay, sweetheart. Are you okay? Are you hurt?"

"I don't know. I don't think so. It all happened so fast. The airbags came out. They stopped us," Melinda said and then started coughing.

In the background of the call, Jack could hear sirens, and it made him feel a little better. He wanted to be there so badly, but he was already doing over a hundred miles an hour. All he could do was drive fast and pray.

"Melinda? Melinda?"

"Yes, Jack."

"Melinda, hang up with me so that you can help the paramedics with Val. Help Val, Melinda. Then call me again when you find out which hospital they're going to take you to. Can you do that, sweetheart?"

"Yes, Jack. I'll call you. Oh God, Jack. Our little baby is hurt. It's all my fault. It's all my fault," and Melinda began sobbing, again.

"Melinda, it's okay. Everything's going to be okay. I'll be there as soon as I can. Just call me back when you know where you're going."

"Okay, Jack. I love you. Please hurry!"

"I love you, too, and I am. I'll see both of you soon."

Jack choked back tears as Melinda clicked off, and he was beside himself with anger that he was on the road instead of with them. All he could do now was drive.

Meanwhile, Melinda could hear the sirens of the paramedics coming toward her from her left, but she still couldn't see anything out of her left eye. She tried to wrench herself around to see, but she was still strapped in with her seat belt. The airbag had thrown white powder in her face, and she found it difficult to breathe.

Suddenly, Melinda's car door was jerked open. "Ma'am, we're here to help you. We need to get you out of the car. Are you hurt anywhere that you know of?"

"No. I mean, I hurt all over, but I don't think anything's serious, except I can't see out of my left eye. My left eye just blacked out on me while I was driving, but don't worry about me. My daughter there isn't moving, but I've seen her breathing. Help her, please!"

As Melinda was pleading with the first paramedic, a second paramedic opened Lisa's door. "Ma'am, what is her name?"

"Her name's Lisa. Is she okay?"

"Lisa? Can you hear me?" The paramedic was immobilizing Lisa's neck while she palpated her head. She soon discovered a large hematoma on the back of her head. As she did, Lisa began to moan and slowly open her eyes. "Lisa, can you hear me?" she repeated.

Lisa responded slowly, but she finally uttered, "Uh, huh."

"Lisa, you've been in an accident. I don't want you to move, just yet. We need to immobilize your head first. Can you feel your fingers and toes?"

"Uh, huh."

"Good. Okay, I'm going to put this brace around your neck. Just try to stay still, and we'll get you out of here, okay?"

"Uh, huh. Mom? Are you okay?"

"I'm here, honey. I'm okay. You do what they say. You're going to be alright. Thank God, you're going to be alright."

"Ma'am, we're going to get you out now. What's your name, ma'am?"

"Melinda Diamante."

"Okay, Melinda. I'm going to put this brace on your neck, as well, and then I'm going to help you out of the car. Then I'll help you lie down on the stretcher. Are you ready?" he said as he fastened the brace around Melinda's neck.

"Yes, but take care of my daughter. Please take care of her first."

"My partner is helping her onto another stretcher. I'm taking care of you, and then we'll get you to the hospital."

"Where are we going? What hospital?"

"We're taking you to Summerlin. It's the closest."

"Okay," Melinda said as she clutched her purse to her chest. As she was settling down onto the stretcher, she fished out her phone and speed-dialed Jack. "Jack? They're taking us to Summerlin Hospital. Val's awake. We're going together. I love you. Please hurry!" She put her phone back into her purse, and as she reclined on the stretcher, she closed her eyes and started to cry.

Once Jack found out the hospital where Melinda and Lisa were being taken, he immediately called Kiersten.

"Kiersten? This is Jack. Melinda and Lisa have been in an accident."

"What? Oh, Jack! Is it serious? Where are they?"

"I don't know how serious it is, but I know the paramedics are taking them to Summerlin Hospital."

"Okay, Summerlin. Are you on your way there?"

"I'm driving in from L.A. Right now, I'm between Barstow and Baker. I'm going to get there as fast as I can."

"Okay, I'll go to Summerlin and meet them. I know you're going to hurry, but drive safe. We don't need two accidents in one day."

"I will, and I'll see you there as soon as I can. Thanks, Kiersten!"

By the time Jack got back to Vegas and to the hospital, Melinda and Lisa were both out of the Emergency Room and had been admitted into the hospital. Lisa was in a regular room, and Kiersten was in the room with her. She had a concussion to go along with a big goose egg on the back of her head. She had some other bumps and bruises, but she would be fine. They were keeping her overnight for observation.

Melinda was another story, altogether. She was in the Intensive Care Unit. They had done a scan of her head to see if there was any bleeding or brain trauma from the crash. What they found was a tumor about the size of a tennis ball. The attending physician said he had called in a neurosurgeon to consult on the findings, and that he would be able to answer Jack's questions after the consultation.

Jack stayed by Melinda's bedside talking with her and holding her hand. The only times he left her were when he went to go check on Lisa. Hospital policy wouldn't allow them to be in the same room, so Jack would trudge up two floors of stairs to be with Lisa while Melinda was sleeping. Kiersten would go down to Intensive Care to be with Melinda. Once Jack was sure that Lisa was okay, he and Kiersten would switch places so he could sit next to Melinda.

It was during this dual vigil that Jack met with the neurosurgeon. He was anxious to hear what the doctor had to say, but it wasn't the news he was expecting.

"Are you Mr. Diamante?"

"Yes."

"I'm Doctor Cavanaugh. I'm the neurosurgeon consulting on your wife's case. Have you got a few moments?"

"Yes, of course. How's my wife? How's Melinda? Is she going to be alright?"

"Let's sit down over here."

Jack didn't like that. All he needed to hear was a simple, "Yes, she'll be fine." You can stand up to hear that. Sitting down meant bad news.

"Mr. Diamante, I have looked at the scans and spoken with your wife. Based on what I see and what I hear, I'm

95% certain that she has what is called a glioblastoma multiforme tumor. It is located in her brain, and that is what caused her to lose the sight in her left eye. I'm also sure it is the cause of her headaches this past year. Her vision is actually starting to come back slowly, but that will be a transient condition."

"So, what do you do? You can operate and take it out or put her on chemotherapy or something, right?"

"Unfortunately, this type of tumor is completely resistant to chemotherapy. It is notoriously fast growing and lethally resistant to any type of treatment. As far as surgery is concerned, that might have been an option had we detected it sooner. If we were to operate now, there's a very good chance that she would not survive the surgery. Even if she did make it through the surgery, we wouldn't be able to get enough of the tumor out to even slow the progress. The average patient with this type of tumor can sometimes survive for up to twelve months, but your wife's tumor is advanced. She most likely only has two to four months to live. I'm afraid that all we can hope to do now is keep her pain under control and give her anticonvulsants to try to control the seizures that will inevitably take place. Your wife is very sick, Mr. Diamante. Do you understand what I'm telling you?"

"It sounds like you're giving up on her! My wife is a fighter! She can pull through! You said you were only 95% sure it was this blastoma thing. You could be wrong!"

"You're welcome to get another opinion, Mr. Diamante, however, I've seen many of these tumors, and I think you need to start thinking about how to get her affairs in order. You're likely to only have her for a short while longer."

Tears began to well up in Jack's eyes. His vision blurred and his quickly swelling eyes began to sting, but nothing compared to the pain of the dagger that had been plunged deep into his heart and soul. It was gut-wrenching. He felt like screaming, crying, and vomiting simultaneously. The walls seemed to close in on top of him, and "two to four months" kept echoing in his head like a monster reverb. How could this be happening? He had turned things around. He was being a good husband and father. Wasn't life supposed to be good now?

"What about my daughter?" Jack stammered.

"Your daughter will be fine. She took a pretty good crack to the head, but she should be up and around by tomorrow."

"Does she know? About her mother, I mean. Does she know?"

"No. I've only told you. I think she should hear this news from someone she loves."

9

Lisa screamed at the top of her lungs. She screamed so loud that her head began to pound. Two nurses came rushing in expecting to see blood flying around the room. When they asked what had happened, all Jack could say is, "Her mother is dying."

Jack had told Kiersten before going into Lisa's room. Kiersten stood dumbstruck and then she had to be helped to a chair in the waiting area. She had a million questions, but Jack had no answers. When Jack steeled himself to go tell Lisa the news, Kiersten made her way down to be with Melinda.

As Lisa wailed and shook from sobbing, Jack had no words of comfort for her. He was as lost as she was. All he knew to do was hold her, but she didn't want to be held. She wanted to fight and lash out at everyone and everything. Lisa had to be sedated just to keep her in the bed. Her mother was dying, and it wasn't fair. She was fourteen years old, and it just wasn't fair.

When Lisa was discharged the next day, Kiersten took her home. She picked up some of Lisa's clothes and belongings so that she could stay with Kiersten at her house while Jack attended to Melinda and talked further with the doctors. However, further discussions with the doctors didn't change the diagnosis at all.

Trying to be a good husband and father, Jack was pulled back and forth between the hospital and home. He wanted to be by Melinda's side, but Lisa needed him, too. He let her skip school the whole next week, but eventually she had to go back. There were meals to prepare, loads of laundry to wash, bills to pay, and transportation to provide. On top of that, Lisa was becoming increasingly tougher to oversee. Kiersten temporarily moved into Jack's and Melinda's spare bedroom to help with Lisa and the house, but Jack continually had to deal with Lisa's outbursts and tantrums. She made life an absolute hell on everyone, yet no one could blame her. Her mother was dying.

Compounding all of this was the fact that Jack was slowly running out of money as the weeks became a month. The costs of living continued uninterrupted, but he hadn't been able to play poker or make any deliveries for Jesse. On top of that, Jack knew that the medical bills were mounting, and his medical insurance was almost non-existent, so he was using his poker stake to keep the medical bills in check. There is no poker players union to provide medical benefits.

Jack decided that he had to start bringing in cash, so he'd make whatever runs he could for Jesse, and he played poker late at night when he knew Melinda would be asleep. He'd finish at about three or four in the morning and go to the hospital. He'd stay with Melinda until about six o'clock, and then he'd go home to take Lisa to school. Once she was in school, Jack would try to get some sleep until it was time to pick up Lisa. Together they would go see Melinda.

Jack would take Lisa home around seven to get dinner, do homework, and eventually go to bed. Jack would return to Melinda at about ten o'clock and then leave at eleven to go play poker and start the whole merry-go-round again. Unfortunately, this was a different carnival, and the rides were more expensive. Jack didn't make a run for Jesse during the first month. In addition, his poker playing suffered significantly, because his mind was usually with Melinda while his body was at the poker table. That scenario meant that his money was often in someone else's pocket.

After six weeks in the hospital, Melinda was moved to a hospice facility. This made visiting tougher on Jack, because it was ten miles farther away from the house than the hospital. The financial pressure also continued to mount as the bills started to fill his mailbox. Jack kept up his visitation routine, though, but now he was playing poker every night, and he upped his errands for Jesse to almost one a week. This was a blessing and a curse. He was able to make more money from Jesse, and his poker playing improved with greater focus, but he wasn't able to spend as much time with Melinda and Lisa as he wanted. He was between a rock and a hard place with no wiggle room.

One afternoon, after about a month of this routine, Jack got a call from Melinda. This wasn't unusual. Melinda would call from time to time when she was awake and Jack wasn't there. This time, though, her voice sounded unusually weak, and she asked Jack to bring her wedding rings when he came later. The hospital had given them to Jack for safe keeping the first night that Melinda was in the hospital.

When Jack got to her room, all of the lights had been turned off except the standing lamp next to her bed, and it seemed to direct all of its energy like a spotlight toward Melinda. The vertical blinds were swaying gently back and forth with the breeze of the air conditioning, and it struck Jack that they looked like mourners silently filing by a casket. The vision made him shudder as he approached her, and he was shocked at how feeble she looked. He had seen her the day before, and while she had been in a steady decline, he had never seen her change so dramatically in one day. She had a faint smile on her face from seeing Jack, but it looked as though she was giving in.

"Hey there," he said. "How's my sweetheart?"

"Hi, Jack," she said dreamily. "Did you bring my rings?"

"Of course. They're right here."

Melinda took the rings in her right hand. She took the small wedding ring, put it on her left ring finger and smiled. She gazed at it for a long time, and Jack was thinking it was the first time he had ever really seen it sparkle. Melinda then took the second ring that Jack had given to her. She held it between her right thumb and forefinger and lifted it up so that the light hit it. It lit up the darkened room, and Melinda smiled, again.

"You know, Jack, I never really realized just how beautiful this ring is until just now. It's a very special ring, Jack. Thank you."

"Oh, sweetie, it's nowhere near as special as you."

"I love you so much, Jack."

"I love you, too. So, so much."

"Jack, will you promise me something?"

"Of course. You want me to bring you something?"

"No. I want you to do something for me. Will you?"

"You know I will. What would you like me to do?"

"Take this special ring that you gave to me. I want you to hold on to it. One day Val is going to need it."

"What do you mean? You want me to save it for her wedding?"

"No. I don't know. Maybe. I just know that one day she'll need it. You'll know when that is."

"Okay. Anything you want."

"Jack, promise me you'll keep it for Val."

"I promise."

With that, Melinda smiled and placed the ring in Jack's hand. She pressed it into his palm, and he closed his hand around hers. He couldn't help noticing how small and dainty her hand was, and he remembered the first time he had held her hand and how wonderful he felt. He didn't feel wonderful now. How he wished he could take her back to high school or when Lisa was born. He wanted to take her back someplace peaceful and happy where nobody thought about dying.

He held her hand as she fell asleep, and his heart broke. The love of his life, the woman he wanted to live with for eternity, was slipping away, and there wasn't a damned thing he could do to stop it! Tears streamed down his face as he gazed at her. Through bloodshot eyes he could see the light dance off of her lustrous, long blonde hair giving her an almost angelic glow, and he kissed each of her eyes one last time.

Jack stayed by her bedside silently holding her hand. If she was going to go tonight, he thought, she wasn't going to go alone. She was going to know on some level of consciousness that she was loved to the end. Jack also made a conscious effort to only think about happy memories. He wanted her room to permeate with nothing but love and happiness. It absolutely wouldn't do in Jack's book to let such a radiant soul pass into eternity shrouded in sorrow, anger, or fear, so he thought about the first time he had seen her in high school. She had a deep tan from a summer at the beach, and he had marveled at the contrast between her bronzed skin and her long, snowy blonde hair. She always lit up any room that she walked into, and people would literally stop and stare at her in awe. He remembered their wedding and how proud he was when the minister announced them as Mr. and Mrs. Jonathan Diamante. He also remembered the day that Lisa was born and the look of rapture and pride on Melinda's face when they handed Lisa to her to hold. He thought about how he could always make her laugh, and he loved to make her laugh, because her face became absolutely seraphic.

As she slept, he saw her smile ever so slightly, and he figured she must be dreaming. He hoped she was dreaming good dreams about ocean waves lapping at her feet or the sunset in her face. She always loved sunsets, he thought. She used to say that they made her happy, because it meant the day had come to a peaceful end.

That night, Melinda came to a peaceful end, and the angels claimed one of their own.

THE TURN

IO

Melinda was buried on a Wednesday, and Jack took up residence in a liquor bottle by Wednesday night.

Tequila became Jack's painkiller of choice, although, in a pinch, Jack would drink anything that was at least eighty proof. He drank it straight from a bottle or a glass. Hell, he'd drink it out of a dead man's skull if it meant that he didn't have to feel the pain in his heart.

Ol' reliable Jack became "Where's Jack?" Jesse stopped giving him errands, because too often Jack would take a detour all the way to the bottom of a bottle. While Jesse sympathized with his friend, he was primarily a businessman, and it would be *very* bad for business to lose one of his shipments. Luckily, that hadn't happened, yet. Jesse had always found Jack when he didn't make his appointment, and there were no losses. Yet. But Jesse couldn't take that chance, so Jack was eventually cut out of the loop.

Life on the home front was even worse. Lisa and Jack fought all of the time. If he was drunk, she berated him for that. If he was sober, she'd pick something else. Her favorite topic to scream about was how he had been gone when they had the accident and how he had abandoned her mother in the months leading up to her death to go play poker. Their arguments usually ended with Lisa screaming, "You didn't even care! You just let her die!"

At first, she didn't really believe it. She had seen him too many times at Melinda's bedside, and she knew he had been there to the end. It was just a convenient way for her to lash out in her grief, but as with any lie, if you say it often enough, it becomes the truth.

Lisa eventually went to live with Kiersten. Jack really didn't want her to go, but he knew they couldn't keep clawing at each other's throats. Each one reminded the other of their loss and pain. Lisa would look at her shell of a dad, and she would scream. Jack would look at Lisa, who every day looked more and more like Melinda, and he would drink. It was a powder-keg soaked in gasoline just waiting for anyone to strike a spark.

Financially, Jack was spiraling down, too. He wasn't playing poker much anymore, and when he did, he usually lost. It was mostly just an excuse to get away from Lisa and drink for free.

Without Jesse's errands, Jack was forced to dip into the money he had received from the sale of Diamond Locksmith and Security. He and Melinda had set it aside for eventual retirement, but Jack figured there would be no retirement without Melinda, so what the hell.

Then the medical bills came due. It was like adding a cruel insult to injury. Jack had put them off as long as he could, but eventually he had to sell the house and anything else that wasn't tied down. He emerged from it all with about eight thousand dollars, a seven-year-old Buick, and Melinda's ring.

The day Jack signed the closing papers on his home was a particularly painful one. He and Melinda had picked it out together. She had furnished and decorated it and really made it a home. To see it used to pay debts seemed to be the final insulting blow to his reeling, alcohol-slogged mind.

Jack left the escrow office, went straight to a liquor store, and bought four bottles of Patron. He had decided to drink himself to death, so he went back to the motel room that he had rented for the week on Las Vegas Boulevard North, not far from the Cashman Field complex where he had watched the Helldorado rodeos sitting on cement bleachers as a kid. He had considered going to the Par A Dice, but he didn't want to see Lauren or anyone else he might know that might try to talk him out of his mission. This motel was about three notches below a dive, so he hadn't spent much on the room. It was pretty dilapidated, and what little bit of furniture and fixtures were there looked like they dated back to the Civil War.

As he came into the room, he put everything he was carrying next to the television on the small desk in front of the bed. He absentmindedly turned the television on, and the evening news began to fill the small room. Jack went into the bathroom to get one of the plastic cups, and once he got the wrapper off, he began to drown himself in the nectar of the blue agave. He sat on the bed and gulped shot after shot out of the plastic cup. Then he started completely filling the cup and drinking it until the cup was drained. The last thing that Jack remembered before he passed out was the news anchor saying that a couple had died in a home invasion robbery. Jack figured he would be joining them soon on a cold slab in the morgue.

Jack awoke in a stupor about seven hours later, and he struggled to sit up on the bed as he tried to remember where he was. The bedspread had been thrown from the bed, and the sodden sheets had him tied in a knot from his thrashing around as he fought his demons. He had finished the first two bottles of Patron and started on the third before he had passed out, but he had been sitting up at the head of the bed watching the television while he drank. Now his head was at the foot of the bed. Jack figured it was time to put the last nail in his coffin when he happened to look at the desk top in front of him. Through bleary eyes he tried to focus on the objects resting on the desk. Lying next to the escrow papers, the check, the last full bottle of tequila, and his car keys … was Melinda's ring. It sparkled even in the dim light of his low rent suicide chamber.

As he looked at the ring, he heard Melinda's voice in his head through the haze of tequila saying, "Take this special ring that you gave me. I want you to hold on to it. One day Val is going to need it."

Jack doubled over in anguish at the memory of that last night with Melinda. He remembered how she had looked up at him and smiled before she closed her eyes for the last time. His cheeks suddenly became slick with tears as he lowered his head into his hands with an anguished grimace on his face. He felt a pain as if he were being eviscerated right there on the sweat and tequila-soaked sheets. "Melinda," his mind screamed, "I can't go on without you. I just can't!"

As clear as if Melinda were standing right in front of him holding his head in her hands, he heard her soft voice say, "Jack, promise me you'll keep it for Val."

Jack wanted to cry out, "I can't do it! I only want to be with you, Melinda. Please let me be with you!" He wanted to end, once and for all, the excruciating agony of losing Melinda, but in a voice that was drowning under the enormous waves of hundreds of gallons of tequila and his last few drops of tears, Jack heard himself say, "I promise." He had no choice but to honor Melinda's last request. He had promised her then, and he promised her now. Then, as the

Vegas sunrise began to peek through the tattered blinds, Jack passed out again on the bed.

II

Jack woke up lying face down on the cold tile bathroom floor. He looked up to see the underside of the plumbing leading to the sink. The bathroom reeked of tequila and what seemed like the rancid smell of Parmesan cheese that has been left someplace hot and dank. Jack pulled himself up on the side of the tub, but then his left hand slipped on something wet and textured. He looked at his hand, sniffed it, made a grotesque face, and shook his head. Somehow, in a semi-conscious state, he had crawled into the bathroom and vomited in the tub.

Jack looked around to get his bearings and noticed splatters of blood on the tile and on the side of the bathtub. He looked down and noticed that his right hand was cut between his middle and ring fingers, but he had no clue how it had happened. His clothes were soaked in sweat and vomit, and he felt as if his insides had been scoured out with drain cleaner and a wire brush.

He looked at his watch for the date and time and realized he had no memory of the previous eighteen hours, but he was alive. Somehow by the grace or animus of God, he was still alive, and if he was alive, it had to be due to his promise to Melinda. He didn't know how he was going to do it, but he had made the same promise to her twice, and he just knew that his soul would be damned for all eternity if he couldn't find some way to stay alive and keep that promise.

From that day on, Jack had a purpose, and he knew he had to be sober, or it would never be fulfilled. He vowed to do everything in his power to keep his promise to Melinda. He would keep the ring safe until his daughter needed it. After that, he affirmed, all bets were off. His sobriety and the necessity of breathing would be renegotiated.

Jack also made a decision about himself. He would go back to playing poker the *right* way. No more drunken all-nighters at the poker table just to wind up paying about fifty-dollars each for "free" drinks. No more playing without a purpose. He was not going to give his money away anymore.

Consequently, he went to the bank and put Melinda's ring and $5,000 in a safe deposit box. The money would be used to stake his comeback when he felt he was ready. The balance would be used for operating expenses in his new start.

However, until he got his mojo back on the poker table, Jack needed income, so he decided to try going back to Jesse to see if he could get his old job back. After about a week to get himself dried out and back on his hind legs, Jack scrounged up his cleanest dirty shirt and headed over to Jesse's house.

When he pulled up to the house, Jack pushed the intercom button at the gate, and a female voice came on, "If you have a delivery, just leave it in the box by the intercom."

"It's not a delivery, ma'am. It's Jack Diamante to see Jesse. I don't have an appointment, but he knows me."

After about fifteen seconds, the gate opened, and Jack drove up to the front entrance. As he did, he marveled at the grounds. Jesse had upgraded his digs from the last time Jack had been there. The lawn and shrubs were meticulously manicured, and there were more bushes and trees. It looked more like a jungle than a part of the desert. The house sported new paint, and what just used to be a circular driveway passing by the front door was now a grand entrance complete with a Spanish style porte-cochere. Jack thought to himself that the self-serve car wash business must be booming. A lot of quarters obviously went into putting a shine on this place. Jack also noted a new security system that would've made the CIA jealous. He watched motion sensitive cameras track his every move, and he wondered why the owner of car washes needed that much security. Jack just chalked it up to Vegas paranoia.

Before he could knock on the door, a very pretty Asian girl with long, dark silky hair opened it and ushered Jack inside. The girl was about half a foot shorter than Jack. She had very delicate features, and she looked to be about eighteen or nineteen years old. As she led the way through the house, Jack couldn't help but notice that the mid-thigh length sheer white negligee that she wore left nothing to the imagination. Her tiny hips rolled back and forth, and her straight raven hair hung down past her waist and swept behind her as she padded along the Spanish-tile floor in bare feet.

When they reached the sliding glass door to the back veranda, Jack could see a huge kidney-shaped pool with a diving board at the far end and a large built-in jacuzzi beside it. These were new additions that had been installed subsequent to Jack working for Jesse. The jacuzzi looked like it would comfortably accommodate ten to twelve people, depending on how familiar they wanted to get with each other. As they walked outside, Jack was momentarily blinded by the sharp glint of sunlight reflected off all of the expensive liquor bottles installed on a portable bar setting next to the jacuzzi.

Jesse was lounging in the bubbling water with three women: blonde, brunette, and redhead with Jesse ensconced in the middle of them. As Jack and the Asian girl neared the jacuzzi, she slipped off her negligee, laid it across one of the wicker chairs, and then she held up her hair as she stepped nude into the bubbling water. As Jack took a seat in a wicker chair at a sunbrella-equipped table next to the jacuzzi, he noticed that all of the women were nude and quite young. The brunette and redhead both had their hair swept up and pinned on top of their heads in curls, and appeared to have barely reached the cusp of legality. The blonde's hair was long and wet, and it clung to her ample chest. It looked like she had emerged from under the water recently. She also looked like she was only sixteen or seventeen, and he shuddered when he thought about Lisa being that age. The brunette and redhead were massaging Jesse's shoulders, and the blonde seemed to be massaging something under the water.

"Jack, boy! How the hell ya doin'? Shuck your clothes and climb on in! We've got room for my ol' buddy Diamond Jack, don't we girls?"

Almost on cue and in unison, they all chimed, "We sure do!"

"Thanks, Jesse, but I came to talk a little business. I'm afraid if I climbed in that water, I might forget why I was here and what I was doing."

"Well hell, Jack, isn't that the point!" and Jesse laughed. Jesse held up a cocktail and said, "Would you like a drink, Jack? Deidre, go get Jack a drink. Tequila, right Jack?" The brunette stood up, and Jack almost swallowed his tongue as he watched the water run down and around her curvaceous physique.

"No, uh, no thanks, Jesse. In fact, that's part of the reason I'm here. I've pretty much been on a bender these last couple of years since Melinda died. During that time, I was no good to you, myself, or anybody else, for that matter. However, I'm getting back in the saddle, and I know you don't owe me anything, but I need work, and I was hoping you could use me."

"Well, sure, Jack. You know I can always use good people I can trust. I can trust you, right Jack? I mean, you were quite a mess there for a while."

"I know I was, but ya, you can trust me. I'll be honest, though, Jesse. I'm not the same as I was before Melinda died. I've been a little rattled, lately, but I won't let you down. I've let too many people down for well over a year, but that me is gone. I don't want to let anyone down, again."

"All right, Jack, then come back by here next Thursday. I've got something that might be up your alley. Come about ten in the morning, and we'll talk some business. Are you sure you don't want a massage, Jack? Sissy here always tells me a story when she gives me a massage, and her stories always have a happy ending," Jesse said with a grin and a gleam in his eye.

"No, no thanks on the massage, but thank you for the work. You won't regret it."

"Okay, Jack, but you *really* don't know what you're missing! Say goodbye to Jack, girls."

Again, on cue, "Bye bye, Jack!"

Jack made his way back to the sliding glass door, and in its reflection, he caught one last glimpse of the depravity going on in Jesse's back yard. It reminded him of the chasm that had ruptured between who Jack was and who he used to be. Jack knew there would be no going back. The sight of that young blonde girl in the jacuzzi splattered a vision in his mind of Lisa in a similarly seductive ambiance, and he swore that he would do everything in his power to ensure that it never became reality.

However, Jack was pleased that Jesse was so receptive and validating of Jack's return to the human race. He felt that working for Jesse and earning some money would help him right his derelict of a ship.

If only Jack's reconciliation afterwards with Lisa had gone as well. Kiersten was supportive and glad to see that Jack appeared to be on the right road, again, but Lisa was having none of it. She blamed Jack for everything, and she wanted him to suffer as much as possible.

Jack had been an absentee father for about two of the most critical years in Lisa's life. He almost quit before he started when Lisa launched into a blistering tirade as he stood in the foyer of Kiersten's house.

"You don't belong here!" Lisa screamed as she came rushing at Jack when Kiersten ushered him inside her home. "You're not my father anymore! Grandma Rose, don't let him in here!"

Wracked with guilt, Jack lowered his head and said, "Maybe I should go. This might not have been such a good idea. I'm sorry, Kiersten."

"That's right! You're sorry, alright! You're the sorriest excuse for a father I've ever seen!" Lisa was shaking as she screeched out her abuse.

"Now that's enough, young lady. This is *my* home, and I'll invite in whomever I damn well please. Jack, you stay. We need to talk. Lisa, as for you, you can stay and listen or you can go to your room, but you will respect my home. There will be no more screaming," Kiersten said with a look lasered at Lisa that said she meant business.

"Bastard!" Lisa mumbled as she ran off to her room.

Jack's head drooped, and he shook his head as he stood there looking at his feet. With a weary resignation he said, "Kiersten, I don't want to cause trouble. I really probably should go."

"Nonsense, Jack. There's been nothing BUT trouble ever since Melinda died, and it got worse when you checked out. Come sit at the kitchen table for a minute. You want some coffee or something?"

Jack said, "Maybe just a glass of ice water, if you don't mind," as he shuffled into the kitchen.

Returning with the water and sitting down next to Jack, Kiersten said, "Jack, I have tried to stand in the gap between you and your daughter, my granddaughter. I have done my best, but that little girl, and she is still a little girl, Jack, that little girl desperately needs her father, and she needs all of you, not just what the alcohol leaves behind. Do you catch my drift?"

"I do, and I swear on Melinda that I've quit that life."

"You can't swear on Melinda, Jack. She's gone. God has her now. Not you. You need to swear on Lisa's life, because that's who you have left, and it's her life that weighs in the balance. If you fail now, I don't know which way that child will go. She has so much pain bottled up, and you're going to feel the brunt of it, but it's time for you to stand up and take it. Otherwise, she'll find another way to deal with it. Drugs, sex, suicide, who knows what she's liable to cling to, but none of it is good, and all of it wants to claim her body and soul."

"I hear you, Kiersten. That's the way I want it. I really do. I don't know if we'll ever have a father/daughter relationship again, but if it's possible, I'll make it happen. I owe that to her. I owe that to Melinda."

"Jack, you owe that to yourself, too. You and Lisa need each other, now more than ever. When you married my daughter, I was convinced that you were no good for her, but all the time you were married I saw how much you loved her, and I came to love you, too. You're like a son to me, and I hated to see you hurt the way you did when Melinda died. We all hurt. I lost my only daughter, but you and Lisa lost the glue that was holding your family together, and you two fell apart when you didn't cling to each other. You need to cling to each other now, but she won't cling to you, so you have to hold on tight enough for both of you. I'll do what I can to promote you to her, but you've got to be everything she needs and more. Be her father and love her unconditionally, even when she hates you back. The truth is she doesn't hate you. She just thinks she does, and the love switch will click on if you're there for her when she needs you and if you don't give up. Don't give up on her, Jack."

Jack stood up from his chair and straightened like he was taking an oath. "I won't. I swear I won't. Thanks, Kiersten. Lisa and I owe you big time!"

"No, you don't," Kiersten said while rising. "That's what family is for. You're all the family I have left, and I'll be damned if I'm going to give either one of you up," Kiersten said as she gave Jack a hug. "You and I need to stay in touch more, and we'll work on this together."

"You've got it, and thanks, again. For everything."

Jack left Kiersten's house with a new hope that things would work out. However, if he was going to *really* have any chance at turning things around, Jack's focus now had to be on getting his mind back into poker shape. Poker would allow him to be self-sufficient, and he desperately needed that. If he was going to climb all the way back up the mountain, he would have to be able to support himself without being involved with Jesse. Something nagged at the back of Jack's mind telling him that Jesse was bent more crooked than before, and Jack really shouldn't be part of it. For right now, though, he ignored it, and he told himself that he needed Jesse's help to resurrect himself. He was grateful that his life seemed to be headed in the right direction.

Unfortunately, he hadn't used his moral compass in so long that he couldn't tell when it was pointing south.

12

Jack eased back into playing poker with small-stakes, easy games and no monumental wins or losses. There were poker tournaments running all over town 24/7. Jack loved playing in cash games against players that had just picked up a couple thousand dollars in a tournament. It was like shooting fish in a barrel.

Tournament players were impatient. That's the nature of tournaments. There is a time limit to each level of required blind bets that players must regularly make. As each time limit expires, the blind bets escalate and force the players to make plays against the odds as their chip stacks dwindle. In a cash game, there is no clock ticking. You play with the odds, and you capitalize on the other players that play against the odds. Through the bad beats and suck-outs, Jack stayed consistent, and he started winning again. Nothing major, mind you, but he was winning and getting the old rhythm back. As his head continued to clear, he began to read the players like he was reading his favorite book.

The more Jack played, the more he slid into the rhythm of the night owls. Las Vegas is, and always has been, a three-shift town, and it caters to the night owls. Those are the people that make their living in Vegas between 10:00 p.m. and 6:00 a.m. Not only are the hotels, strip clubs, bars, restaurants, gas stations, and grocery stores open 24/7, but so are dry cleaners, liquor stores, florist shops, pharmacies, pizza delivery, you name it. If you want anything, you can probably get it 24/7 in Vegas.

Like all of the other night owls, Jack would hang out after playing poker in one of the many restaurants or bars that catered to the third shift workers: places like the Peppermill, Bootlegger, Port Tack, and Starboard Tack. These places were always open, and they offered breakfast, lunch, dinner, and drinks at any time of the day. The night owls would get off around 6:00 a.m. and go eat dinner or have cocktails the way nine-to-fivers did around six or seven in the evening.

All of these places were relatively dark inside with few if any windows. It kept the illusion that normal nocturnal activities, both casual and carnal, were still being conducted at night rather than after the sun had risen. While the nine-to-fivers were preparing to start their work day and getting kids ready for school, the night owls were drinking away a bad night at work or performing various mating rituals with varying degrees of success.

It was in this upside-down adult petting zoo that Jack met Abigail "Abbie" Duncara. Abbie was a poker dealer at the Golden Nugget. Like just about everyone else that Jack met these days, they met at a poker table on the graveyard shift. She was dealing, and Jack was playing. Jack noticed her right away. She was hard to miss with long flowing auburn locks that usually bounced down her back in loose curls, wispy bangs that swept down into and around her eyes, a dash of freckles across her nose and cheeks, the greenest of eyes, and exquisite curves in all the right places. She was a stunning woman that looked more like twenty-six rather than her age of thirty-six.

What captivated Jack most of all was her warm Southern charm. Abbie hailed from Savannah, Georgia, and like all true Southern belles, she drew out every syllable of every word. Single syllable words became two syllable emotions. Whereas another woman would say, "I like it here," Abbie would slowly drawl, "Ah like it he-uh." The words would drip with honey and bourbon and sounded like an auditory wet dream to Jack.

Abbie had gone to the University of Georgia to get her Mrs. Degree, and she had found what she thought was suitable husband material in her junior year. He was in law school at UGA while she was getting her undergraduate degree in Art History. They graduated the same year and got married in June after graduation. He accepted a position with a big law firm in Atlanta, and they settled into married life. Unfortunately, as Abbie would later explain to the judge presiding over their divorce, "That boy never could keep his pecker in his pants." Numerous affairs with interns and other lawyers doomed their marriage. The marriage lasted six years, but it was never really viable from day one.

After her divorce, Abbie discovered that a bachelor's degree in Art History qualified her for a position as a culinary delivery engineer, a group visual-reverie performance artist, or adult hospitality and service consultant. In other words, she could be a waitress, stripper, or call girl. She chose waitress, but after a year of hand-to-hand combat with customers, cooks, and management, she decided a change was in order.

She and her girlfriends had taken a trip to Vegas right after her divorce was final, and it had captivated her. She had been banking her alimony and decided to use it to stake a move.

When she got to Vegas, she quickly decided that she didn't want to continue waitressing, so she signed up at a school for poker dealers and started a new life. Her new career as a poker dealer had all of the advantages of waitressing with none of the disadvantages. She got to meet new people all the time, had a non-smoking environment in the poker room, wasn't constantly cleaning food stains off her uniform, and nobody pawed her in the poker room like they did the cocktail waitresses. All in all, she enjoyed living and working in Las Vegas.

The only wrinkle to Vegas for her was that her father had ties to organized crime when he was alive. He had actually been an enforcer for the Gambino crime family back East. This created some interesting circumstances for Abbie. She had been sheltered by her mother away from that life after her parents had split up when she was twelve years old, but anyone that knew her through her father knew to keep their hands off. Consequently, she could sometimes make certain inquiries through people she had met on her father's side of the fence. In turn, she would pass on information of interest to those same people anytime she came across it. It was an arrangement that blossomed in the shady realms of Vegas.

Jack and Abbie had become good friends over the last nine months. Jack felt like he could talk to Abbie about anything and often had. They were close but not intimate, although, it was not for a lack of Abbie being receptive. Jack just wasn't ready for that type of relationship. However, he dearly loved Abbie's company and loved to talk to her. He especially liked when she'd had a drink or two and she pronounced his name "Jayack, hun." He was also Jayack, hun, when she was concerned about him. When she said it, it sounded like doves cooing to Jack.

Being with Abbie was comforting, but it also made him miss Melinda.

After a long night of poker, Jack and Abbie had made their way to the Bootlegger and were watching the morning news over drinks. She was drinking Southern Comfort and Coke, and he had a Sprite. Jack hadn't quit drinking completely, but he had severely curtailed it, especially if he was going to see Lisa later. They were sitting at the bar leaning on the video poker machines, but neither one was playing, and they had drifted into a quiescent silence until Abbie spoke up.

"Jack, hun, where are you? You've got this dreamy look in your eyes. You look peaceful, but sad, too. Was it somethin' I said?"

"No, Abbie, I'm sorry. My mind just floated back to another time. It seems like another life, now. I really apologize. I'm sitting here with a beautiful woman and a good friend, and I wind up thinking of my late wife."

"No apology necessary, Jack. I'm not here to compete with her. I know you loved her very much, and I wouldn't dare try to tell you to forget her. You shouldn't. You have a daughter that didn't know her as well as you, and she deserves to know her momma. I'm just wonderin' if there might be room in that dream for me, too, Jack, hun."

"You are, Abbie. You are. Frankly, you've been a much better friend to me than I deserve." Jack was going to say something else, but the news anchor caught his attention.

"Our top story this morning, the death toll attributed to the home invasion robbers, dubbed the High Society Gang, now climbs to seven as another husband and wife were tortured, murdered, and robbed last evening. Their bodies were discovered bound in chairs in their home by a family member last evening. Metro Police Department officials are not saying if they have any leads or if they are close to catching the gang which is now believed to be responsible for eight robberies along with the seven murders. All have been home invasion type robberies of wealthy families. All of the victims have been tortured and robbed, but it is unclear at this time if the murders were intentional or a byproduct of the torture going too far. Metro officials are urging everyone to lock their doors and refuse entry to anyone they do not know."

Jack turned from the television. "Two more people murdered by home invaders. What the hell is this place coming to?"

"I don't know, hun, but I do know that it's got all the bigwigs down at the Nugget spooked real good." Abbie stood up and turned to Jack, "I'm fixin' to head home, Jack. I know you probably haven't had a good home-cooked meal in quite some time. How 'bout you come over and let me fix you some breakfast? I make a mean omelet," she said with a wink.

"I appreciate it, but I've got to take a rain check on that. I have some business I have to take care of before I meet my daughter for lunch. We're actually starting to be able to communicate without clawing each other's eyes out."

"All right, Jack, but this isn't the first rain check you've asked for, and you know it never rains here in Vegas but once in a blue moon. If I have to wait till it rains to get you to come over, I'm liable to just dry up and blow away!" she said with a grin.

Jack laughed. "Now I certainly wouldn't want that! I promise to cash in these rain checks sometime soon. Maybe I'll invite you over, and I'll cook for you."

"Oh, lordy! This I've gotta see! Jack Diamante with an apron on! Be still my heart!" Abbie said as she fanned her face and pretended to faint with a grin on her face.

"Hey, don't laugh. I'm a pretty good cook when I'm properly motivated!"

"Well, you tell me the proper motivation, and I'll pony up," she said with a nod of her head.

Jack chuckled and said, "Okay, you've got a deal."

"Well, okay, Jack, hun. Ya'll take care."

"You too, Abbie."

Jack stood up and embraced her tightly, almost like he was holding on for dear life. He breathed in deeply swelling his chest and pressing in closer to Abbie. He loved the smell of her hair and the way her silky auburn tresses soothed his face. Her curves seemed to melt into his chest and arms, and it felt so natural. Then he smelled it. Honeysuckle. At first, he thought it was his imagination playing a cruel trick on him, but no, it was honeysuckle, and for some reason it didn't seem odd or out of place. It just was, and it was just right.

Jack cocked his head a little to the right and nuzzled his nose into her hair and close to her neck. When he felt his jeans begin to get a little taut, he suddenly realized he'd been holding Abbie a little too long and a little too tight. He grinned sheepishly and blushed as he released her. "I'm sorry, Abbie. I guess I just lost myself for a minute there."

"Jack, hun, you can lose yourself in my arms anytime you like, and I'll hold you as long as you hold me."

Jack blushed, again, and chortled, "I'll remember that."

"You see that you do, Jack, hun," Abbie said with a sly grin and a wink.

With that, the two night owls flew their separate ways into the glare of the Vegas morning sun.

13

Jack pulled into the convenience store to get some gas. As he walked away from the pumps and toward the store entrance, he looked up into the clear blue sky. It was a beautiful Sunday morning on the first of December, and the weatherman had said it was going to get up to seventy degrees that day. "Another day in paradise," Jack thought, and he was really looking forward to seeing Lisa. The ice had started to thaw somewhat between them, and he felt like he was making some real progress toward the day when the two of them would once again feel like a family.

As Jack stood in line to pay the attendant, he happened to notice the front page of the Review-Journal on the stack by the register. There screaming out at him were the pictures of Tobias and Elena Moscowitz. Jack grabbed a copy of the newspaper and read how they had been brutally tortured and murdered at what was believed to be about seven o'clock the previous night, and he suddenly realized that this was the couple that the newscaster had been talking about earlier.

Their hidden wall safe had been left open and stripped bare.

Toby and Elena had been found by their son at about nine p.m. after they failed to answer their phones. Both were zip tied to chairs facing each other in the living room. Elena bore the most torture marks having sustained multiple deep lacerations across her arms, legs, and face. She died on the way to the hospital of cardiac arrest due to massive blood loss. Toby was dead at the scene having had his throat opened from ear to ear. The crime scene described by the reporter read like something out of a slaughterhouse.

Evidently, the High Society Gang had somehow disabled the security system prior to entering the home. The front door had been forced open, but no alarm had been triggered. From there they rounded up the elderly couple and zip tied them to the chairs. Police speculated that they tortured Elena until Toby gave the location and combination of the safe, and then he was quickly killed in order to leave no witnesses.

Jack turned the newspaper back to the front page after reading the story in utter disbelief. He looked at their faces and remembered the last time he had seen Toby when he picked up Melinda's ring. Such a gentle old man. Jack couldn't believe that Toby and Elena had been so brutalized and were gone. It sickened him to think about what they had been through, but he couldn't imagine Toby being uncooperative and forcing the robbers to resort to torture in order to get him to tell them anything they wanted to know. Jack knew that Toby adored Elena and would've done anything to protect her.

Jesse had called about four in the morning. and said he needed Jack to come to the house no later than nine, so after pumping the gas, Jack drove to Jesse's house, but he was preoccupied with the story in the newspaper. All the way to Spanish Trail, Jack wondered why Toby would've held out and let Elena suffer so much. It made no sense at all. Jack barely registered a response when the guard at the gate waved him through, and as Jack pulled into Jesse's driveway, he was still shaking his head in wonder at the viciousness and ruthless disregard for human life exhibited by these killers.

Jesse appeared to be alone in the house. He was standing in the den with the only illumination being the faint ambient sunlight that was filtering in through the shears hanging over the back sliding door in the kitchen and the glow of the fifty-inch flat screen television that was screen-split into four security monitors. Jesse had a tumbler full of scotch and ice cubes in his hand that he frequently sipped from while he nervously stared at the monitors. He motioned for Jack to follow him into the dining room, and then he began pacing furiously by the dining room table as Jack stared at him. On the table were two envelopes—one large manila padded envelope 11 x 14 inches and another letter-sized envelope that looked to be full of cash. With a rupture of agitation, Jesse handed both envelopes to Jack.

"Here, Jack. This big package needs to go to Santa Barbara. The address is on this slip of paper. It has to be there no later than four o'clock. You hear me, Jack? Four o'clock!"

"But Jesse, I was gonna meet my daughter for lunch. Can I deliver it later or tomorrow? We're just starting to get to know each other, again."

"NO, JACK!" Jesse shouted almost hysterically. "This gets delivered today! You hear me? Four o'clock! No later! Don't screw this up, Jack!"

"But what about my daughter? I promised her."

Jesse slammed his drink down on the table splashing scotch and ice all over the table and floor. In a rage he screamed, "Jack, I don't give a rat's ass! Take her with you, for all I care! As long as she doesn't handle the package, she can ride along. Make it a father/daughter outing. Whatever! Just deliver the damn package on time! There's ten thousand dollars in the other envelope. Buy her something. Smooth it over. Use your imagination, but get it done with no screw-ups! You hear me? This is important! No screw-ups, Jack!"

"Okay, Jesse, I'll do it. No problem. You can count on me."

"Good. Oh, and make sure that you rent a car. Your car's leaving oil on my driveway. I don't want that piece of shit breaking down and being the reason that you don't make it there on time."

"Okay, you've got it."

Jack didn't waste any time getting out of Jesse's house. He quickly got into his car, fired it up, and threw it into gear before Jesse could have any second thoughts. As Jack wheeled around the circular driveway, he tried to remember if he had ever seen Jesse this wired before. Jack had seen him on cocaine several times, and it had a profound effect on Jesse's mood. While coke couldn't be ruled out as a contributor, it seemed to be more a combination of worry and anger.

No, not anger. It was more like infuriation foaming into rage. Whatever it was, Jesse was really hyped up, and for the first time, Jack didn't see Jesse as his life-long friend. He was somebody else, and Jack couldn't put his finger on why, but regardless of the reason, it had Jack really spooked.

Jack had plenty of time to pick up a car and make the delivery. That was of no concern to him. However, he didn't want to have to cancel on Lisa. He had worked hard over the last six months, with Kiersten's help, at being dependable for Lisa. If he said he was going to do something for her or with her, he had kept his word. However, he knew he *had* to make the delivery. Plus, this was an opportunity to really score a big payday, and he absolutely needed it. He was stepping up his poker game, and it required a bigger stake. If all went to plan, this might be the last delivery that he'd "have" to make for Jesse. He really wanted to be free of him and just be able to play poker. While Jesse had been a big help towards getting back on his feet, Jack knew that Jesse was bad news in the long run. He could see Jesse getting busted for some of his shenanigans, and Jack didn't want to get caught in the fallout.

Jack's only solution was to take Lisa with him, but trying to figure out a way to get Lisa to come along, though, was going to be tough. She and Jack still weren't on the best of terms, even though they had come a long way. It would probably be classified as a mutual cease-fire. She usually made plans with her friends on the weekend, and she would have to break them if she was going to go all the way to Santa Barbara with Jack. While Jack wanted to spend time with her, he knew that right now her friends came before "dear old dad," so he would have to entice her with something she wanted more than her friends. "This is *not* going to be easy," he thought.

As he was driving along Paradise Road heading back to his apartment, he happened to notice one of the exotic car rental shops that were popular with the tourists. They loved to cruise the Strip for a night or weekend in a big Mercedes convertible, a decked-out Hummer, or even a Lamborghini. These rentals were expensive, but for many tourists it was part of the Vegas "experience."

Jack suddenly slammed on the brakes. It hit him what would entice Lisa to abandon her friends and come along. Even though she had her driver's license, Lisa had no car of her own, so she could only drive her grandmother's Kia or Jack's old Buick on a limited basis. However, she had a love affair with powerful cars that wouldn't quit! Jesse had a vintage "Smokey and the Bandit" Trans Am that he had let Jack borrow one day. Jack had taken Lisa to the movies in it and let her drive it home to Kiersten's house. Lisa squealed practically the whole way home!

Jack figured he would rent something special and offer to let Lisa drive it some on their road trip. She'd get a big kick out of that. Maybe on the long drive they could get a few things worked out. Maybe they could be close, again. Maybe it really could turn out to make some special father/daughter memories that would last a lifetime!

Jack pulled into the rental lot.

14

When Jack pulled into the driveway at Kiersten's house to pick up Lisa, she was waiting for him outside. She was seventeen now, and she stood long and lean. She was taller than Melinda had been, but she had her mother's comely figure, piercing blue eyes, and long blonde hair that hung almost to her waist with side-swept bangs and bouncy curls. She was dressed in jeans and a royal blue sleeveless turtleneck top that set off her eyes.

Jack had called ahead and told her that he had a surprise for her. When she saw Jack behind the wheel of the rental car, her jaw dropped and bounced a couple times on the cement. Jack had pulled up in a racing red Ferrari Testarossa. It was going to set him back about eighteen hundred dollars with the mileage costs to rent it for the day, but it was worth every penny to him to see that look on her face of pure amazement and ecstasy.

When he pulled up to a stop, he revved the engine three times for emphasis. Lisa hopped up and down and clapped with an excited smile full of teeth. "Daddy!" she exclaimed when Jack crawled out of the car. "What are you doing driving THAT!"

"Well, Val, I promised you lunch, but I need to go to Santa Barbara, so I thought we'd have lunch there. I also thought that you might like to drive this baby on the way down there. Of course, if you have other plans . . .," he said with a twinkle in his eye.

"Are you kidding?! I can cancel my plans! My friends are going to be sooo jealous! Santa Barbara, here we come!"

Without hesitation, Lisa clambered onto the black leather of the passenger seat. Kiersten had come outside to see what all the commotion was about, and she winked at Jack and gave him two thumbs up. Jack revved the engine a few more times for emphasis and to hear Lisa squeal.

It was music to his ears. He hadn't seen her act this happy since before Melinda's death. It reminded him that she really was still a little girl, even at seventeen years old. "Yup, worth every single penny," he confirmed to himself.

They hit I-15 headed south toward the California state line and opened up the Ferrari. Jack had the radio tuned to a classic rock station, and Deep Purple began blasting out *Highway Star*. When Ian Gillian began to wail, "Nobody gonna beat my car. It's gonna break the speed of sound," Jack sang along and punched the accelerator. The Ferrari jumped up to 120 miles per hour in a heartbeat. Lisa squealed, "YAAAAA," at the top of her lungs, and Jack just grinned.

Jack told Lisa that they would switch driving when they got to Primm and crossed into California. He figured there wouldn't be any Highway Patrol in the wasteland between Primm and Baker. He wanted to let her open up the Ferrari and enjoy driving it, but he also didn't want to get an astronomical ticket.

About thirty miles outside of Vegas, Lisa started to revert back to "Angry Lisa."

"So, how come you still live in that grungy apartment, Dad, if you can afford a car like this? You'd think you'd have a little class and get a nicer place."

"Val, don't start in on me. This is supposed to be a fun outing. I rented this Ferrari as a special treat just for you, but it's only for the day, and it wasn't cheap. Besides, you know your mom's medical expenses wiped me out. I'm still trying to recover."

"Yeah, your drinking didn't help, either."

"Okay, you're right. It did make things worse, but I've really got things under control now."

"Yeah, right."

"Let's not go there. Let's see if we can just have a fun day together, okay?"

"Yeah, whatever."

About ten miles outside of Primm, Lisa tried to recline her seat a little, but it wouldn't move. "Geez, you pay a bunch of money for a car, you'd think the seat would work!" She reached around behind her seat and pulled out the large envelope that Jack had stashed there. "What's this, Dad?"

"Don't mess with that, Val. That's just a package that I have to drop off in Santa Barbara. I'm being paid to deliver it safe and sound."

"Wow! This is heavy," Lisa said as she pulled it out. "So, you can afford this car because you're delivering this? What is it, drugs?"

"Val, I said leave that alone. It's not yours, and it's not mine. I don't know what it is, and I don't want to know. I've been entrusted with it, and I don't want anything happening to it," Jack said as his voice began to rise.

"Nothing's going to happen to it. It's not like I'm going to throw it out the window. Chill out! I just want to peek!"

Before Jack could do or say anything, Lisa had opened part of one end of the envelope and reached in. When she pulled out her hand, she gasped. "Daddy! Look at these jewels! They're enormous!"

"Val! What're you doing?" Jack almost hit the car next to him in the other lane as he tried to grab the envelope. When his fingers touched it, he pulled, but Lisa was still holding onto it, and the envelope slashed open, spilling some of the contents into Lisa's lap.

"Oh my God, Daddy! This is a huge necklace, and it looks like there's blood all over it!"

Hearing the alarm in Lisa's voice, Jack pulled over to the side of the road. When he looked at the necklace in his daughter's lap, all the blood drained from his face. He threw open the door, stumbled out, and fell to his hands and knees in front of the car retching his guts out. The sunbaked asphalt of the emergency lane burned and blistered his hands, but all he could think about was the sight of the blood-stained Slezy Bogov necklace in his shaking daughter's lap.

Jack could hear Lisa screaming as his head started to clear. He spat several times trying to get the taste of vomit out of his mouth. Then he haltingly climbed to his feet, wiped the grit from his hands on his pant legs, and opened her door. By now she was sobbing. As carefully as possible, he picked up the remnants of the envelope from her lap doing his best to keep the necklace and other jewels cradled in the bubble wrapped interior of the envelope without touching them. The last thing he wanted was *his* fingerprints on these witnesses of torture and death. Once the envelope was off her lap, Jack helped Lisa out of the car. Using his handkerchief, he retrieved all of the jewelry that had fallen onto the floorboard and seat of the car.

Bewildered by this turn of events, Jack knew that he was in a fix. His best friend Jesse was involved somehow in these home invasion murders. He absolutely wasn't going to go through with the delivery, but what should he do? He couldn't go back to Jesse. The people perpetrating these robbery/murders obviously had no compunction over killing people, and Jesse was either one of them or in it up to his eyeballs. Either way, Jack and Lisa would probably end up taking a dirt nap in the desert somewhere if he contacted Jesse.

Jack considered calling the police, but then he remembered that *he* was involved with attempting to transport stolen items out of the state. Items stolen from a double homicide! For all he knew, that made him an accomplice, and he had absolutely no desire to spend the rest of his life in prison!

Jack also knew they couldn't stay where they were. Any moment now, a Nevada Highway Patrol cruiser was liable to come sailing down I-15 and stop to see what was going on, so Jack got Lisa back into the car and drove to Whiskey Pete's Casino in Primm at the state line. He figured they could easily blend in with all of the tourists bouncing back and forth between Vegas and Southern California. Right now, Jack needed to disappear.

When they pulled into the parking lot, the red Ferrari stood out like a rose among weeds. The lot was full of minivans and the land yachts favored by the Geritol brigade. However, Jack decided he couldn't risk a nosy valet finding the jewels, so he parked the car in the parking deck and set the alarm hoping that the Ferrari's low-slung profile would help to hide it.

Walking into the casino, Jack suddenly felt like everyone was staring at him. Every face was strange, and he felt like a pariah. Jack had been in casinos almost all of his life and ordinarily felt comfortable in them, but it suddenly seemed like he was the last person standing without a chair when the music stops at a cake walk. In the din of the bells and sirens emanating from the slot machines, Jack decided this was no place to think clearly, so he and Lisa went to the coffee shop.

Jack picked out a booth that was away from everyone else, and they sat down. The waitress brought menus and two glasses of water. Lisa kept her mouth shut while they perused the menus, but soon after the waitress took their order, Lisa couldn't contain her curiosity any longer. "Daddy, why were you taking that package to Santa Barbara?"

"Because Jesse Brizetta paid me to make a delivery, Val. I didn't know what was in the package, nor did I want to know. I was just supposed to drop it off."

"Why do you think there was blood all over that necklace?"

"Because the people that owned it were murdered."

"How do you know?"

"I know, because I've seen that necklace before. It was shown to me by the owner who was a very dear friend of mine. He and his wife were killed last night by the High Society Gang. I read the story in the newspaper this morning."

"Oh, my God! You knew them?"

"Yes, and I've got to figure out what to do."

"Call the police! Give them the necklace, and let them handle it!"

"It's not that simple, Val. It's not that simple," Jack mumbled as he shook his head and rubbed the back of his neck.

The waitress delivered their food, and they ate in silence. Jack looked over at Lisa several times trying to gauge her head, but she wouldn't look up at him. When they were finished, Jack led Lisa to the registration desk where he got a room. As they rode the elevator up, Lisa asked, "Why are we getting a room? Are we staying here tonight?"

"I don't know. Maybe. Right now, I just need a quiet place to think. I have an idea, but I don't want to be talking about it with strangers around."

When they got to the room, Lisa made her way to the bathroom and closed the door. Jack sat down on the bed, leaned forward, and put his head in his hands. The quiet of the room allowed him to focus, but all he could think about was how Jesse had to be involved with the murders, and now Jack was, too. To make matters worse, Lisa had been interjected into this wicked turn of events, and he had to figure out some way to protect her. If only he hadn't brought her along. If only she hadn't opened the package. If only he had hidden it better. If, if, if. If only he could talk to someone that cared and would help him.

Slowly he pulled out his phone. There was only one person that he felt he could trust right now. One person that might be able to help him. As he punched in the number, he said a silent prayer that the phone would be answered.

"Hello?"

"Abbie, this is Jack. I need your help."

15

Jack had learned from their conversations that Abbie was connected on both sides of the law. She had also dated a criminal lawyer for a while, and they were still good friends. Jack was hoping she could find out what his options were before he talked to the police. He also considered going back to Jesse, again, but he decided that he just couldn't risk it. As much as he disliked the thought of prison, he liked dead even less. Plus, Lisa was involved. It not only complicated the circumstances, but now taking his chances with Jesse was out of the question. Risking Lisa's life was simply not an option for Jack.

Abbie called him back after about an hour. She was all business, and most of the Southern drawl had drained from her voice. "Jack, I talked to Michael. I also talked to a detective with Metro, and he talked to the District Attorney. The consensus seems to be that you need to get back here as soon as possible. Jesse's gonna find out you're off schedule as soon as your deadline passes in Santa Barbara. Michael believes that you can get full immunity if you cooperate. They want this High Society Gang in the worst way, so that necklace is your get-out-of-jail-free card, especially if it has prints on it or you can tie Jesse to the crimes."

"So, where do I go?"

"Go to Michael's office. I'll text you the address, and I'll meet you there."

"Okay, I'll be there in about an hour and a half." Armed with a plan, Jack and Lisa grabbed their things and checked out.

The drive between Primm and Las Vegas is usually about forty to forty-five minutes. Jack did it in thirty. He wanted to make sure that he got Lisa back to Kiersten's house before going to the attorney's office in order to keep her identity out of the investigation. He also wanted to stop by his place. He had left the .38 revolver he usually kept strapped to his ankle back at his apartment, because he was going to the Left Coast of California. He didn't want any complications traveling with Lisa. Plus, he wasn't carrying a trunk full of cash, so he wasn't worried about being hijacked. Now, however, he wanted it back where it belonged.

Jack had returned the Ferrari early, so the rental only cost him half of what he had expected. That left him with about $9,000 of Jesse's blood money. He decided to keep the money with him instead of stashing it. In Vegas, cash is king, and he had no idea if he might have to grease some palms, buy some muscle, or bail himself out of jail. In any case, just like his pistol, it was better to have it and not need it than to need it and not have it.

Since he had dumped the high-priced wheels, he arrived in his own Buick beater at the office of Michael James, Attorney-At-Law, at Third Street and Bonneville right next to A-1 Bail Bonds. He marveled at how convenient it seemed to have a bonding service right next door, but he was hoping that he wouldn't require their services after this meeting.

Inside the office, Abbie first introduced Jack to Michael. Michael was in a tailored gray suit that looked like it cost about six months' worth of rent for Jack. Michael was quite handsome with sparkling blue eyes, and Jack could see why Abbie would've been attracted to him. Michael was in his late thirties, and with his brown hair slicked back, he looked every bit like a high-priced, predator lawyer. Jack hoped that he was as skillful and intimidating as he looked.

Next, Abbie introduced Richard Allen, the District Attorney. Allen was an ultra-conservative looking black man. He was in his early forties, but he looked much older. His head was shaved to conceal a receding hairline, but he had a close-cropped beard that was peppered with gray throughout with a round gray patch the size of a quarter just under his chin. He wore a dark blue suit, light blue broadcloth button-down shirt, and a burgundy tie that made him look like he had just stepped off the cover of GQ Magazine. He had silver wire rim glasses that were in stark contrast to his shaved head that shined like it had been waxed. He kept fidgeting with his glasses, however, like they didn't fit right or belonged to someone else, and it gave the impression that he was more like a fussy accountant than a big-time district attorney.

Lieutenant Vincent DeLuca, head of Metro's Homicide Division, was up next, and he exuded confidence and masculinity. Also in his early forties, his tall, muscular build filled out his navy-blue sport coat, khaki pants, red tie, and tan loafers, and he was all business. With a swarthy look and deep brown eyes, he reminded Jack of an Italian lothario. Even though he had a hard, menacing air about him, he still had a smile on his face creating dimples that almost reached up to his dark brown mustache. His straight dark hair was combed back to his right, but it kept falling down into his eyes forcing him to periodically smooth it back into place. He struck Jack as a hard-edged sort that didn't get pushed around by men, but was silky enough to talk a nun out of her knickers. Still, Jack felt that besides Abbie, he could probably trust DeLuca the most. Certainly, much more than the two lawyers.

Lastly, Russell Kosten, a CSI technician was introduced. He was built heavy on a medium frame, but he had a cherub's face that seemed a perfect fit with his curly blond hair. His cheeks were red, like he was blushing or wind-burned, but they never changed color.

Jack shook everyone's hand, but he was upset that he couldn't talk to Michael in private first. He wanted to know what he should or shouldn't say before he bared his soul and transgressions to total strangers. Not that he had ever met Michael before, either, but he figured if Abbie vouched for him, that was the Good Housekeeping stamp of approval.

They all sat down in a conference room at a large cherry wood table surrounded by matching bookcases filled with volume upon volume of impressive looking law reference books. On the table was a crystal pitcher of ice water ringed by ten crystal tumblers on a large silver tray, and everyone sat in matching cherry captain's chairs. Enveloped in this overt display of money and order, Jack was extremely uneasy.

Allen opened the conversation. "Jack, Abbie tells me you think that you have a piece of jewelry that was owned by the Moscowitz's and that it has blood on it."

"I don't think. I know. Toby Moscowitz showed the necklace to me at his jewelry store. He said that it was his wife's and that it was one-of-a-kind. I would know it anywhere, and I've got it. As for blood, it looks like blood, but I don't know that for sure."

"Where is it?"

"Here in this bag."

"Okay, give it to me. I'd like our Mr. Kosten to take a look at it."

"Hold on, now," Michael interrupted. "My client hands over nothing and says nothing more until we understand each other. He gets full immunity on any and all charges. He produces the necklace and tells you what he knows. That's it! Understood?"

"Yes, of course. Now let's see the necklace."

"Say it out loud so everyone can hear and it's clearly understood, Richard."

"Jack Diamante has full immunity from any and all charges related to the necklace, murders, and robbery. Do you want that in writing, too?" he said with a bit of disgust.

"Actually, I would, but for now we can proceed with everyone as witnesses."

Michael nodded to Jack, and Jack smiled. He liked the way that Michael had put Allen in his place. He felt a little more at ease with Michael, so he carefully lifted the remains of the padded envelope out of his gym bag with the necklace wrapped inside.

"Mr. Kosten, if you would, please take the package, photograph it and the contents, remove the contents, and ascertain if in fact there is blood on the necklace," Allen instructed.

Kosten took the package wearing blue Nitrile gloves and took multiple photographs of the package and contents. He then swabbed one of the jewels with luminol and confirmed that there was blood present on the necklace.

Satisfied that he had some significant evidence, Allen asked Jack to continue his story.

With a conflicting combination of dread and relief, Jack said, "Jesse Brizetta gave me this package and asked me to deliver it to this address in Santa Barbara." He handed the slip of paper that Jesse had given him to Lieutenant DeLuca and continued, "I was supposed to deliver it by four this afternoon. When I had almost reached Primm, I pulled the package out from under the seat, and it accidentally tore open. When I saw the contents, I knew exactly whose necklace it was. I also knew that the Moscowitzs had been killed from a newspaper story that I read this morning. I wasn't sure what to do, so I pulled over at Whiskey Pete's to figure out my options. I may have been delivering the necklace, but I had nothing to do with their murder. They were good friends of mine. It was obvious, though, that Jesse was involved somehow, so I couldn't go back. That's when I called Abbie and asked her to talk to you guys." Jack made a point of not mentioning that Lisa was with him. He figured the less she was involved, the better, but he knew that they could probably be identified by the waitress, the front desk clerk, and who knows how many other people. He just hoped that the necklace and his story would be enough to satisfy them.

"Jack, how did you get involved with Brizetta in the first place?"

"Jesse and I go way back to Junior and Senior high school. We've been friends for a very long time."

"But surely you knew he had to be dirty, and yet you never said anything. Why?"

Jack looked down slightly and shook his head. Then he looked up and said, "All lies and jest, still a man hears what he wants to hear and disregards the rest."

"Is that something from Henry David Thoreau?" Allen said with a pretentious look. "No," Jack said with a grin. "Simon and Garfunkel."

DeLuca snickered, and Allen looked at him with a scowl. "Alright, Jack," Allen said. "That's probably all we need for now, but I want you on record with a sworn statement. I'll arrange for you to meet with a court recorder. Kosten, you get that necklace to the lab asap. I want fingerprints and every bit of DNA you can find on it. You call my office as soon as you find out anything." Kosten nodded, sealed the necklace and envelope in evidence bags, and left.

Lieutenant DeLuca came over to Jack and gave him his business card and told him, "Mr. Diamante, you give me a call if you think of anything else. This is the first real break that we've had on these bastards, and I don't want them slipping through our fingers."

"Lieutenant, Jesse's got to find out pretty soon that I didn't make the delivery. When he does, he's gonna be pissed. He'll probably come looking for me like he has in the past thinking I got drunk or something. If he gets wind that we've talked, he may just disappear. Should I try to contact him?"

Allen butted in, "Not on your life, Jack! He could just as easily come after you. In fact, Lieutenant, I want Jack transported someplace safe and out of the way where we can get his statement recorded. Have one of your men take him to the Rio through the back entrance. We've got a suite there that we can use. I want him under wraps, understand?"

"Got it. I'll take care of it myself. Jack, looks like you're coming with me after this."

"I drove here, so I'll follow you over there."

Michael had Jack's immunity paperwork typed and printed. Allen and Jack signed it before they left, and then Jack was on his way to the Rio. When he arrived there, he was met by Detective Patrick McGreer. McGreer then escorted Jack up to the suite and stayed there as a bodyguard. He also told Jack that a court reporter was supposed to meet them there in a little while. Allen wanted Jack safe, sound, and hermetically sealed away. So far, Jack was the only link between the murderers and the victims, and Allen didn't want to take any chances on losing him.

As much as Jack tried to relax, he absolutely knew that Jesse was going to find out pretty soon, if he hadn't already, that Jack hadn't made the delivery. Jesse had seemed very anxious to have it delivered as soon as possible, and Jack knew that Jesse would be checking up on him.

Moreover, Jack knew that Lisa's involvement couldn't stay a secret forever. She had handled the necklace, and her fingerprints were probably slathered all over it. The only saving grace was that Jack doubted that she had ever been fingerprinted previously, so she wouldn't show up in any database. Still, the Metro CSI personnel were probably good enough to figure out that the prints belonged to a young female, so it was only a matter of time before the cat got let out of the bag.

16

Lisa had wanted to go with Jack to the attorney's office rather than be dropped off at her grandmother's house. Kiersten was out grocery shopping and running some other errands, so Lisa was alone at the house, and while Jack would've preferred that Kiersten be there with Lisa, he absolutely didn't want anyone else knowing that she was involved. That meant that Lisa stayed put, but as much as she tried to relax, she kept thinking about the necklace soiled with blood stains lying in her lap. She could imagine the screams of the woman as they tortured her, and she decided that she had to get out of the house or lose her mind imagining it over and over again.

She decided to take a walk around the neighborhood to clear her head. Jack had told her not to call any of her friends, but in her mind that didn't mean that she couldn't talk to them if they were home. After all, he just said that she couldn't *call* them. Lisa changed into some shorts, a tee shirt, a red fleece hoodie with UNLV on the front, and her running shoes and headed out about four-thirty.

It was a typical Las Vegas December afternoon. The sky was pale blue without a cloud in it. The air was dry, and the sun shone warm on Lisa's face. That is until she stepped into a shadow. Moving from the sunshine to the shadows seemed to drop the temperature twenty degrees, especially with the breeze that was stirring up little dust devils in the neighborhood. The wind would swirl the dusty streets and sidewalks suspending the sediment and wayward trash for about two or three seconds and then disappear, only to resume thirty feet away.

After walking around the neighborhood for about half an hour, Lisa was frustrated. She had gone to several of her friends' houses in the neighborhood, but none of them were home. They were all still out at the mall or at the movies, so she decided to go back. Unfortunately, Kiersten lived in the western portion of Peccole Ranch. That is the uphill side, and Lisa had walked downhill, so now she had a long uphill trudge in front of her.

The sun had seeped down behind the Spring Mountains while she had been walking, so it was now considerably colder than when she had started. The warm breeze from earlier now seemed more like an arctic blast. It bit right through the skimpy clothes that Lisa was wearing, and it was raising goose bumps all over her arms and legs. She started to jog to warm herself up a little and get back faster. Lisa never liked the cold, so getting back someplace warm became a priority.

Fifteen minutes later she was breathing heavy and started to slow down. As she turned the last corner, she could see one of the smaller neighborhood kids talking to somebody in a dark blue van. The little girl started pointing at her as she walked up the slope toward Kiersten's house. The van then slowly started driving down the street approaching her. Lisa stopped walking while she tried to see into the driver's side of the van. She could see people inside, but she didn't recognize anyone.

When the van pulled up, the passenger window was tinted so dark that Lisa couldn't see in, but the window slowly rolled down about half way. A strange voice said, "Hey, Lisa, your dad sent us to your grandma's house to pick you up. He wants to see you right away. Hop in." Then another man she didn't know rolled open the sliding side door to the van from the inside and motioned for her to get in. This other man was muscular and wearing jeans, a blue tank top, and flip flops with tattoos on both arms. He had long, greasy red hair that was parted down the middle, four days' worth of facial scruff, and looked like two-hundred and twenty pounds of trouble.

Lisa turned to the person in the passenger seat and said, "My name's not Lisa. That's another girl. I live back that way," she said turning and pointing behind her. When she turned back around, the second man from inside the van was suddenly in her face with his hand over her mouth. He grabbed her around the waist with his other arm and picked her up like a sack of potatoes. She tried to scream and began to kick her legs trying to stay out of the van. She kicked at the sliding door violently and bit down on the man's hand. Without making a sound he quickly moved his hand about six inches from her mouth and then viciously back-handed her across the face. Jesse then got out of the passenger-side door, and he held a folded switchblade in front of her eyes while the other man returned his hand to covering her mouth. Jesse pushed the release button on the knife, and it snapped into place with a metallic thwack! Lisa's eyes were wide with terror, and she flinched when the knife snapped out. Icy cold, Jesse said, "We can go for a ride and talk, or I can slice your throat right here. What's it gonna be, Lisa?"

Lisa stopped kicking, and the red-haired gorilla lifted her into the van. Once seated, she was gagged, her hands were zip tied behind her back, and her feet were zip tied, as well. Jesse shut the sliding door and climbed into his seat. The driver, who looked like the twin of the muscular red-headed man, then made a U-turn and quickly exited the subdivision.

Jesse turned in his seat and looked at Lisa. Lisa's eyes were full of tears, but when she saw Jesse the second time without the switchblade in her face, she suddenly recognized him. She had met him once previously when Jack had borrowed Jesse's Trans Am, and she had gotten a bad vibe from him then. Now those feelings had been confirmed, and she bit down hard on the gag while closing her eyes.

"Now, now, Lisa, I just want to talk," Jesse said smoothly. "We can do this pleasant, or we can do it nasty. If you answer my questions, and I don't think you're lying, I'll let you go. If you don't answer my questions or if you lie to me, then my friend here is going to hurt you. He may hurt you badly. If you understand me, nod your head." Lisa hesitated and then nodded yes. "Good. I need to know about your dad. I need to know what he's been doing and where he is. I know he was planning to meet you earlier, so tell me, did he pick you up? Now remember, I'll know if you're lying. Nod yes or no. Did he pick you up?"

Lisa hesitated, again, not knowing if she should tell him the truth. She knew that Jesse was using her to get to her dad, and she didn't want to help him, so she shook her head no.

Jesse looked into her scared blue eyes, and when Lisa looked the other way, he nodded to the other man. Quick as a flash the man slapped Lisa across the face with his open palm. The slap of skin on skin barked sharply, and Lisa's head spun. Her long blonde hair flew across her face and became wet and tangled with her tears and sweat. Lisa started to silently sob into the gag.

Her tears overflowed the banks of her eyelids and flowed like a river down her face soaking her hair even more.

Jesse took the switchblade and used the tip of the ominous blade to scrape the hair from in front of her face, exposing her eyes and tear-soaked cheeks that were beginning to swell from the two vicious blows. Her lower lip was split and had started to bleed. Jesse looked at her with a steely gaze and said, "I told you he would hurt you if you lied to me, and, Lisa, that's the best it's gonna get. It's all downhill from here unless you start giving me some truthful answers. Now, your dad picked you up. Did he take you with him on his trip?"

Lisa glared at Jesse and nodded yes slowly. The other man looked at Jesse, but Jesse shook his head no. "Okay, now we're getting somewhere," he said. "Just a few more answers, and this will all be over. Did he take you to California with him?"

Lisa looked bewildered. Her eyes darted from Jesse to the man next to her and back to Jesse. She didn't know how to answer or even if she should answer. They had headed to California, but they never made it. She didn't want to be hit again, but she couldn't decide what to do.

When Lisa didn't answer after about three seconds, Jesse nodded to the man next to her. Slipping his hand into his right pocket, the man pulled out a butterfly knife, and with a couple flips of his wrist, the sharp blade was pointing towards Lisa. Her eyes opened wide in terror as he moved the thumb of his hand holding the knife up to within a quarter inch of the razor-sharp tip, and with a swift, smooth motion, he flicked his wrist at Lisa's left leg and slit the flesh on her bare thigh. It opened a cut about three inches long and a quarter inch deep. Lisa screamed at the top of her lungs, but the gag still muted her desperate shrieks. Blood began to leak from the wound and ooze to the seat. Jesse tossed a dirty rag to the other man, who held it on her thigh to staunch the flow of blood. Sobbing now and starting to feel light-headed, Lisa looked into the red-headed man's face, and he grinned at her.

Then he licked his lips like a serpent, and she screamed, again, turning away.

"Look at me Lisa," Jesse said. When Lisa wouldn't turn, Jesse screamed, "I SAID LOOK AT ME!" The other man grabbed her head and twisted it to face Jesse. "I told you it would only get worse. Roby, here, can be a very bad man when he wants to be, which, of course, happens to be all the time!" Jesse said and then laughed. "Now answer my question. Did you go to California with your dad?"

Lisa immediately started shaking and nodding her head yes and no. Roby raised his knife, again, but Jesse raised his hand and stopped him. He peered into Lisa's eyes and saw raw fear. He didn't know what yes and no meant, but he didn't think she was playing. She was too scared.

"I'm not sure what you're trying to tell me, so I'm gonna take the gag off of your mouth, but if you scream or lie to me, I'm gonna have Roby drive that knife right through your leg and nail it to the seat. Do you understand me?" Jesse said with fire in his eyes.

Lisa nodded yes, and Jesse motioned for Roby to pull her gag down. When he did, Lisa wanted to peel the paint off of the van with her screams, but she bit her tongue so she wouldn't. In fact, she bit so hard it started to bleed in her mouth, and she started to gag on the copper tasting liquid.

"Alright, now. Did you go to California with your dad?"

Through the tears and the blood and the pain, Lisa stammered out, "We left, but we only made it to Whiskey Pete's."

"Did he have a package with him? It was a large padded envelope. Did he have it with him?"

"Yes."

"Did he open it?"

"We didn't mean to," Lisa sobbed. "It just came open. That's why we stopped. He didn't know what to do." Lisa clenched her eyes and lowered her face behind her bedraggled hair.

"Is that when you came back?" Jesse asked. Lisa nodded yes. "Where did you go when you got back into town?"

"He took me to my grandma's house," Lisa said without looking up. "Where did he go after that?" Jesse asked.

Lisa shook her head no. Roby grabbed her sweat-soaked hair behind her head, yanked back violently, and shook her head like a rag doll. "Answer his question, bitch!" Roby pulled back on her hair even more and showed her the knife, again.

"I don't know," she pleaded. "He dropped me off and left me!"

"Where do you *think* he went," Jesse growled. "I'm getting impatient with these half-assed answers, so spit it out!"

Roby let go of her hair, clapped his left hand over Lisa's mouth, and made another shallow slice on her other thigh this time. Lisa screeched in agony, but her cries were smothered by Roby's big hand. She continued to cry out futilely, hoping someone would hear her, until Roby used his fist to drive the butt end of the knife into her solar plexus. Lisa doubled over desperately trying to suck in air, but no air made it down her throat. She felt as if her lungs had stopped functioning, and she wondered if she would ever be able to breathe again. She urgently wanted to fill her lungs so she could scream, but no air arrived.

"That's enough for now, Roby. Lisa, you're trying my patience! You've just had the wind knocked out of you. Don't try to suck air in. Exhale and you'll be able to breathe again. And when you do, I want answers!"

Lisa couldn't figure out how exhaling would bring more air in, but she did as she was told, and miraculously she was able to breathe again. It seemed like hours since she'd been able to breathe, and she sucked in mouthfuls of precious air in between sobs. She prayed that they would stop and let her go. How long were they going to keep torturing her? She remembered seeing the floor of the van when she got in. It was bare metal covered with a combination of receding blue paint, streaks of rust, and patches of a crusted reddish-brown substance that she now realized must have been blood, and she registered the revelation that she definitely wasn't the first to bleed profusely in the van. Then she remembered how Jack had said the old couple had been tortured before they died, and the truth dawned on her that they probably weren't going to let her go at all.

"Now, can we get back to where we left off? Where did your dad go with the package?"

With tears, snot, and blood running down her face, Lisa looked up through her matted blonde hair and glared at Jesse. "You're not going to let me go anyway, so why should I tell you anything, you son-of-a-bitch!"

"Because, you little whore, I can have Roby drag this out all day and night. I can have you begging me to kill you, or I can make it all go away. Besides, if your dad still has the package, I can make a deal for you, and for that I need you alive. So, you see, it's in your best interest to help me. Now where was he going?"

"I don't know for sure. He didn't tell me, but I heard him talking on the phone about possibly meeting a lawyer and the cops. That's all I know," Lisa sobbed and went limp. She didn't know if she would be given a stay of execution or if she had just sealed her fate.

17

Jack couldn't relax in the suite. He was concerned that the CSI group would somehow identify Lisa from the necklace, and the last thing he wanted was for Lisa to be exposed. To make matters worse, Detective McGreer kept looking at his watch as if he had somewhere to go, which made Jack even more fidgety. Lieutenant DeLuca had assigned McGreer to baby-sit Jack until relief was sent, but it was obvious to Jack that McGreer didn't want to be there. It was as if he was expecting trouble and didn't want to be around when it happened.

About twenty minutes after they arrived in the suite, there was a knock at the door, and McGreer went to answer it. Looking through the peephole first, he broke into a big grin and opened the door. In walked the court reporter. She was dressed in navy blue slacks with a cream-colored blouse and navy-blue blazer, and she carried a small suitcase. She was almost platinum blonde, although the hair close to her neck was still a light brown. Her hair was styled smooth and straight in a perfectly coiffed bob style that tapered longer in front, ended in a slight curl forward about three inches below her jawline, and shined all over. Her hair was parted on the left side and tucked behind her left ear with just a wisp of bangs in front, and she seemed to ooze sophistication.

As soon as she came in, she looked at Jack sitting in one of the chairs, and she stopped abruptly just inside the door. A big smile swept over her face, and she said, "Hi, Jack. Long time, no see." It was Julie McKenna.

With the light brown curls replaced by straight blonde hair and her sophisticated appearance, Jack didn't recognize her, at first. She had put on about ten to twelve pounds that seemed to have gone to her hips and bust. It gave her curves that hadn't been there the last time Jack saw her in high school. A few crow's feet placed around the eyes completed the metamorphosis.

After about three seconds of awkward silence while he studied her intently, Jack's face softened from confusion to guarded recognition, and he said, "Julie?"

"So, you do remember me. I was afraid from the blank look on your face that I had become a complete stranger."

"Forgive me, Julie. I obviously wasn't expecting to see you, and you look so different with blonde hair and such a more, I don't know, polished and professional look. It's good to see you! You look great! How are you?" Jack asked as he walked over to her and gave her a brief hug.

"Thank you. I'm doing well. And you?"

"Fine, I guess. Well, not right now, really. I'm battling a boat load of trouble. I guess it's the trouble that brings you here. I assume you're the court reporter that Allen said he was sending?"

"That's me. I guess I'll set up over at the table."

With McGreer's help, Julie assembled her equipment at the table and had Jack sit down.

She had him raise his right hand and agree to tell the truth in his statement. Jack made a full statement as he did in Michael James' office. However, Allen had sent along some more questions about Jesse, Jack's relationship with Jesse, Jesse's connection with the necklace, ownership verification, etc. that he wanted to make sure were included in the statement.

McGreer asked the questions that Jack failed to answer on his own. As in his recollection of events in previous statements, Jack left out any references to Lisa, but he made those parts vague enough that he could insert her back into the story if it became necessary without risking perjury.

When they were done, McGreer excused himself to use the bathroom. Julie got up, stood seductively close to Jack's right side, and looked down at him. With a small coy smile, a slow half wink of her right eye, and a slight cock of her head, she said, "I'm glad he finally left. Now raise your right hand, again, Jack." Jack did as he was asked, and Julie took her left hand, cupped it around the back of Jack's raised hand, slid it under the front of her blazer, and pulled it in to her left breast. Jack could feel that she wore nothing under her blouse, and every red blood cell in his body began to pump a little harder. Actually, they pumped a lot harder. "Mmm, that feels nice, Jack. I have fond memories of those nights we spent long ago behind the Gate to Paradise when we were young and silly. I especially remember our first time there. Do remember that night, Jack?"

"Oh, I remember it vividly. I'm sure I'll remember that night for as long as I live."

"You know, Jack, I think you and I need to get reacquainted. Whad'ya say, Diamante? Are you up for a randy trip down memory lane?"

"Uh, sure. Why not?" Jack was apprehensive and worried that McGreer would see them, but he didn't worry enough to remove his hand. In fact, he was starting to brush his fingers slightly against the silky-smooth blouse. He pressed in a little more with his hand and felt an expectant nugget push back.

"It's funny that Jesse is the cause of you and me running into each other, again. I'll have to say thanks when Metro catches him," she said with a sly grin.

They both heard the toilet flush and the bathroom door handle unlatch, so Julie let go of Jack's hand, and he slid his hand down her blouse, finally resting it on his knee. Jack felt like he was eight shades of red when McGreer returned to the room, but Julie kept her cool. "So, Jack, if you think of anything else that might be important to your statement, you know like something you feel you need to share with me or if I can help you find that gate, give me a call. You know, sometimes it gets hard … to remember everything important, I mean. Here's my card," she said handing him her business card with her cell phone number written on the back.

"I, I, I will," Jack stammered. He was shocked that Julie acted so brazen with Detective McGreer right there. Her looks may have become more sophisticated, but she was still not shy at all about stating precisely what she wanted and how she wanted it. He remembered *that* little revelation from days gone by, too! Jesse had once said about Julie that, "You can take the girl out of the trailer park, but you can't take the trailer park out of the girl." Of course, at the time, Jesse had meant it as a compliment. Jack shook his head at the thought.

When Julie had left, McGreer asked, "A little history there, Jack? You two seemed to know each other pretty well. Plus, what did she mean about finding a gate?"

"We went to high school together, and I haven't seen her since then. She really does look a lot different than she did back then. It was a big shock to see her here. Oh, and the gate was just a little inside joke about something back in high school," Jack said, hoping McGreer wouldn't press the issue. Seeing Julie and having her come on to him shook Jack up and stirred up old memories and emotions. Long dormant primal hormones were being revived, and Jack was unprepared for the sudden infusion, although, he wasn't exactly lamenting the experience. However, Jack was relieved when McGreer let it pass without further explanation.

It was almost six o'clock, and Jack was exhausted. He normally slept during the day, especially when he had played poker the night before, but the day had turned out to be anything but normal. The long hours without sleep and the day's events had drained him, so when McGreer decided to turn on the local news, Jack went into the bedroom and collapsed onto the bed.

Jack took his phone out of his pocket and set it on the nightstand next to the bed. As he laid there with his head on the pillow, Jack thought about calling Lisa to see how she was holding up, but before he could reach for the phone, he passed into the sweet twilight zone of exhausted sleep. He was soon dreaming of Melinda and Lisa. They were at Fantasy Park, and Lisa was climbing in the rocket ship and then swooshing down the slide with her blond hair swirling behind her as Jack and Melinda waited to catch her at the bottom. Lisa loved the rocket ship and the whale, but her favorite was the old locomotive with all of its nooks and crannies to explore. She used to climb all over that locomotive for hours, and she loved when Jack would play hide-and-seek with her on it. Melinda would stay on the ground while Jack would scramble after their spunky ball of energy. Jack could remember creeping in and out of tight spaces looking for Lisa and how she would squeal and giggle when he found her. Just the sound of her laughter would cause Melinda to whoop and clap in joy. Jack loved to hear the two of them having fun.

Just as Jack was reaching out to pick up Lisa, he heard a rumbling noise as if the locomotive were starting to move. Lisa looked up at him funny as if she could hear it, too. Lisa started to drift away from Jack, and she reached out her arms for him to pick her up, but she kept getting further and further away. Slowly the dream faded away, and he realized that his phone was going off. He had turned it on vibrate and set it on the night stand next to the bed. Now it was doing a little dance as it rumbled next to the digital alarm clock that read 9:15 in glowing red numerals. Jack picked it up, and through bleary eyes he recognized Lisa's number.

As he started to say hello to Lisa, Jack heard her scream, "Daddy!" and then there was silence on the line.

"Val? Val! What's the matter?"

"You know what the matter is, Jack? My package didn't get delivered. That's what the matter is." Jack suddenly recognized Jesse's voice on the line, and his blood ran cold. "You remember the package I gave you, Jack? You remember the ten grand I gave you to deliver that package, Jack? Well, my guy in Santa Barbara said you never showed. I said to myself that can't be. Jack wouldn't make a mistake like that. I know, because I remember him telling me, 'No problem. You can count on me.' You remember saying that, Jack?"

"I remember. Where's my daughter?" Jack demanded.

"Oh, she's right here. Of course, she can't come to the phone right now. She's a little tied up at the moment." Jesse looked back in the van and smiled at Lisa squirming against the gag and her bonds. "You see, she and I have been having a real enlightening conversation about you and my package. When I heard that you didn't show, I thought maybe you got shit-faced on me, but then I remembered that you were gonna pick up your little girl. I figured what the hell. Maybe she knows what's going on, so I found her and invited her for a ride. You know, to kinda get reacquainted. At first, she didn't want to talk, but with the right motivation, she got downright chatty. These friends of mine are great motivators. In fact, they've been motivating people into giving them all kinds of things, including the jewels your daughter found in MY PACKAGE!" Jesse screamed into the phone.

"Jesse, damn it, if you hurt her, I'll—"

"Shut up, asshole! I'm talking here! It's not a question of whether or not she gets hurt. She's *been* hurt, Jack. Now it's a question of whether or not she survives, and that's up to you. You see, she also told me that you were thinking of going to the cops. I sure hope you weren't that stupid, Jack. That would really piss me off to think that my ol' buddy Jack would actually do me that way."

Jack put his fist over his mouth, and the lines on his forehead deepened as he tried to retain his composure. He knew Jesse could be pushed, but he couldn't push too hard with Lisa's life hanging in the balance. "Sorry to disappoint you, ol' buddy, but the cops have the necklace. However, they don't have the rest of the jewels that were in that package. I do, and they're safe and sound. Whad'ya say I give you those jewels, the ten grand you gave me, and an extra ten grand, and you give me my daughter. Then we can all be friends again. How's that sound, Jesse?" Jack said as he closed his eyes and said a silent prayer to no one in particular.

"Jack, that necklace was worth a shit load more than ten grand. Even hot, it's worth at least ten or twenty times that amount. As for being friends again, I think that ship has sailed, ol' buddy, but I'll tell you what I'm gonna do. I'll give you a choice. You can bring me the necklace and the jewels, or you can bring me the jewels and a hundred thousand dollars. You bring me either one of those two ransoms in twenty-four hours, and I'll give you your little skank of a daughter back."

"Jesse, you can't be serious! I don't think the cops will let me have the necklace back, and it would take me at least a month to get that amount of money put together. That's if I could get it at all!"

"It's either the money or the necklace plus the jewels, but I'll tell you what. I'm feeling generous, so I'll give you forty-eight hours. Otherwise, Jack, my friends are gonna think of all sorts of new games to play with your daughter, and let's just say they have *very* lurid imaginations when it comes to playing games with fresh young girls. I wouldn't waste any time, Jack. This one looks like a bleeder. You've got until nine o'clock Saturday night. I don't think she's got much staying power, Jack, so don't be late. Call me when you're ready, and we'll take care of our business."

Jesse thumbed the end button and threw Lisa's phone up on the dashboard of the van. Lisa's sodden hair fell over her face in strings, and blood was now starting to drip down to her chin and turn strands of her blonde hair to ginger as her bottom lip had opened up again when they forced the gag back into her mouth. Jesse said to her, "Well, little girl, let's see if your old man loves you or not. Frankly, I don't think he's got the stones to face me, but we'll see."

Jesse reached into the glove box and pulled out a cylindrical container of Morton salt. "Here, Roby, why don't you make sure that the princess doesn't contract any infections from those nasty cuts on her legs."

Jesse tossed the container of salt to him, and Roby's face slowly broke into a depraved grin. He opened the spout and poured a generous amount of salt into his right hand. "This won't hurt a bit," he said as he started to grind it into Lisa's cuts. Lisa's eyes nearly exploded out of her head, and she screamed as loud as the gag would allow. Tears began flooding from her eyes.

Roby started to laugh as he continued to rub salt into her wounds and said, "Damn, Jesse, I lied again. I have such a bad habit of doing that!"

"Well hell, Roby, I guess I'm gonna have to put you in time out for that when we get home," Jesse said with a mock look of disapproval. Then all three of the men started laughing, and Jesse backhanded the driver's right arm. "Toby, let's go to the warehouse. We'll stash her there and then head to my house. On second thought, if Jack's been talking to Metro, then he's told them where I live. The house is no good. Drop me off at the condo instead."

"You got it, boss," Toby said still smiling. Then he half turned is head and said, "Hey Roby, don't forget her busted lip. You don't want to miss a spot."

"I'm thinking of making some new spots, too," Roby said as he made his eyes go wide, and they both started laughing, again.

"Now, now, boys," Jesse said. "I need her in relatively good condition until I get satisfaction from Jack, so no more fun and games. After that, you have my permission to play with her all you want."

When they arrived at the warehouse complex off Industrial Road, they circumnavigated the maze of rusted out dumpsters and stacks of broken wooden pallets. They twisted their way around to the back and stopped in front of a derelict, solitary warehouse-looking building. Many years ago, it had been white-washed with the name Lamb Liquidators overlaid in big black block letters. However, time and the desert sun had been cruel to the paint job, and large patches had peeled away exposing the cinder blocks beneath.

Roby jumped out of the side door of the van and approached the roll-up door. Looking around furtively, he produced a key, unlocked the padlock, and raised the door with a loud clatter. Toby drove the van inside, and Roby turned on an overhead light that consisted of a single 60-watt bulb hanging from a wire suspended over a wooden chair with slats for a seat.

Besides the chair in the middle of the expanse, there was a ramshackle wooden table placed against a side wall with a pegboard on the wall behind it. The pegboard looked like the type that held tools in somebody's garage, but this one had all manner of weapons hanging from it, including shotguns and various handguns. Other than that, the building was barren inside. It was about three-thousand square feet of cement floor and various musty smells.

Toby pulled up close to the chair and jumped out of the van. He roughly pulled Lisa out by her arms while Roby lowered the door behind them. After putting Lisa in the chair, Toby cut her bonds and then zip tied her hands and legs to the supports of the chair.

Jesse came around to face Lisa carrying a dirty blanket that he had retrieved from the van.

He wrapped it over her shoulders and around her legs. "There. That's so you don't freeze in here. I can't have you kicking off on me before I need you to get your dad."

Lisa started mumbling and mouthing words into the gag, so Jesse pulled it down a bit. "I need to pee really bad," Lisa half sobbed.

"So, pee. Look at that cement floor around you. Do you seriously think you're going to make it look any worse?" and all three men started laughing.

Lisa looked down at the floor around her, and she could see dried pools and splatters of what looked like blood. It was all over the floor surrounding her. She started to scream, but suddenly a strange smelling rag was stuffed over her nose and mouth. Lisa shook her head, but she couldn't escape the hand that held the rag. Slowly her vision started to narrow and blur until it went completely black.

18

Jack looked at his cellphone as if he was trying to make it tell him where Jesse had taken Lisa, and he noticed that Kiersten had texted him. The message said, "Jack, I'm back home. You can bring Lisa over whenever you like." Jack figured Kiersten was safe and hadn't been around when Jesse snatched Lisa. He counted that as a blessing, but he wasn't looking forward to telling her that her only granddaughter had been abducted by a psychopath and that he was the cause.

Before he called Kiersten, Jack had to get out of the hotel. Exiting the bedroom Jack saw Detective McGreer watching a Miami Vice rerun. He hoped Crockett and Tubbs had him enthralled.

"Hey Detective McGreer, I'm heading downstairs for some cigarettes. You want anything?"

McGreer gave him a dismissive wave of his hand. Some detective, Jack thought. He didn't even smoke. Fifteen minutes later, Jack was driving West on Flamingo Road when his phone rang.

"Hello?"

"Jack, hun, it's Abbie. Are you all right?"

"Abbie, Jesse has my daughter. He said if I don't give him the necklace or $100,000, he's gonna turn Lisa over to those mongrels that have been doing the home invasion tortures! I've gotta get that necklace back from Allen!"

"Won't happen, Jack. Allen wants those guys in the worst way. He figures you and that necklace are what he needs to make his case, and he's not lettin' go of either one of you."

"Well, he doesn't have me anymore, Abbie. I bolted when I got the call from Jesse. I'm not sitting in some hotel room while he's got Lisa."

"Oh, dear God. Jack, hun, where are you?"

"I'm driving up Flamingo right now."

"Well, I gotta tell ya somethin' else, then. There's a price on your head, Jack. Jesse punched a ticket on you for $20,000. The only caveat is the clock doesn't start tickin' for forty-eight hours. I'm guessin' that's how long he gave you to save your daughter. Jack, hun, he's planning to pay your contract with your own money."

"Shit! I never thought he'd go that far. Well, that seals it. He's not going to give me Lisa. He just wants his money and then it's adios muchacho! By the way, how do you know all this? What gives you this pipeline of information?"

"Well, Jack, let's just say that my daddy was known to work with certain businessmen of the Italian persuasion back East, and I grew up around some of the families and got to know a lot of the kids. This led me to become acquainted with some other business owners here in Las Vegas that don't exactly belong to the Chamber of Commerce. I stay in touch and pass them interesting tidbits from time to time. They help me out from time to time. It's a mutually beneficial arrangement. One foot on both sides of the line, remember?"

"Ya, I know. You just never cease to amaze me, that's all. Just when I think I've got you figured out, I see another facet."

"Jack, hun, if you had me all figured out, it wouldn't be as much fun!"

"I agree, but that conversation has to wait for another time. Right now, that rat bastard has my daughter, and he wants me dead. I guess I should've expected this. If you lie down with dogs, you get up with fleas, and I've been lying with this dog for way too long."

"What do you plan to do, Jack?"

"I don't know, yet. I don't have the necklace, and I don't have $100,000, but somehow, I'm gonna make this work. I have to. I'm not going down without a fight, and I'm not leaving Lisa at the mercy of those animals. If I have to just open up on him, I will. It would be better to go down with guns blazing instead of offering Lisa up for the slaughter without a whimper. Who knows, I might get lucky."

"Jack, hun, don't do anythin' rash, now. We'll figure this out."

"I'm not saying that's plan A. I hope it's plan Z, but I guarantee you that I will have a plan. I won't just sit on my hands."

"Okay, well let me know if I can help, Jack."

"I will, and thanks, Abbie."

Jack hung up the phone and realized that he was now heading North on I-215 and had driven almost clear to the turnoff to Redrock Canyon. He veered off the freeway at the Charleston Boulevard exit, made a left off the ramp, and headed for the canyon. When he neared the entrance to the canyon loop, he slowed down, made a U-turn, and stopped beside the dark, quiet two-lane highway facing back toward the valley. He got out of the car and leaned against the grill. The heat from the engine permeated through the hood and warmed him from beneath while the cold desert air tried to cool him from above.

Jack figured it was time to call Kiersten. He still didn't know what he was going to do, but he owed her the courtesy of keeping her at least somewhat informed. He certainly wasn't going to tell her the whole story. Who knows? Maybe she had $100,000 that he didn't know about.

Kiersten picked up on the first ring, "Jack?"

"Hey, Kiersten. Listen to me carefully. I've got horrible news. Lisa's been kidnapped."

"WHAT! By who? I thought you had her! Is she alright? Oh my god! My little Lisa! How do you know this? What do you know?" The questions came out like .45 slugs from a Tommy Gun, each one hitting him rapid fire in his gut.

"I dropped her off at your house while you were gone. Somehow these people found her and took her after that, and they want $100,000 in forty-eight hours to let her go. They said they'll kill her if they don't get the money."

"Oh my God, oh my God, oh my God! Jack, you don't have that kind of money, do you?"

"No, I don't, but I'll figure something out. I have to."

"We've gotta call the cops and get Metro in on this!"

"They're already involved."

"You don't think they'll actually hurt her, do you?"

"Unfortunately, these are some nasty people. There's no telling what they'll do."

"How do you know these are people that might hurt her? Jack, are you telling me everything?"

"Of course! The cops told me they know these people. Listen, I've got to call the cops back and start working on this. The moment that I know anything else, I'll call you, okay?"

"Okay. Don't you dare keep me in the dark on this! My god, Jack what are we going to do?"

"I don't know, yet, but I'm sure the cops will find her and bring her back safe and sound. I've gotta go. I'll call you."

After Jack had hung up, he shook his head at all the little lies he had told Kiersten. She deserved to be informed, but he didn't want her knowing everything that he knew. Of course, that last lie was a whopper. He never believed in a million years that Metro would ever bring Lisa back to him in one piece. He knew Jesse too well. Jack didn't believe that Metro could outsmart Jesse. After all, they had failed to catch him or even link him to the High Society Gang. Plus, he knew Jesse would never go down without an all-out, blood-bath fight, and he would take anyone and everyone with him, including Lisa.

Perched up high above the valley he looked out and surveyed the lights of Vegas. The valley was crisscrossed with ribbons of sparkles that marked the major thoroughfares with the Strip and downtown rising up and outshining the rest. It looked like a giant bowl full of diamond necklaces and tiaras.

Jack sometimes came out here at night to clear his head and think. Save for an occasional coyote howling, he was sure to be alone, and it always seemed to give him a different perspective on whatever was troubling him, just like it was a different perspective on Vegas.

Las Vegas existed most of the time under cloudless skies, but it was nearly impossible for Jack to see any stars in the night sky when he was in the valley due to the brightness of the lights. The vertical beam emitted from the Luxor, for instance, could be seen from hundreds of miles away and had been acknowledged by NASA shuttle astronauts from space. There was just too much civilization in his face to recognize reality.

However, peering from up above the lights revealed a totally different paradigm. The night sky was full of twinkling stars and the lights below seemed like spectacles in an intricate menagerie. Even the Stratosphere Hotel, a stoic concrete and glass behemoth that towered over the valley floor, seemed like a child's toy to be picked up and rearranged on a whim.

It was here that Jack began to contemplate his predicament in earnest. Whatever he did, he couldn't jeopardize Lisa's life, yet he figured that Jesse had plans to kill them both. He didn't believe any amount of money would change Jesse's mind about that, but he had to try.

Maybe the money would buy him some time, though. Jesse surely loved money.

However, if the money wouldn't change his mind, then Jack had to entertain other methods of persuasion and acquisition. Jack considered himself to be pretty good with a handgun, but he knew that he would be out numbered at least three to one, if the newspaper reports were to be believed. He didn't like those odds. A shotgun would be no good, because he had to assume that Lisa would be present at the exchange, and he couldn't afford a stray pellet from a scattergun. Jack knew he could probably procure a small sub-machine gun. He had the money, and it seemed as though Abbie might have the contacts, but that presented the same problem of collateral damage as a shotgun. A high-powered rifle with a scope would probably be the ticket, but Jack had never been a hunter, and he had no experience as a sniper. He even entertained the notion of hiring his own hitman as a sniper, but if Jesse caught wind of that plan, he could just outbid him and seal Jack's fate. Besides, even with Jesse's money, Jack had less than $20,000 for talent that would cost twice that amount. He needed a crack marksman that worked for cheap and couldn't be bought. Jack laughed at himself when he realized how improbable and silly that sounded.

That brought Jack back full circle to handguns and close quarters combat. Maybe the threat of gun play alone would compel Jesse to release Lisa back to Jack, he thought. Probably not, though. Jesse and his associates were obviously no strangers to violence and death. The use of force faded back to plan Z.

Jack vowed to himself that he would do everything in his power to rescue Lisa, even if it meant trading his own life. Of course, he preferred making Jesse trade his life. The trick was going to be how. How could he get Lisa out of harm's way and live to tell about it? Two things were painfully evident. He didn't have the necklace, and he didn't have $100,000. "Minor details," Jack thought as he rolled his eyes.

He thought about pawning or selling some of the other jewelry that he still had stashed. He figured that Jesse wouldn't miss a few pieces until later when Jack was hopefully very far away. The problem was that any pawn broker with $100,000 to lend on the jewelry would be much too savvy to touch any of it. Even the greedy ones wouldn't dare soil their beaks in that carcass.

Then he heard a voice. At least it sounded like a voice. It was ethereal but insistent.

Jack shook his head. It sounded like, "Promise ... promise." He figured it must just be the dry desert breeze whistling through the canyon, but it became clearer and repeated itself until Jack could distinguish the words. "Jack? Will you promise me something?" the voice whispered.

"Melinda?" Jack said hesitantly.

"Jack? Will you promise me something?" This time the voice was louder.

Jack knew the voice had to be in his head: a free roaming memory floating through his brain like a willow-the-wisp. Still, he had to answer. "You know I will."

"Take that special ring that you gave me. I want you to hold on to it. One day Val is going to need it."

Jack remembered the promise that he had made to Melinda, and almost reflexively he said, "I have the ring, Melinda. I didn't let go of it. I have it for Val."

"Jack? Will you promise me something?"

Jack's eyes started to tear up. It was painful to have this voice in his head. It was a forlorn ghost-in-the-machine repeating the words of a memory that had all but faded into the mist of lapsed memory, but it sounded so real that it hurt. Melinda sounded so real. He desperately wanted to hold her in his arms and have her tell him that everything was going to be all right. As he held his arms to his chest, wishing she were wrapped in them, his voice choked, but he dutifully repeated the words that he had spoken the first time to his beloved Melinda. "You know that I will. What would you like me to do?"

"Jack, Val needs my ring today. Take my ring and go get our little girl. Go get our Valentine, JACK!" The name "Jack" echoed through the canyon twice and then went silent.

Jack stood up stock straight. His eyes were as wide as silver dollars and his lower jaw hung slack like a limp bag of hammers. He jerked left and right looking over both shoulders.

All he saw was the darkness, and all he heard now was the breeze rustling through the sagebrush.

Had the voice been real? Had he really heard Melinda? Did it really matter? The voice was right. Today was the day Melinda had foreseen. Jack could sell the ring and hopefully buy Lisa's freedom. Somehow, he had to make it work!

19

Lieutenant Vincent DeLuca was having an argument on the phone with District Attorney Richard Allen. "I know he's a material witness, but I don't have the manpower to babysit him twenty-four seven. I've got Detective McGreer over at the Rio with him now, but I can't spare him to be Diamante's roommate, not to mention the overtime involved with something like that."

"Vincent, without Diamante, we don't have a case. He's the only one right now that can put anyone in possession of that necklace besides the victims. If we lose him, we're almost back to square one."

"No, we're not, Richard. We now have a subject for our focus. Our manpower would best be allocated on surveillance of Brizetta, rather than protecting Diamante when he probably isn't even in jeopardy. Frankly, if Brizetta was using Diamante to ferry his stolen property around, then Brizetta's no Einstein, so if we stick to him, he's going to stumble. When he does, we'll be there to catch him before he hits the ground."

"I don't agree. I think he's too valuable to our case, so I'm telling Sheriff Ballard that you need to keep Diamante under wraps. He'll authorize whatever manpower you need. Recruit patrolmen if you have to, but make sure he stays put!"

DeLuca looked up when Terry Robertsville, the lead detective on the High Society Gang case, burst into his office.

DeLuca stopped his conversation, covered the receiver, and said, "What's wrong?"

"Diamante left the Rio."

"Are you shitting me?"

"I shit you not, boss. McGreer said Diamante told him he was going downstairs to get some cigarettes, but he never came back. After about twenty minutes of waiting, McGreer said he figured he'd better go look for him in case something happened. He described Diamante to the gift shop cashier, but she said no one by that description had been to the register in the last half hour, so he went out to look for his car, and it was gone."

"Damn!" DeLuca said and shook his head. He uncovered the receiver and said, "Richard, I've got to call you back. Diamante's disappeared."

"WHAT? What do you mean he's disappeared? I thought you had somebody with him. How did he get away, dammit?"

"I don't know. I was just told about it. Give me a couple minutes and let me see if I can straighten this out."

"You'd better straighten it out, DeLuca! Right now, he's our whole case! Dammit to hell!"

"I'll call you right back," he said and hung up.

DeLuca suddenly focused back on Robertsville. "What the hell's going on? Did McGreer say anything about where he might've gone?"

"No, he said Diamante told him he was just going for cigarettes. He said he kinda heard him talking in the bedroom right before he left, like he was on the phone, but he couldn't tell what was being said."

"Shit! Get a squad over to his apartment to see if he went there. Meanwhile, I'll call somebody that might know where he went. Check back with me in about five to ten minutes."

"You got it, boss."

DeLuca pulled out his cellphone and opened up his contacts list. He scrolled down to "Abbie Duncara" and hit send.

"Hey, Vinnie."

"Abbie, we've got trouble. Jack bolted the Rio."

"I know. I just got off the phone with him a little while ago."

"Where is he? Why didn't you call me?"

"He's driving, but I don't know where. Jesse Brizetta called him. He kidnapped Jack's daughter. Jack's pissed and worried sick about her. Jesse wants the necklace for Lisa, or he said he'd kill her."

"Jack's not getting the necklace back. I hope he knows that. It's not even up for discussion."

"That's what I told him."

"So, where's he going? What's he gonna do?"

"Don't know."

"Shit!"

"Yeah, shit is right. His daughter means the world to him. He might just try to go after Jesse on his own, but I don't think he's got a clue where they're keeping her."

"That's the best news I've heard, so far. Hopefully he doesn't know where they are. If he decides to go after them, he'll only get himself and his daughter killed. If Brizetta really is involved with this High Society Gang, Jack's in over his head. They're sadistic and brutal. Can you get him to call me? Maybe I can talk some sense into him."

"I'll try."

"Try real hard, Abbie, and let me know if you find out where he's gone."

"Alright."

DeLuca watched the call disconnect from his phone just as Robertsville came back into his office. Robertsville looked at DeLuca with expectant hope in his eyes, but DeLuca just shook his head no.

"Damn. The squad said he wasn't at his apartment. I was hoping you had good news."

"All I know is that he's driving somewhere. Brizetta kidnapped his daughter and called him. He wants the necklace back for the daughter, which ain't gonna happen, so now Diamante's in panic mode. Damn that McGreer! I told him not to let Diamante out of his sight. Now we've got a loose cannon running around. Alright, get an APB out on Diamante and his car. The details are in the file. They are not to arrest. They are merely to detain until I can get there. Go. Get it out. Oh, and tell McGreer to get his stupid ass back in here!"

"I'm on it."

Jack was coming down Charleston Boulevard from Redrock Canyon. Golden Earring's *Twilight Zone* was blaring from the radio. "I'm falling down a spiral destination unknown, double-crossed messenger, all alone," echoed through the car, through Jack's head, and out into the night. He knew exactly how the mythical character in the song felt. It was more than helplessness. It was helplessness with consequences. Lives hung in the balance, and Jack had put them there with no backup plan.

As he passed the Redrock Casino on the right, the strains of *Dixie* shattered Jack's reverie.

He had recently changed the ringtone for Abbie from a common jingle to the Anthem of the South. It seemed appropriate, and he immediately knew it was her. He had begun to think of her more and more as "his" Southern belle. "Hey, Abbie."

"Hey, Jack. Metro's lookin' for you now. I don't know what you've got planned, but I'd call in and at least square things with them. Otherwise, any plans you have better include evading every cop in the valley."

"Oh, geez. That's just what I need is to make the most wanted list. I guess when it rains, it pours, doesn't it?"

"It does seem like that, Jack, hun. Metro doesn't take too kindly to skipping out of their protection. They get kinda surly when you make them look bad, if ya know what I mean. My suggestion is to call Richard Allen. You've probably got the most leverage with him. If you can convince him to give you a pass, maybe at least part of the heat will let up. He'll be able to call off Metro."

"Okay, I'll give it a shot. Thanks for the heads-up, Abbie. I owe you one."

"You owe me nuthin', Jack, hun. Friends do for friends. You be safe, and don't do anything crazy. You can't help your daughter if you get yourself killed or arrested."

"Well, I think I've figured out a way to get the money I need, but I've gotta figure out a way to handle Jesse. It's obvious he wants me dead, and he'll figure Lisa may as well go along for the ride in the hearse. Damn his black heart to Hell!"

"I'll second that motion, Jack. So, got any ideas?"

"No. I feel like a one-legged man in an ass kickin' contest, and I'm wearing a roller skate."

"I wish I could help you more, sugar."

"You've already been a huge help, Abbie. I feel better from just talking to you. I'm treading water in this ocean of shit with sharks circling, but every time you call, I feel like a lifeline is being thrown out to me. Thanks. You always make me feel like I can do this."

"Jack, hun, I'll always be here for you. If you haven't figured that out, then know it now. I'm not goin' anywhere."

"I know that, Abbie, and I couldn't ask for a better friend. Thank you. I'd better call Allen now before some cop sees me and wants to get promoted. I'll stay in touch."

"You better, Jack, hun, cause you don't want *me* doggin' your trail!" Abbie said with a mock threat in her voice.

Jack laughed and said, "I don't know. If I knew you were after me, I might let you catch me!"

"That sounds like a plan I'd like to try, Jack, hun."

Jack laughed, again. "When this is over, we'll have to have a drink and discuss it in more detail," he said with a smile.

"It's a date, sugar. Take care, Jack."

"You, too, Abbie," Jack said. He clicked off the connection, looked at his phone like it had suddenly grown a tail, and he shook his head. Things seemed to be changing between him and Abbie, and he realized that he liked it. For now, though, he needed to focus on Lisa and Jesse. This was *not* going to be easy.

DeLuca was about to call Abbie when she called him. "Vinnie, it's Abbie. I couldn't get hold of Jack. Either he has his phone off or he wasn't getting reception. I left him a message to call me back."

"Damn it! Alright, Abbie. Thanks for trying. If he calls you, tell him to call me asap."

"No problem, Vinnie. Think nothing of it." When Abbie ended the call, she thought to herself, "Think *absolutely* nothing of it, Vinnie," and she smiled.

DeLuca smiled as he laid his cellphone on his desk. The choice of putting McGreer, his biggest screw-up, on Diamante's babysitting detail had unexpectedly paid dividends. Now he could focus on catching Jesse and leave finding Jack to patrol officers. However, he had to schmooze things with Allen. He didn't want Sheriff Ballard crawling up his ass over witness protection. He figured if he could just mollify Allen long enough, he could catch the High Society Gang and all would be forgiven and forgotten. The question was how to do it. That's when Allen called him.

"DeLuca, it's Richard Allen. I just got off the line with Jack Diamante. He wants us to let him freelance rather than keeping him under wraps. I know that will please you, but are you sure he won't get in your way or jeopardize what we've got now on the case?"

"If he's smart, he won't get in our way."

"So, you're not concerned about the kidnapping of his daughter and him mucking up your investigation if he tries to go after her?"

"Look, the sign on my office door says Homicide. If she gets killed, then I'm interested. Otherwise, she belongs to someone else. Now, do I want to see that she gets back safe? Sure, but that's not my priority. Catching Brizetta and the High Society Gang is my priority, and I can do that most effectively if I'm focused on Brizetta. If Diamante gets in my way, then I'll arrest him for obstruction."

"Alright, then, but I want you to continue to reach out to him. He's still our best link to Brizetta, especially with his daughter being kidnapped. They'll probably stay in touch, and we need to know what's going on."

"Makes sense. I'll keep trying to reach him. Plus, I've got Abbie Duncara trying to contact him for me, as well. He'll hopefully listen to her and call me."

"Just don't let this opportunity get away from us. We've got to get these maniacs off the street, and this is our first big break. Don't let it slip away!"

"I won't. I want these guys as bad as you do. I'll keep you up-to-date."

"See that you do, Lieutenant."

DeLuca hung up his office phone and smiled. "I love it when a plan comes together," he said to himself.

20

Jack had thirty-six hours left when the bank opened up the next morning. He was the first customer in the door, and he headed straight for the bank manager, Lou Gangi. Jack had been a long-time customer at this particular branch dating back to before he had started Diamond Security. Lou greeted him warmly with a handshake and grabbed his keys when Jack told him that he needed to get into his safe deposit box. Lou didn't even check Jack's identification. He just had him sign in and took him into the vault area where the safe deposit boxes were located.

Jack had his key hanging on a chain around his neck under his shirt. He pulled it out and gave it to Lou. Gangi unlocked both locks, pulled out the box, and took it to a private cubicle. There he placed it on a small table and left Jack alone. Once Jack knew he was alone, he opened the lid to the box. Ensconced inside were Melinda's ring, ten thousand dollars, and two derringers chambered in .45 Colt/.410. Each derringer was loaded with two .410 #000 buckshot shotgun shells. Each shell contained five lead balls the diameter of a .38 caliber bullet.

The derringers weren't particularly accurate beyond thirty feet, but up close they were devastating. Of course, they really didn't have to be highly accurate. They threw a lot of heavy lead into the air and were highly concealable. Jack had found that he could conceal both of them between his butt cheeks as long as he didn't have to walk too much. It wasn't the most comfortable location, but he had once been told by an undercover detective that it was one place that rarely got searched. He figured that he would be searched when he met Jesse, but he calculated that he could smuggle both guns into the meeting. He would also have the snub-nose .38 that he kept on his ankle, although he was sure that they would find that and confiscate it.

No matter. They would have to find something, or they would keep looking until they did.

With the deposit box emptied and his business finished at the bank, Jack had someone else he needed to see: Dixon "Dix" Phillips. Dix Phillips had the largest pawn brokerage in the state of Nevada. He would loan money on anything of value. He was also probably the only pawn broker locally with enough cash on hand to be able to give Jack the $100,000 that he needed without blinking an eye.

Dix's pawn shop was on Main Street in downtown Las Vegas. Most tourists think the Strip is Main Street, but that's Las Vegas Boulevard, which is five blocks east of Main Street, and it's a totally different world. In fact, most tourists don't know that the Strip is not even in Las Vegas. The Strip starts at Sahara Avenue and proceeds south. The City of Las Vegas city limits start on the north side of Sahara Avenue, so the city proper sits in the opposite direction.

When Bugsy Siegel opened up the Flamingo Hotel in 1947, it was purposely built several miles south of the city limits in order to keep the city politicians' hands out of the mob's pockets. Every casino downtown had to grease the palms of the local politicians and cops, but out in the unincorporated part of Clark County, the mob operated unhindered for many years until the county government woke up and noticed that Las Vegas Boulevard South was sporting new hotels and casinos. Anxious to pump up the tax revenue base, they rolled out the red carpet for the "boys." The Sahara, Desert Inn, Sands, Flamingo, Tropicana and others all had cross streets to the Strip named after them.

Downtown was different. The cross streets to Las Vegas Boulevard and Main Street were named after famous pioneers. John C. Fremont, Kit Carson, Jim Bridger, Meriwether Lewis, and William Clark, among others, all lent their names to the streets of downtown. So while the Strip was a star-spangled tribute to the mob, downtown was all about the pioneers: Las Vegas pioneers like Benny Binion, Joe W. Brown, and Dixon Phillips.

Dix was never a casino owner. He just owned everyone that worked in the casinos. With his pawn shop close by on Main Street, it was a short walk for any downtown casino worker to go pawn a watch or ring until payday. Of course, if you didn't have anything to pawn, Dix made you a loan that bit deep into the flesh of many casino workers. That left them beholden to Dix, and there were only a few ways to pay him that didn't include cash. In the '60s and '70s, there were many scams run on the casinos at Dix's behest in order to pay off his loans.

These days, Dix didn't bother with loan sharking. He had made his millions, and he was content to fleece the rich in a legitimate fashion. Many professional athletes left behind their Super Bowl or World Series rings in Dix's pawn shop. There were even a few actors that left behind Academy Award "Oscar" statues. It was all for a price that made Dix Phillips famous and infamous. If you had a high-end pawn, Dix was the man you had to see and hated to see, because Dix had the money, but you paid the price.

So it was with mixed feelings that Jack made his way through the wrought iron gate guarding the door into the Dixon Phillips "Pawn Shop and House of Pain." He would've liked to be anywhere else, but there was nowhere else to go. The shop was poorly lit and smelled of old dust, old carpet, old sweat, and old menthol cigarettes. Dix was standing behind a glass display counter filled with handguns, and he was thumbing through a numismatic magazine when Jack came in. He was a short man and had a round belly that protruded out almost like he was pregnant. His wavy gray hair was parted just over his left ear and combed over in an attempt to cover his expanding bald spot. It wasn't successful. His ears and nose seemed over-sized for the rest of his head, and he bared some gold crowns interspersed with some rotten choppers when he smiled at Jack. He looked like a jack-o-lantern two weeks after Halloween.

"Hey there, Dix."

"Hey, Jack. Long time no see. Whatcha' been up to?"

"Same old same old. I've got some business for you, Dix."

"Yeah? You come back to pawn your watch, again? You know, I think I've worn that watch more than you have!"

"Ha! You may be right! No, I've got something special today, and I need your best price."

"Something special, huh? Well, let me see it."

Jack pulled out the box that held Melinda's ring. When he opened the box, the ring sparkled, even in the dingy light of Dix's shop.

Dix whistled and said, "Good God, Jack, where did you get a ring like that? You weren't exaggerating when you said it was special. Look at that fire!"

Dix pulled out a jeweler's loop and turned on a small lamp on the counter. When the ring was placed in the light, the room lit up as if there were laser beams passing through a kaleidoscope.

"That was my wife's wedding ring. Just before she died, she made me promise to keep it for the proverbial rainy day.

Well, Dix, it's coming down in buckets outside, and I need every nickel I can get for it."

"I see. It's a beautiful ring, Jack. Are you looking to pawn it or sell it?"

"Sell it. I won't need it after this."

"Alright, then. Let me do some figuring. I'll be right back."

Dix left the ring on the counter under the light and went into the back room. He emerged holding some papers inscribed with handwritten notes, an electronic scale, a micrometer, and a calculator. After removing the three stones from their settings, he took measurements and weighed each stone. Dix consulted the papers several times and worked the calculator. It appeared as though he was arguing with an imaginary partner in his mind as he shook his head and mumbled to himself. After several minutes of this intracranial conference call, Dix cocked his head slightly to the left, and then he nodded his head. Finally, he wrote a figure on a piece of paper and slid it over to Jack.

"That's what I'll pay for it, Jack."

"$50,000? That's all? Dix, this ring was appraised at $250,000 when I bought it."

"I hope that's not what you paid for it."

"Of course not, but still it's got to be worth more than $50,000," Jack lamented.

"It is. Retail I could maybe sell it for $80,000 to $100,000. But, then again, maybe I couldn't. The Russians have been dumping diamonds on the market, Jack. Why, I don't know, but they've driven the prices down, and I've got to make a profit. I normally would have offered someone else $40,000 and maybe gone as high as $45,000, but you're a friend, Jack, so no screwing around. That's what I can give you. You're welcome to shop it around, but I doubt anyone would give you more even if they could."

Jack knew he was right. No one else had that kind of cash to throw at just one purchase.

As much as he hated to admit it, he was stuck with Dix's offer and only had about half of the money that he needed.

"Alright, Dix. I'll take it. I really don't have much choice."

"Fine. Let me lock up the shop, and I'll get the money out of the safe."

Dix trundled over to the entrance and turned the locks in the steel reinforced door. Then he made his way back into the office, and Jack could hear a heavy door squeal open and then shut with a hefty oomph. Dix then returned to the counter with a large cash box that he opened to expose wrapped stacks of one hundred-dollar bills.

As Dix counted out the money, Jack started wracking his brain for a way to turn $50,000 into $100,000 in about thirty-four hours. It seemed like an impossible task given the time limit. As Jack silently loaded the money into the gym bag that he had brought, he noted with a grim shake of his head that it was only half as full as it needed to be. He had to think of something!

As Dix was unlocking the front door, he said, "Hey Jack, you gonna cruise the NFR with some of that money?"

"Huh? What's that?"

"The NFR, Jack. You know, the National Finals Rodeo? You gonna cruise the rodeo in some fancy boots and hub cap belt buckle? Maybe you could pick up Miss Amarillo and turn her into Miss Behavin'!" Dix said with a mangled, toothy grin while his scraggly eyebrows danced up and down.

"That's it! The rodeo! Thanks, Dix! I owe you for that!"

"Owe me for what?" Dix said with a quizzical look as Jack bolted out into the blinding Vegas sunlight.

21

"Hello?"

"Abbie?"

"Yes. Is that you, Jack, hun?"

"Yeah. Have you been working the last couple of nights?"

"Sure. I'm working tonight, too. Why?"

"Has there been any decent action there at the Nugget?"

"Sure has. It's been downright crazy. All the good ol' boys are in town, and they all want to play poker after the rodeo. We've been running extra 2/5 games, a 10/20 limit game, and last night we even opened up a 100/200 no-limit game."

"That's the one I'm interested in. Do you think they'll open up a big game like that tonight?"

"I don't know, Jack. It all depends on who shows up and wants to play."

"If it looks like there's a decent chance that game will get going, will you call me? I've GOT to get in that game. If it doesn't go, I'll have to play at the Bellagio, and there are too many sharks in the water there. I don't want to be a part of that pissing contest. I just need to make money."

"Jack, if you want in that game, it's gonna be expensive. The minimum buy-in is $5000, but nobody bought in for less than $20,000 last time. There's at least $200,000 on the table at any given time and usually more. Management has put on extra security around the poker room just in case."

"That's what I'm looking for, Abbie. I need that table to be rockin'! I've got about $50,000 to work with, and I need twice that much to have a chance at getting Lisa back."

"Jack, hun," Abbie said as her voice got softer and mellower, "I know you've got to do this, and I'll help you any way I can, but that table's no picnic. I've seen a whole slew of players get chopped up pretty good. The Duke's been there every night along with a few others that have been feasting on the tourists."

"Thanks for the heads-up, Abbie, but I really have no choice. I'm short of the $100,000 I need. I could maybe fudge $10,000, but I can't show up with only half the money. For me to get Lisa and get out alive, Jesse has to think that I know nothing about the contract and I'm buying my daughter back. If I'm $50,000 short or $100,000 short, it's all the same."

"All right, Jack. I'll call you as soon as I know somethin'."

"Thanks, Abbie. You're a peach!"

"That's what I keep tellin' ya, Jack, hun."

With Plan A starting to take shape, Jack started to lay the foundation for Plan B just in case he couldn't get the money together. He had about thirty-two hours left, so Jack made some phone calls, got something to eat, and headed back to his apartment.

On the way there, Jack got the uneasy feeling that someone was following him. He didn't like carrying around that much cash, but he didn't really have anywhere to stash it, so he decided to stash himself.

Jack called Richard Allen. He had talked to him the night before after he had talked to Abbie, and he had squared things with him. He had convinced Allen that he was better off making moves unfettered rather than being locked in a hotel room. Now he wasn't so sure, so he arranged to stay downtown at the Nugget with Detective McGreer, again. That way he could get some sleep before he started playing while someone watched his back. A game like this would start after that night's rodeo, maybe eleven or midnight. It could easily go twelve hours or longer, and he needed to be sharp.

As he packed what he needed into another gym bag, he looked around the dingy expanse that had been his home for the last eighteen months. He noted that there really wasn't anything in his apartment that would distinguish it as being his. There were no pictures of him or family, no personalized belongings, really, that could identify him, and he mused that if he died in the next day or two, no one would even be able to tell that he had been here, much less where he'd gone. Except, of course, the landlord would wonder where he'd gone when the rent was late.

Then Jack thought about when he had tried to drink himself to death. He had been in a similar nondescript hovel. Back then, he felt like he had nothing to live for and nobody cared if he lived or died. Now he was fighting for his life and for Lisa's life. Everything hinged on Jack. He also knew, this time, that Lisa and Abbie would dearly miss him if he didn't make it through this ordeal. Even Kiersten cared wholeheartedly whether he lived or died. It was an ironic twist that wasn't lost on Jack, and he vowed to stay alive long enough to see that his daughter was safe. He was hardly convincing, though. Deep down he wasn't sure that he would be able to keep that vow to himself.

22

Jack pulled into to the parking deck of the Golden Nugget around four-thirty in the afternoon. He had arranged for Detective McGreer to meet him on the fifth level, but he didn't know where on the level he would park. He wanted to be as close to the elevators as possible to reduce his exposure, but the closest parking space available was twelve spaces away, and there was a support column blocking his view of the elevator. He wanted better visibility, but it was the best he could do without getting substantially further away.

McGreer had been told to meet Jack at his car, but Jack didn't see him anywhere in the deck. He glanced over to the gym bag with the $50,000 inside. He took out another $5,000 from Jesse's money and put it inside. The balance he left in his coat pocket. Then he moved the bag from the passenger seat to down between his legs on the floorboard. That much money filled Jack with trepidation, and he didn't want to take any chances.

A tap, tap, tap on the driver's window made Jack bolt upright in his seat. His blood pressure rocketed, and his eyes bugged out as he swiveled his head in the direction of the tapping. McGreer's face was about three inches from the glass and plastered with a big grin. "A little jumpy, Jack?" McGreer said with a chuckle.

Jack opened the car door and said, "No, I always break my neck like that when somebody taps on my window.

Where did you come from? I didn't see anyone when I drove in."

"I was hunched down in my car when you pulled in. I wanted to make sure it was you before I gave away my position. I'm sorry if I startled you. Well, maybe not all that sorry. I owe you for skipping out on me last night. You should've seen your face!" McGreer started laughing, again, as Jack got out of the car.

"Very funny," Jack said, but he was relieved to have McGreer there. Jack leaned back into the car, unzipped the bag on the floorboard, and ascertained that the money, a spare shirt, and one of the derringers were inside. That determined, he grabbed the money bag and left the other one in the back seat.

The two men made their way to the parking deck elevator and down to the ground level. On the way to the hotel room elevators, Jack felt like everyone they passed in the halls were all looking specifically at him. He felt conspicuous carrying a gym bag while McGreer walked next to him with nothing. It seemed obvious to Jack that McGreer looked like a bodyguard. "So much for blending in," he thought, however, they made it up to the hotel suite without incident.

Once they were in, McGreer did a cursory check around the suite, and then Jack threw his stuff into the bedroom. He wanted to get some sleep, but he was still pretty wired, so he sat down with McGreer in the living room and watched the evening news on television.

Jack felt a little sheepish being with McGreer after the incident at the Rio, so he decided to clear the air. "Hey, McGreer, no hard feelings about skipping out on you, huh?"

"Naw. For some reason the lieutenant didn't chew my ass out. Surprised the hell out of me. I've got a daughter, too, and I know I'd be going out of my mind, so I'll cut you some slack. I sure hope you get her back."

"Thanks."

A follow-up story on the Moscowitz murders came on, and McGreer started to quiz Jack. "So, you knew that couple pretty well?"

"I knew Toby Moscowitz pretty well. He was a good friend and past customer of mine when I owned a security business. I had only met Elena once, but Toby talked about her constantly."

"Damn shame. Those sons-of-bitches really treated them rough. Are you meeting them here tonight or something?"

"No. I've got to try to get $100,000 together to pay the ransom for my daughter. I've only got half of it, so I'm buying into a high stakes poker game here to try to get the rest of it."

"Is that what's in the bag? Fifty grand?"

"Yeah, a little more actually, but it won't mean a thing if I can't get it all."

"I heard Brizetta put a contract on you."

"Where'd you hear that?"

"Oh, word gets around. You didn't know?"

Jack started to get a little uneasy and decided to play dumb. "News to me," he said with a quizzical look on his face.

"I figured that's why I was here: to make sure you stayed upright."

"I requested that someone watch my back while I get some rest before the game. I've been up a lot lately, and I need to be sharp, but keeping watch over this money can be nerve wracking. Speaking of which, maybe you could turn down the TV some. I'm gonna see if I can get a little sleep."

"Sure thing, Jack," McGreer said as he thumbed down the volume on the remote.

Jack went into the bedroom and closed the door. He pulled back the comforter on the bed and put the bag on top of it. The next thing he did was check to make sure that the money was okay. As a precaution, he pulled the .38 out of his ankle holster and put it under the pillow. He knew that DeLuca had assigned McGreer to help him, but the detective seemed like he knew more than he should have, so he decided to not take any chances. He locked the bedroom door, and after kicking off his shoes and taking off his sport coat, he crawled into the bed with the bag of money under the covers with him and his head resting on the pillow over his revolver.

Just for a little insurance, he took the derringer that he'd brought in the bag and stuck it in the front right pocket of his jeans. It felt a little uncomfortable, and he wasn't sure if it would affect his ability to sleep, but he was more concerned about someone trying to relieve him of the burden of having to carry around all that money. He needn't have worried about sleeping. Even though he thought he heard McGreer talking to someone on the phone, he soon drifted off.

It was a little after ten when Jack's phone woke him up by playing "Dixie."

"Hey, Abbie."

"Hey, Jack, hun. All right, Sweetie, it looks like you're on for tonight. There's already a list building. I had my manager put you on the list. The Duke's on it already along with three others. I expect they'll be openin' the table up within an hour."

Jack took note of the use of "Sweetie." He knew that it was more than Southern charm or flirting. It was affection, and he liked it. It made him smile, and for a moment, he forgot the dire circumstances that surrounded him.

"Thanks, Abbie. In that case, I'm going to head down in about thirty minutes. I don't want to miss the table call. When do you go on tonight?"

"I go on at midnight."

"Okay. I'm sure I'll see you tonight."

"You better, Jack, hun!"

Jack chuckled. "I'm sure it will be impossible to miss you. You light up every room you enter."

"Oh, Sweetie, I think the same about you."

"Abbie, I wish we were having this particular conversation under different circumstances."

"Me, too, Jack, but at least we're startin' to have these conversations. I've been waitin' a while for this, and I'm all for it. Well, enough small talk. You get yourself ready. This won't be easy, so good luck."

"I know. Thanks!"

As Jack hung up, he really wished he had said more. He hadn't felt these emotions since Melinda had died. Then he reminded himself that he could only focus on one thing at a time.

Even though his goals were to free Lisa and stay alive, he couldn't let those thoughts cloud his judgment or perception. It couldn't be about love lost or found. Tonight had to be all about poker.

Before leaving the bedroom, Jack changed into the fresh shirt. It was a button-down oxford blue dress shirt that was open at the collar. Then he slipped his tennis shoes on and topped it off with his navy-blue sport coat. He put the derringer and his other shirt in the gym bag with the money. Then he zipped up the bag, grabbed the handles, and started for the door when he remembered his revolver. He shook his head at his forgetfulness, snatched it from under the pillow, and slid it back into the ankle holster.

McGreer accompanied Jack down the hall to the elevators. On the ride down, neither man spoke. It wasn't elevator etiquette that kept them quiet, though. Both men simply realized that tonight was heavy and no conversation could lighten it. The elevator let them out into one of the back hallways, and they made their way out onto the casino floor.

Jack appreciated the escort. Carrying $55,000 in his gym bag seemed like a low-profile maneuver, but it was also risky, and he wanted no interruptions or problems between his room and the casino cashier. This was his stake for tonight, and his hopes for rescuing Lisa rode on this money, his playing skills, and hopefully a big bucketful of luck. It would be difficult enough to pull off this miracle without also worrying about being robbed.

As they rounded the last corner, the cacophony of the slot machine bells, the shrieks and groans of players, and the calls of the dealers like carnival barkers filled the atmosphere, but Jack was oblivious. People squealed at the roulette table as Jack walked by with the detective, but he was focused only on his journey. He had to get to the cashier and then to the poker room unmolested. Then he could relax. That is until the cards were in the air.

Suddenly, someone stepped in front of him, and Jack jumped like a scalded cat. McGreer quickly stepped between them, but Jack's tunnel vision quickly widened, and he recognized Abbie.

Relieved, Jack said, "It's alright, detective. She's with me."

"Damn right, I am!" she said wrapping her arms around Jack's neck. Abbie was in heels and only two or three inches shorter than Jack at this moment. "Jack, hun, this is for luck," she said, and she kissed him on each cheek then pulled his head down and kissed his forehead. "But this, Sweetie," she drawled, "is for me," and she pressed her mouth to his. As their tongues slowly danced together, Jack placed his right hand at the nape of her neck and eased his fingers into the silken locks of her long red hair. He clutched a handful of her hair and pulled her head back slightly as his tongue searched the inner recesses of her mouth. It had been years since Jack had kissed a woman like this, and he realized in that moment that he was ravenous for Abbie's touch. He wanted to devour her and have her devour him. His left hand was holding the gym bag, and he brought it to the small of her back and pulled her as close as he could get her. They stayed in this embrace for what seemed like hours to Jack.

As their lips parted, Jack opened his eyes and looked into Abbie's slowly opening emerald green eyes. "Oh, my gawd, Jack, hun. We have *got* to do that again when no one's lookin'!"

Jack burst out laughing still holding Abbie in his arms. "I totally agree," he said with a wink and a smile, "but right now they *are* looking, and I have to get to work." With that, he squeezed her to his chest, gently pressed his lips to her lips and then kissed her forehead before releasing her. Then he nodded to McGreer and continued with his trek to the casino cashier.

McGreer grinned as they walked and said, "Now *that* was intense!"

"I have a feeling that might be the most civilized and understated experience that I have in the next twenty-four hours," Jack said with a sense of foreboding.

Meanwhile, as Abbie watched Jack and McGreer walk towards the cashier's cage, a very large, Nordic-looking man eased up behind Abbie while her eyes remained riveted forward. He had thinning white hair, a white goatee and mustache, and he was almost a foot taller than she was. Even when wearing a XXXXL dark blue sport coat over an open-necked white dress shirt and gray slacks, it was easy to see he carried a rock-solid two-hundred and eighty pounds plus on his towering frame. He looked like a cross between Hulk Hogan and Richard Kiel, the actor that played Jaws in the James Bond movie. He gently put both of his massive hands on Abbie's shoulders surrounding her neck. He bent down and whispered into her left ear, "Is that him? Is that the guy?"

Without flinching or turning around, Abbie said, "Uh huh. That's him, alright."

"How much is he carrying in that bag?"

"About $50,000."

"Nice. Is that cop going to stay with him while he plays?"

"No. He's supposed to leave after he delivers him to the poker room."

"Good. That'll make it easier. Well, I'd better go get what I need. This squares us."

"This squares us," Abbie said.

While the man disappeared, Abbie never turned around. She just kept her eyes locked on Jack and McGreer. As her shoulders and neck cooled where the large man had placed his hands, Abbie shuddered and said to herself, "Tonight's gonna get very real, very soon."

THE RIVER

23

As Jack entered the poker room, he felt the aura of all the famous poker players that had played there previously. Men like Doyle "Texas Dolly" Brunson, Thomas "Amarillo Slim" Preston, Daniel "Kid Poker" Negreanu, Chris "Jesus" Ferguson, and Scotty "The Prince of Poker" Nguyen. They were the ghosts of poker tournaments and cash games past. They had all won and lost there, but he wondered if they had ever played for their lives or the lives of their family. It was a daunting thought, and it sent a cold chill up Jack's spine.

Jack knew that the game of poker was a microcosm of the game of life. It's about survival. Your chips are your life's blood. When your chips are gone, your life is over. When playing a hand, like most situations in life, you're risking some of that life in the hopes of gaining more life, so the risk must be acknowledged and embraced if you are going to maintain control of the hand and your life. If you don't, you lose control, and someone else makes your decisions for you. So, the never-ending objective is to maintain control, but in life, just like poker, control is an illusion. Just when you think you've got the game of life figured out, a card is turned that you weren't anticipating. Your trips meet a straight, your straight meets a flush, and your flush meets a full house.

Unfortunately, the bad beats in life sometimes don't leave you breathing to tell the sad tale.

Jack realized he was facing a rigged game with Jesse, but it was the only game he had, and he had to win. Lisa's life and Jack's soul were in the pot. They were all in and didn't have many outs, but Jack still had cards to play. If he played them right, and with some help from Lady Luck, maybe he and Lisa could escape unscathed against the monumental odds. The problem for Jack when it came to Lady Luck was, he had never trusted a woman that only came around when things were going good. Such was his conundrum.

As he approached his seat at the poker table, Jack tried to see if he recognized anyone else. He carefully put down his racks of chips and placed the first stack of black $100 chips out in front of seat number three. Then he started unloading stack after stack of $100 chips. When he was finished, he had stacked $35,000 worth of chips in front of him. Behind the stacks of chips, he placed two tightly wrapped packets of $100 bills for a total of $55,000. When he was done, the gym bag was empty except for the derringer and a soiled shirt. He put the bag in his seat, but he didn't dare leave his place at the table.

Normally Jack would hold some of his stake back to cover any contingencies or until he had a feel for the table. Every smart player keeps something off the table for "just in case." It's a way to hedge your bet against elimination by a bad beat. Tonight, though, Jack sensed that his opportunity to make his score might come unexpectedly, and he wanted all his money on the table when it came. Jack had also concealed the $10,000 from the safe deposit box in his car.

That, along with the $4,000 in his pocket, was his escape money if he was able to free Lisa and get away from Jesse. If he was unable to free Lisa, then Jack figured that having the extra money wouldn't really matter, anyway. Some tow truck jockey would probably find the stash and figure he'd hit the jackpot when he picked up Jack's Buick from the Diamante murder scene.

As the players began to take their seats, Jack recognized a few faces. The first familiar face was Stevie Moore. He looked like some skinny kid off the street that no one would give a second look. Stevie had stringy black hair that hung past his ears in waves, and it always looked like he had combed it with an egg beater. He wore his usual jeans and tee shirt with the logo of some local punk band on it, and he wore dark rimmed glasses that always seemed to have tape on one of the hinges.

Stevie was a local grinder like Jack. Jack didn't consider him to be a bad player, but he never seemed to play well at the right time. He had the nickname of Rabbit, and that's what everyone called him that knew him. Most people didn't even know his real name. To them he was just Rabbit.

Stevie told everyone that he was called Rabbit, because he was always "chasing tail" and "humped like a rabbit." What Stevie didn't know was that everyone called him Rabbit, because he tended to lose his stake too fast in the big games and had to run away. In either case, no one called him Stevie; he was just Rabbit.

Rabbit came walking over to Jack carrying one rack with $5,000 in chips. It was the minimum buy-in and typical of Rabbit. "Diamond Jack! How's it shakin,' big guy?"

"Hey there, Rabbit. I see you came to a gun fight armed with a knife."

"Yeah, well, maybe I'll do a little slice and dice tonight! I haven't seen you all week since NFR came to town. It looks like you cashed in your life savings for tonight. What gives?"

"I've been busy, but I couldn't let you fleece these cowboys all by yourself. I heard the NFR had brought in some big fish, so I brought out all my bait."

The National Finals Rodeo, or NFR, is the World Series of rodeo. It is sanctioned and organized by the Professional Rodeo Cowboys Association, has been held in Las Vegas every year since 1985, and brings together the best of the best in all rodeo events for ten days.

It also brings in every rich ranch and farm owner in the United States, along with some from other parts of the world, and they bring their families, girlfriends, and lots and lots of cash.

Each night for ten nights they hold a brand-new rodeo, and after each rodeo, these farmers, ranchers, and cowboys—real and otherwise—like to do three things: 1) get laid, 2) get drunk, and 3) play poker, not necessarily in that order. If they don't bring their wives or girlfriends, or sometimes even if they do, the local call girls are ready, willing, and able to accommodate the first item on the list. The hotels and casinos make sure they are over-stocked with Crown Royal and beer to accommodate the second. For the third item on the list, the poker rooms roll out the red carpet and Jack, Rabbit, and the other local players welcome the sheep in for the slaughter.

Now, that's not to say that these good ol' boys are poor poker players, but most of them are thinking about doing item number one while they're doing too much of item number two for them to do well at item number three. It all makes for a profitable week for the girls, hotels, and local players. All of them can smell blood in the water, and the feeding frenzy lasts as long as the cowboys do.

"Good luck, Rabbit," Jack said, "unless you're in a hand with me, of course!"

"Back at'cha,' Jack!"

The next person that Jack recognized was the Duke of Downtown. The Duke was setting up in seat six in all his splendor. He was wearing a gray fedora with a wide black band, a charcoal gray pinstripe zoot suit, black shirt, and a blood red tie and matching braces. He got his nickname by prowling the downtown casinos of Vegas dressed to the nines, usually in a Roaring 20's motif. In his mid-forties with blonde hair, trim, and handsome, he looked like a GQ model that had stepped out of a time machine or off a movie set. And he always carried cash. *Lots* of cash. He never walked into a poker room with less than $10,000 in hundred-dollar bills. It didn't matter if he was playing high stakes or low. He always put it on the table, and tonight he brought a satchel full of it.

The tourists have all heard of him either by word of mouth or through the internet, and they love to watch him play. They especially love to play against him. The Duke is a bit of a self-promoter, and he loves the spotlight. Tales of his adventures away from Vegas are legendary and probably exaggerated, but he does make a good show, and Vegas tourists *love* a good show. So they sit with him at the poker table like lambs in the lair of a wolf. You see, even at a $1/$2 no-limit table, the Duke sets the limits.

Most poker rooms in Vegas have an upper limit on the buy-in at a table in addition to the usual minimum buy-in. A typical $1/$2 game usually has an upper limit buy-in of $200-$500. That way, prospective players aren't scared away by one player with a large stack of chips. The casino doesn't care who wins in the poker room. They just want the players playing to collect the maximum rake each hand; the rake being the casino's share collected from each pot.

However, downtown Las Vegas is another world. Downtown is where it all started. The World Series of Poker began and flourished downtown at Binion's Horseshoe. Benny Binion was a poker player, and loved a good poker game, so his poker room had no maximum limits on buy-ins. It created many epic poker games between some of the greats. Many of the other downtown poker rooms followed suit.

Texas Holdem is the gold standard of poker games. There are other poker games played in Vegas poker rooms, like Omaha and Stud, but Texas Holdem is king. Each hand starts with a shuffle and cut of the deck that predetermines the order of the cards for the entire hand. However, while the order of the cards has been set in stone, the fate of each hand is anything but sealed. Each stage of the hand offers the players new information and the opportunity to change fate, but nothing is certain until the last card is revealed. At that point all wagers must be surrendered, and the rewards or penalties are meted out.

In the first betting round, players are dealt two "hole" cards face down. Only the individual player knows his own hole cards, and it is very guarded information. The next betting round is called the "flop" where the top card in the deck is "burned," meaning set aside, and the next three cards are exposed in the middle of the table and used as community cards for all players to use.

Another card is burned in round three, and a single card, called the "turn," is exposed and joins the first three in the middle of the table. The last betting round is called the "river," and it proceeds the same as the turn thus putting five cards in the middle of the table for all the remaining players to use, along with their hole cards, to make their best five-card hand. After all the betting is concluded, the remaining players "show down" their hands, and the dealer pushes the pot to the winner.

Limit Texas Holdem has preset limits for any betting round, but in No-Limit Texas Holdem, the only limit is the amount of chips or cash that sits on the table in front of each player. Most players in a $1/$2 No-Limit game will play with a minimum of $100 to a maximum of $500, and that is sufficient for most games. However, when the Duke sits down and pulls out $10,000 or more in stacked hundreds, all the other players know the stakes have just changed. It is either ante up, or get out of the way for the next player. And there WILL be a next player.

Crowds start to form around the table as everyone wants to see if someone, anyone, can separate the Duke from his money. They rarely do.

You see the Duke seldom plays a hand. He has been known to sit at the poker table for hours without playing a hand. The Duke plays pocket aces, maybe pocket kings, and rarely anything else. Most everyone knows this, so you would think that when he raised a hand, everyone would run for cover. Just the opposite happens. When the Duke plays, everybody plays. Everybody wants a piece of the Duke's cash, so they will play any two cards and pray for a miracle. Then the Duke cleans up. That doesn't mean that he wins every hand. He just rarely loses anything significant, because he usually knows when to get away from cracked aces. It is the tourists that don't know how to get away from the second-best hand.

The Duke's satchel was full this night. He pulled out $50,000 and put it on the table. The rest he left in the satchel at his feet. The set-up dealer cashed in $30,000 for chips and left the rest on the felt. The Duke silently stacked his barrels of chips without looking up. He seemed intent on making sure every last chip was perfectly ensconced in its rightful place.

The rest of the players started to sit down, but Jack didn't recognize anyone else. Most of them were wearing cowboy hats and expensive boots. All of them were carrying black $100 chips—the coin of the realm in games like this. Most had bought in for at least $20,000 with a couple at $50,000. Two of the good ol' boys had "custom sweaters." A sweater is a friendly observer that sits behind the player. A custom sweater is a woman that's wearing more money in jewelry, clothes, and/or breast enhancements than the high stakes buy-in.

Jack calculated that there was at least $300,000 on the table with more available on black Am Ex cards plus whatever the Duke had kept behind. He only needed about a third of it, but Jack figured it was going to be tough sledding. Even with $55,000, he reckoned that he couldn't be involved in too many wild hands. He decided to bide his time until he knew he had the best of the table, and then he had to pray that he got paid off.

Play started with one card dealt to each player with the high card to determine the starting position of the dealer button. The Duke pulled a king and was given the button. The two players to his left put out the small blind of $100 and big blind of $200 to start the betting. With that the game began in earnest.

After a couple of hours, things had been relatively quiet. For the most part, the tourists hadn't played poorly. Most of the players were about even. The player to Jack's right in seat two was down about $5,000, which seemed like the number of Crown Royals that he had consumed. The player in seat two had become the Drunk in seat two. He was definitely keeping the waitresses busy.

It was here that Jack sensed a change. Maybe the liquor was finally having its way with the tourists. Maybe they were getting tired. Maybe they had a wife, girlfriend, or hooker waiting for them. Maybe, just maybe, it was Abbie's presence in the room as she moved from table to table. Whatever it was, the tourists started to loosen up. They started playing more hands and throwing money around.

In what seemed like a matter of a few minutes, two of them had busted out. Jack got about $8,000 from them. Even Rabbit carved out about $1,500, but the Duke took the lion's share. He had about $70,000 in front of him, and Jack was up to about $60,000.

Abbie caught Jack's eye as she was tapping into another table, but someone else caught his eye, as well, and Jack froze. Walking over to Jack's table was a mountain of a man with thinning white hair, a white goatee, and a white mustache. He was carrying $20,000 in chips and homing in on Jack's table like a guided missile. As he prepared to sit down in seat eight, he looked over at Jack, and Jack pretended to be interested in his own stack of chips.

It wasn't the size of the man that had Jack spooked; it was the size of his reputation, and his reputation was more capacious than his stature. Jack knew him only as "the Fixer." He was known as the Fixer, because if you had a problem with someone and you had enough money, he fixed your problem. That usually meant somebody appeared on the missing person list.

Jack had seen him in poker rooms before and knew him to be a good player, but for him to be at Jack's table, at this particular time, while Jack had a big contract on his life, well, it was too much of a coincidence for Jack not to pay strict attention. Besides, every time Jack looked up, it seemed that the Fixer was looking right at him. Jack decided that he was safe as long as he stayed close to the poker table, but that meant no bathroom breaks or strolls to stretch his legs. He could stand up and walk around a little to loosen his legs, but he dared not leave the crowded confines of the poker room without providing an opportunity for his demise.

Regardless of the new wrinkle in the table dynamics, Jack had to put the Fixer out of his mind. He was nowhere close to the $100,000 that he needed, and the sand kept slipping through the hourglass. Jack only had about twenty hours left, and that's if Jesse kept his word. Prior to this latest twist of events, in spite of Jesse's sordid character, Jack had felt that he could always count on Jesse to shoot straight with him. Now he was sure that he couldn't trust Jesse at all. Jack already knew that Jesse planned to have him killed, and he was losing confidence in either trying to buy or shoot his way out of whatever trick bag Jesse planned to throw over him.

As the hours passed, Jack became more and more morose. Nothing seemed to be going his way. He hadn't really been losing. He kept floating between $45,000 and $60,000, but he wasn't making any headway, either. It was four in the morning, and more tourists had busted out or left a significant amount of their chips on the table. The Fixer was up about $5,000, Rabbit had doubled up to $10,000, but the big winner, so far, was the Duke. He had managed to drag enough pots to swell his stack to about $90,000.

Jack's only moments of diversion occurred when he saw Abbie working in the room. Whenever he was out of a hand, he would try to locate her. When he did, he would marvel at how beautiful she looked even in her dealer's uniform. Several times he caught her looking his way, and she would smile a smile that warmed Jack's whole body. It reminded him of when Melinda would do that to him in high school classes, and he liked it so much that he would purposely try to catch her eye and make a funny face just so he could see that smile again and again.

Whenever Abbie would deal at Jack's table, she would maintain a professional demeanor, but several times she would purposely touch his hand when she pushed him a pot. Every time she did it, Jack's blood pumped a little harder. One time when she was pushing him a pot, he could tell she was going to touch his hand, so he turned his hand palm side up and lightly stroked his index finger against her downward facing palm. He saw her bite her lip slightly. Then he saw her eyelids descend ever so slightly as he did it quickly twice more. His body began to flush with excitement, and he was glad that he was seated at a table that covered him from the middle of his chest and downward. Standing up would definitely have been a mistake at that point!

At the end of Abbie's last thirty-minute down on his table, Jack was back up to $60,000, although he couldn't really remember how. That's when he knew that she was a distraction. She was a gorgeous, auburn-haired, green-eyed vision of red-hot loveliness type of distraction, but a distraction just the same. He wasn't happy to see her go, but he knew he should've been. Jack could ill afford to be haphazard in his thoughts or actions.

"Boy, she's a looker, ain't she?" the Drunk said with a leer.

"Yes, she is," Jack said snapping back to reality.

"Yesiree, Bob! I wouldn't mind climbing in between those legs and giving her the ride of her life!"

Jack felt like punching the Drunk square in the face, but he thought better of it. The Drunk had been a non-stop chatterbox that Jack had been ignoring, so he let it slide. As obnoxious as he was, the Drunk was still a pretty fair poker player, and Jack didn't want to give him any advantage by letting him get into his head. Besides, he knew Abbie could handle any drunk, including this one, and she wouldn't give him the time of day. Still, he couldn't help feeling protective over her.

At six o'clock, Jack was up to $75,000. He figured if he could drag one or two more big pots, he would have his $100,000. His goal was within sight, but then over the next two hours he went card-dead. The deck went absolutely stone cold on him. It seemed that 90% of his hole cards were nothing but unsuited rags. The few times that he would get decent hole cards, like ace/king or a medium pair, the flop would blow them to pieces. He never lost big, but it was like he was attached to an I. V. tube, and the other players were slowing siphoning out his blood.

By eight o'clock, Jack was back down to about $50,000, and the table was showing signs of possibly breaking up. Another one of the tourists had left, but there was no one on the list to take his place, so seat ten was now vacant. That left Jack, the Duke, Rabbit, the Fixer, the Drunk, and four weary tourists left in the game. Abbie was back at the table dealing, so Jack hoped that she would bring him some luck and staunch the flow of chips away from his stack.

So far, the Duke had had his way with the table. His stack had more than doubled to about $115,000. Rabbit was still at about $10,000, and he was feeling full of himself having doubled up. Jack figured Rabbit might take his winnings and leave any minute.

The Drunk was in the midst of a very bad two-hour run just like Jack, but he had suffered far worse. He had taken some bad beats and made some questionable losing calls that conspired to cause him to lose all his original $20,000. However, the Drunk had reloaded back up to $20,000 and ordered more Crown Royal.

The four tourists were down to about $25,000 combined. Jack gauged that they weren't likely to make much noise or stay much longer. They all looked pretty whipped.

The Fixer was up to about $40,000, and he seemed as fresh as when he had first claimed his seat. He hadn't been eyeing Jack as much, but Jack was trying not to appear interested in him, so he wasn't really sure just how closely he was actually being watched. It made his skin crawl sometimes to think that he was under some magnifying glass, so he tried to think about it as little as possible. Still, he couldn't help but realize that, like it or not, he was being observed very closely by a very serious predator. It made him feel like a wounded gazelle that had just seen a cheetah lying in the nearby grass.

While the Fixer had taken several breaks, Jack had remained at or around the table. He was determined to remain in the perceived safety of the poker room. There were still plenty of witnesses, even at 8:00 am, and while Jack had persevered to remain nestled in the sanctuary of the poker room, it hadn't been easy the whole time. The cocktail waitresses were regularly bringing plenty of drinks to the table. Jack knew that he couldn't load up on liquids, but he had had a couple of beers and a bottle of water early. Around six o'clock, the dam was about to burst, so Jack grabbed an empty beer bottle from an abandoned table and sat back down. There he stealthily relieved himself into it. Again, he was thankful for the large poker table and closed armchair in which he was seated. Jack would've sworn that he saw the Fixer grinning at him as he took the near full bottle to the trash can in the poker room. Jack thought the bastard probably knew EXACTLY what he had just done and was tickled with himself that he had forced Jack to do it. "Asshole!" Jack thought.

With the game winding down and really becoming a four-man struggle, Jack knew that he needed things to go his way very soon. Otherwise, he was going to have to take his game somewhere else, and he knew that exposed him to the Fixer. Plus, he didn't know if there were any big games still running that late in the morning. His time was running out, and he swore he could hear the tick-tick-tick of an old wind-up egg timer running down to zero.

With the exception of the Drunk, the tourists weren't going to add much to any pot, and while Rabbit had $10,000, he would probably leave before anyone could get their hands on it. No, the game was really down to the Duke, the Fixer, the Drunk, and Jack. While there was still plenty of money on the table, the Duke held most of it, and he rarely got tied up in big pots unless he really felt like he had the best of it.

Given this set of circumstances, Jack decided that he needed to greatly widen his selection of playable hands down to small suited connectors, suited aces, unsuited connectors, etc. He was going to have to ambush the Duke and hope that he got paid off big, and the only way to do that was to come out of left field at him. He didn't like breaking away from his strategy of staying tight and laying traps, but it was really his only chance to win enough money to make his plan work and save Lisa. He knew he would be playing right into the Duke's hands, but he had no other choice. He said a silent prayer to the poker gods to send him some luck.

Jack put out his $200 big blind. Abbie dealt the cards, and Jack quickly peeked in at his cards while the other players were receiving theirs. His heart sunk like a lead weight and hit bottom when he spied seven/deuce off suit – the worst two starting cards in Texas Hold 'em poker. That was definitely not what he meant by a playable hand! He realized then that his prayer should've specified that he wanted *good* luck. Too late. It seemed the poker gods weren't going to give him any help after all.

Jack's mind wandered for a moment as he thought of Lisa, Jesse, Abbie, and the astronomical odds he faced trying to pull off this gambit. With his mind off his awful starting hand, he noticed the pungent bouquet of the poker room in the wee hours. It was a combination of the stale beer in the bottle sitting in front of him, cigar smoke wafting in from the adjacent casino floor, a faint wisp of honeysuckle emanating soft and sweet as a baby's sigh from Abbie as she scanned the players for action, the musky odor of sweat mixing with cheap cologne, and the foul aroma of whiskey, cigarettes, and coffee breath coming from the Drunk each time he exhaled.

With a heavy sigh and a slight shake of his head, he wondered to himself, "How has everything had come to this?"

24

The tourist under the gun on Jack's left folded. The next player looked at his cards, grunted, and folded, also. The Duke called. "Called?!" thought Jack. "The Duke *never* just limps into a pot!" Jack couldn't have been more shocked than if Abbie had suddenly grown a second head! He'd never seen the Duke limp. He'd never even *heard* of the Duke limping into a pot. He always raised or folded. Even from the small blind, Jack could never remember the Duke ever just calling the blind. Jack was so mesmerized by the Duke's play that he barely noticed Rabbit, the Fixer, the other tourists in seats nine and one, and the Drunk all call the big blind in turn. In fact, he was so bewildered by this aberrancy that it took Abbie to bring him back to the here and now.

"Jack, it's your option," she said. "Check or raise?"

Jack looked at his hole cards again just to make sure that they hadn't magically changed. Nope. They were still the seven of spades and deuce of clubs. Jack tapped the table signaling that he was checking his hand.

Jack's mind was so consumed with the Duke that he didn't notice that the Fixer seemed to be staring two eye-holes right through Jack. Truth be told, it was less like he was staring through Jack and more like he was seeing something beyond him, and that something definitely had the Fixer's attention.

Snap, snap, snap! Abbie crisply thumbed three cards face down on the felt after silkily burning the first. Deftly she scooped them up, turned them over, and spread the flop. Jack couldn't believe his eyes. Of all the unlikely miracles! The flop had just come out seven of hearts, seven of clubs, and eight of diamonds; Jack had made trip sevens on a rainbow flop. His lowly seven/deuce had just become a monster! IT WAS UNBELIEVABLE! The poker gods had not only smiled on Jack, but they had patted him on the back and sent the massage girl over to him on a comp for a full body massage. This was beyond mind blowing! It was the break that Jack had been praying for, and it had arrived gift wrapped and camouflaged in the unlikely guise of seven/deuce.

Trying his best to look uninterested, Jack paused a moment after the Drunk had checked before he tapped the table twice signaling a check of his own. He figured there was no need to give away his position with a bet. Besides, he wanted to see how the Duke and the others reacted to the flop.

Much to Jack's glee, the Duke reached for chips. There was $1,260 in the pot after the rake, and the Duke casually pushed out $3,000. Typical Duke gambit, thought Jack. Jack figured he must be slow-playing aces and decided it was time to push out the savvy players with an over-bet. Then he'd suck in the tourists and relieve them of their chips. Jack knew what the Duke knew that the tourists would sometimes chase anything no matter how bad the pot odds. If everyone folded, the Duke would just take down another pot. At least that's what Jack was hoping the Duke was thinking.

Rabbit got a disgusted look on his face while eyeing the Duke as if the Duke had just thrown up on the felt. Jack gathered Rabbit must have a piece of the flop and wanted to play, but Rabbit thought better of it and folded. Jack knew that he was in way over his head with only $10,000 and wouldn't want to waste 30% of his stack on a draw with less than two to one odds. It was the smart thing to do, but Jack knew Rabbit, and he knew it pissed Rabbit off to fold his hand.

The Fixer, on the other hand, calmly called. Jack wondered if maybe he had a seven, as well. If he did, Jack was in trouble, because the Fixer's kicker *had* to be bigger than a deuce.

Then Jack began to think that maybe he had a straight draw. If so, the Fixer could be calculating that the Duke was bluffing. In any case, the Fixer was in, and the plot thickened along with the pot. If his opponent didn't have the case seven, then Jack figured that he was still in command.

The tourist in seat nine folded, but the tourist in seat one on the button called the $3,000.

Jack surmised that it was probably just a position call hoping to see a magic card appear that would turn his likely small pocket pair into a full house. If the tourist had trips, Jack felt he would've raised the bet.

The Drunk called, which didn't surprise Jack in the least. If he had any draw at all, he was now getting almost three and a half to one odds to stay in the hand. The Drunk was probably going down a bad road, but Jack knew that the Crown Royal could be driving the bus by now. In fact, Jack mentally welcomed the Drunk's extra $3,000 into the pot like a spider welcomes a fly into the web.

Now it was Jack's action. He looked at his hole cards, again, like he wasn't sure whether or not he should call. What he was really thinking was whether or not to raise. Jack knew that this could be the hand that would change everything. He had an extremely shrouded hand that still had some risk. There was a draw on the board, and the Fixer could easily have a seven with a better kicker than Jack. No,

Jack figured this was no time to raise. He wanted a little more information. If a straight card were to hit on the turn and the Fixer or someone else made an aggressive bet/raise, then Jack could get away from the hand without too much inflicted damage.

If an ace came out, Jack decided it would probably give the Duke a full house, and, again, he could go away quietly. If none of that were to happen, however, then Jack assumed that the Duke would bet out. He would be confident that his aces were still best. That's when Jack would strike!

Jack called and let himself smile the tiniest of smiles.

25

Snap! Jack quickly looked at the other players to see if they were as intent on this card as he was. All eyes were on Abbie's hand as she slowly turned the card. All eyes except ... except the eyes of the Fixer. His eyes were riveted on Jack. Jack quickly blinked and diverted his eyes back to watch Abbie's hand turn the card.

And there it was. Jack couldn't believe his luck was holding out! Sitting there face up on the felt next to "his" two sevens was the trey of hearts. That paired the other heart on the board, but it did nothing to complete the straight draw. It did, however, add a flush draw to the mix.

Jack snuck a sideways glance at the Drunk to see his reaction to the turn card. All he saw was a face flushed with Canadian whiskey, but what he heard told a different story. "Well, that's a shitty little card! I check," the Drunk said as he downed the rest of his Crown.

"Uh, oh," Jack thought. Act strong, you're weak. Act weak, you're strong. Jack's mind buzzed with the thought that the Drunk had been playing pocket treys and just hit his magic card for a full house. "Now what?" he thought. Jack had thought about making a sizable bet to isolate the Duke, but then he had decided to check, calculating that the Duke would bet out again making the pot bigger. If the Fixer folded, Jack would re-raise the Duke. If the Fixer raised, Jack would fold. All his calculations centered on the Duke and the Fixer. Now the Drunk had reared his ruddy head and become a Crown Royal pain in the ass! Jack had one move only.

"Check."

The Duke looked down at his stack contemplating quietly. He tapped the top of one of the barrels of chips with his right forefinger. Tap, tap, tap. Then he started cutting out chips.

With a little over $16,000 in the pot, Jack expected the Duke to come out heavy, again, hoping to drive out the draw chasers. The Duke didn't waver as he pushed chips to the center.

"Twenty thousand."

"Atta baby, Duke," Jack thought. Jack knew this bet would define the hand. If the Fixer has a seven, he will raise, and then Jack will fold. If the Fixer folds, then Jack has the only other seven. Then it's down to the tourist and the Drunk, and only the Drunk worried Jack. If the Drunk was in, then Jack was out.

"Call," said the Fixer.

"Call?" Jack was bewildered. Why not raise or fold? Was the Fixer still on a draw? If he was, why would he call with less than two to one odds? Jack knew that the Fixer was a player that wouldn't make a mistake like that. Unless. Unless he had two draws. Suddenly it made sense. The Fixer must have played suited connectors of hearts. He had a straight and flush draw. He was still drawing with fifteen outs. The Fixer was slightly behind the odds, but he probably figured that the size of the pot was worth the stretch. It was getting late in the game, and there probably wouldn't be many more pots like this, if any.

The tourist quickly folded, and the action was on the Drunk. Jack expected him to push the rest of his chips into the middle. Instead, the Drunk looked at his hole cards, mumbled, "Shitty little card," and tossed his cards into the muck.

"I guess it was a shitty little card," Jack silently mused.

With $56,000 in the pot and $47,000 in front of him, it was nut cutting time for Jack. If he believed the Duke had a pair of aces or kings, Jack only had one play. If he believed that the Fixer was still on a draw, Jack only had one play. If he wanted to save Lisa's life, Jack only had one play. Jack only had one play.

"All in," Jack said. With both hands, he pushed all his remaining chips towards the center. Then he picked up the bundles of cash and placed them next to his chips. With a deep exhale, he squared his jaw, smiled, and looked the Duke boldly in the eyes.

The Duke looked calmly back at Jack for five long seconds. Then he looked at the hoard of chips and cash that Jack had pushed. Normally he would've asked for a count of the chips and cash. It would've given him information and a chance to think. Instead, he just slowly looked down at his stack and said, "Call."

In that instant, it seemed as though a hush enveloped the room. Unbeknownst to the players at Jack's table, what was left of the other players and dealers in the room were watching their table. With the Duke's call, there was suddenly over $150,000 in the pot. Word had quickly spread, and all the other games had stopped as all eyes were riveted on this hand.

The focus was now on the Fixer. He had about $17,000 left, which meant that he was getting big odds to call. Jack was praying that he would fold. He didn't want to see him catch his draw card. The Fixer looked at his hole cards, and with a shake of his head, the Fixer picked up his cards, flicked his wrist, and sent the cards floating in the air like two miniature helicopters landing gently in front of Abbie.

"YES!" Jack screamed in his head. "I gotcha, Duke! I finally caught you with your pants down!"

Jack dramatically turned over his seven/deuce, and he couldn't have been prouder. Jack thought to himself that this was going to be his finest moment. Jack had sucker punched the Duke! He had flopped a monster hand with a lousy seven/deuce. He laid the trap, baited it, exalted as the Duke stepped in it, and then watched with utter rapture as the Fixer's cards went floating into the muck. Now he wanted to bask in the moment. He wanted to bathe in it, splash around in it, and then smear it all over his body like a healing balm. He couldn't get enough of it. It was all he could do to keep from screaming in ecstasy!

While Jack was reveling in his "moment," all eyes turned to the Duke. The Duke smiled. It was a knowing smile: a self-satisfied, totally pleased, pernicious smile. He smiled as if he had planned and executed all of this with a deft and whimsical scheme in his mind—Jack's lousy hole cards, the miracle flop, the innocuous little trey on the turn, and even Jack's current nirvana. All of this orchestrated by the man they called the Duke of Downtown.

He blinked once, and with a look of amusement, the Duke uttered one word. "Boat." With that one word and a flip of his wrist, he turned over pocket eights, and every molecule of oxygen was sucked out of the room.

26

Jack was stupefied. His moment was suddenly gone. Now he couldn't breathe. One instant he was practically orgasmic, and the next he's wondering who hit him in the gut with a sledgehammer. All of the blood had drained from his face. He looked like a corpse. He felt like a corpse. Jack started to think that maybe he was a corpse. Maybe the Fixer had done his job already, and this was his introduction into Hell.

"Step right up, ladies and gentlemen!" the demonic carnival barker shouted. "Come right this way! See the arrogant fool as we tease him mercilessly. Watch with glee as we dangle redemption at his fingertips and then rip it away from him. Howl with laughter as he twists and spasms at the end of a noose that he tied himself!" Jack's head felt light and began to swoon with the images he was conjuring.

It was only the soft drawl of a familiar female voice that brought him back from his reverie of ruin. It was that sweet combination of honey, bourbon, and doves cooing. "Jack, hun, I'm fixin' to deal the river. Are you all right?" Abbie. Sweet Abbie.

Jack nodded slowly, and grasping the poker table, he stood up. If he was going down, it would be on his hind legs, but he couldn't even muster the strength to utter the ubiquitous phrase, "One time," because he knew that there was only one card in the deck that would change this sequence of horrors from reaching its inevitable conclusion.

By now, every player and dealer in the entire poker room was standing, craning their necks to see the final act of this Greek tragedy. People were pointing and shaking their heads. They had all heard the basic gist of the wicked turn of events, and they wanted to witness the carnage beside the road first hand as they slowly drove by the hideous wreck.

The poker room manager had by now come over and was standing behind Abbie. In a firm and resolute tone, he said, "Okay, Abbie, burn and turn."

With that, Abbie slid the top card of the deck from her delicate hand to its resting place under the mountain of chips and bundled cash – the mountain that had seemed long, long ago to Jack as though each chip and hundred-dollar bill was engraved with his name. The mountain that seemed like Mount Everest and he Sir Edmund Hillary. The mountain that would save his daughter and redeem his battered, misbegotten soul. Now that mountain seemed like a burial mound sitting beside his grave and waiting to be shoveled in on top of him.

Snap! The river card crisply landed on the soft felt surface of the table. Then Abbie slowly exposed Jack's fate and quickly slid the card into place. En masse, the players and spectators drew in a final breath, and then the whole room erupted at once. "SEVEN!" they all screamed. The seven of diamonds did a large cannonball into the river and set off an explosion the likes of which hadn't been seen downtown since the last World Series of Poker had been held in these ancient, hallowed gambling halls many years ago! Players, dealers, and cocktail waitresses were all slapping backs, shaking heads, and raising a clamor of whoops and hollers that had the whole casino wondering who the hell had just struck it rich!

Only three people in the room were silent–the Duke, Jack … and the Fixer. The Duke just sat there slowly shaking his head. Meanwhile, the Fixer was looking around at all the mayhem like he was trying to calculate his next move. His eyes seemed to scan each person—who was laughing, who was not, who was moving forward, who was moving back, and who might get in his way.

Jack sat back down in his chair–actually more like collapsed into it. He couldn't believe his dumb luck. He couldn't believe that the last seven in the deck, the case seven, the seven of diamonds, El Siete de Diamante, no less, had miraculously elbowed its way up onto the table and smiled at him. It was just like when Lisa used to climb up onto his lap when she was a baby, all full of spunk and beaming from ear to ear as if she had just been crowned the Queen of Sheba.

She would smile real big and reach for Jack's nose and then … "LISA!" Jack shouted, as he snapped out of his day dream and remembered his baby girl was nearly grown and her life teetered on the brink of destruction.

Abbie was pushing the gigantic pot in front of Jack as he bolted upright. She looked up into his bloodshot, terror-stricken eyes and said, "Go get her, Jack, hun. Take this money and you go get that precious daughter of yours!"

Jack and the poker room manager hurriedly started racking all the chips and gathering the cash from the humongous pot that had ended the game. It took over five minutes to gather it all up and rack it. Jack put the bundles of cash in his gym bag, but he was going to need a carrier for all the racks of vitally important chips. As they were finishing, the manager motioned for one of the security guards to come over. "Escort Mr. Diamante to the cashier's cage and see that he gets back to his room or off the property safely."

"Yes, sir!"

Rabbit came up to Jack as he was getting ready to leave. "Hell of a catch, Jack," Rabbit said shaking his head. "Hell of a catch." Jack smiled, shook his own head, and then shook Rabbit's hand. He tried to say something, but all he could do was exhale as if he had still been holding his breath. His arms hung limp by his sides, and the gym bag that had seemed so light coming in was now so much heavier. Thankfully, Jack thought, it was about to get heavier still.

Jack, Abbie, and the poker room manager finished loading the racks of chips onto a rolling cart. Jack had tipped Abbie $1,000 at the table, and now he palmed five black $100 chips to the poker room manager as he shook his hand. Then Jack noticed that the Fixer was no longer at the table. His seat was cold and empty, and his chips were gone. He looked around the room, but he didn't see him anywhere.

"Damn!" Jack thought. He had slipped away during the entire ruckus, and a sense of dread shot through Jack. Somewhere in the mist of the neon madness, the Fixer waited for him.

27

Jack and the security guard stood silently in the elevator. The guard looked like he should be playing defensive tackle for some team in the NFL. He was like a one-man crowd in the tiny elevator, and Jack felt puny next to him. He had a gold nameplate on his massive, uniformed chest that said Terrance Heyne as he stood at "parade rest" with his red hair crew-cut "high and tight" and a determined scowl on his face. Straining for every inch of ascension, the elevator ground to an uneasy halt on the fifth level.

As the doors slowly opened and the smell of exhaust fumes rolled into the elevator, Heyne peered outside into the enclosed parking deck as if he expected a platoon of Marines to assault them. It was eerily dark for being after nine in the morning. It seemed as though some of the fluorescent lights were out, and those that were working only gave a ghostly glow.

Seeing nothing but the rows of parked cars, Jack tentatively exited the elevator behind Heyne. However, even with the imposing guard leading the way, Jack felt a cold sense of dread shoot through him. Somehow the shadows seemed darker and larger than normal. It was almost as if the dark was alive and trying to swallow what little light existed there.

As the elevator doors shut behind them, Jack couldn't see his car. He remembered when he had parked it the night before that the sight line between his car and the elevator was obstructed by the support column. Jack hesitated, but he took the lead and began walking around the column to where he knew he had left his car. Without hesitation Heyne dutifully followed behind him. Step by step they approached Jack's car, and as much as he tried to choke down the feelings, Jack's antennae were screaming, "Something's wrong here!" Jack tried to reassure himself. "Only forty more feet. Thirty more feet. Twenty more feet."

"Have you got your keys, sir?" asked Heyne.

"Yes. Yes, I do," replied Jack as he rummaged in his pants pocket. Then as he was looking at the keys in his right hand, he heard a sickening crack, and Heyne fell unconscious into Jack's back. Jack careened forward, but he managed to catch himself before he hit the cement floor. Still clutching the gym bag that held Lisa's freedom, he turned and found himself staring into the muzzle of a gun.

For a moment, all Jack perceived was the abyss of death formed by the gun's barrel.

Then he noticed the large fist that gripped the handle. That fist was attached to an arm, and the arm was attached to a body, and the body supported a face. The face of . . . the Drunk!

"Hello, Jack. Fancy meeting you here. That was one helluva suck-out hand you played. Can't really say I've ever seen anything like it. I'll bet you're feeling pretty lucky, eh Jack? Well, I'm the lucky one. You see, I get to take all that money and then collect on the contract for killing you, because you can't pay the money. Isn't irony a bitch? Or is that a paradox? I get those two mixed up. Maybe it's an ironic paradox," the drunk said with a big grin.

"You don't understand! You can't do this! Please! I can't give up this money! They'll kill my daughter if I don't pay them!" Jack stammered as if he was flustered to utter confusion. He was really stalling and trying to figure out how he could get to the revolver strapped to his ankle. He knew the Drunk had the drop on him, and it would take a major distraction to give him the time necessary to get to the .38 and try to shoot his way out of this ambush. It was a daunting objective that would take one-part opportunity, one-part skill, and ten parts luck. He didn't like his odds.

"Oh, I understand perfectly. I understand that I'm holding the gun, so either you give me that bag of money and I let you live another thirty minutes while we go someplace a little more private, or I shoot you now and take it anyway. Frankly, at this point, I really don't give a rat's ass. So, what's it gonna be, Jack? You know we all gotta go sometime, but you actually get a choice. Now or later, Ja—"

Pop! It sounded like someone had smacked a soft pillow with the palm of their hand.

Instead, a muffled small caliber bullet had entered the Drunk's left temple, scrambling his brains as it ricocheted around inside his skull, and dropped him like a sack of dirt. Another pop and this time a spray of blood emerged from the far side of the Drunk's head as he lay on the cold, bare cement with the bullet skittering under a car. A quickly growing pool of blood formed on the cement as it flowed from the Drunk's mouth, nose, and temple. Jack sucked in a gulp of air and took a step back as the fingers of blood reached for his shoes.

Emerging from behind a silver SUV and unscrewing a silencer from his pistol was the Fixer. As he approached Jack, he looked down at the draining corpse that was the Drunk.

"Hello, Jack. Allow me to introduce you to the late Carl Jarretson, formerly employed by Jesse Brizetta to make sure you quit breathing. Boy, he did like to talk, didn't he, Jack?"

Jack snotted his nose as he tried to stifle a sudden laugh. Wiping his nose with the back of his hand, he grinned and shook his head. "I must be one sorry son-of-a-bitch to be facing death and laughing at your jokes. I suppose now YOU want my money before you kill me, too."

"No, Jack. I just came for you."

"Well, then do it! Just do it, dammit! I'm through begging!"

"You don't understand, Jack. I came *for* you. Abbie asked me to watch over you. I owed her a favor, so here I am. You better get a move on. Jesse's not a patient man, and there's likely to be more out there like this guy looking to cash in on your ticket. Also, you probably ought to tighten up your security. Somebody clued Jarretson into where you were parked. I followed him out of the poker room, and he came directly here. He was laying for you, so he had to have inside information."

"I don't know who could've told him. I didn't even know where I was going to park before I got here."

"Well, then, you better play your cards close to the vest. Somebody's got a line on you. By the way, that really was a helluva suck-out! I've never seen anything like it, either," the Fixer said as he shook his head.

"Thanks. What were you playing? I didn't think you'd fold with that big of a pot. I put you on suited connectors. Maybe nine/ten of hearts."

"That's exactly what I had. I figured two all-ins meant somebody had filled up. The best I could muster was a flush if I hit. No sense in just making the pot bigger for somebody else."

Now it was Jack's turn to shake his head. He couldn't believe his good fortune. He couldn't believe Abbie had provided a guardian angel! "Tell Abbie thanks for me," he said.

"Tell her yourself. Oh, and by the way, Jack, you really ought to let her make breakfast for you."

Jack's mouth opened slightly, and then his jaw dropped the rest of the way as the Fixer walked away chuckling. "Why that little minx!" he said to himself. Then he gathered his wits, gathered the bag, and got into his car. With a screech of his tires, he was headed out of the parking deck and racing into the glare of the morning Vegas sunshine.

28

Jack drove south on Boulder Highway. He made a few stops after leaving the Nugget to tie up some loose ends. As he passed Sam's Town and the neighborhoods of his youth at the eastern side of the valley, his mind drifted back to more innocent times. He remembered trick-or-treating throughout his neighborhood as a kid without having to be watched over by a parent. He remembered riding his single speed bicycle to baseball practice when he was ten years old.

He would ride three miles to practice and three miles back on Eastern Avenue two or three times a week during baseball season. His glove would hang on the handle bars, and he never had a bit of trouble with traffic. Jack figured now a kid would be lucky to get a hundred yards going down Eastern on a bike without getting run off the road.

Jack also remembered how people did things for each other and watched out for one another. People never locked their doors. Bikes and toys left in the yard never disappeared. Pets that wandered away from home were always fed and returned to their owner.

At the entrance to the subdivision where Jack grew up lived Redd Foxx, a famous comedian that worked in Vegas a lot. Since he worked nights, Jack never remembered ever seeing the man, but he always liked and respected him for an unselfish act of kindness bestowed upon the neighborhood kids.

The school bus stop was right on the corner where Mr. Foxx lived. At the beginning and end of the school year, it was often 100 degrees or more, so Redd Foxx had a water line run from his house out to the corner and had a drinking fountain installed for the kids. He didn't have to do it. He was just being a good neighbor, but it left a big impression on Jack.

Now, innocent people were being murdered in their homes for their possessions, and defenseless children were being kidnapped and tortured. Lisa had been kidnapped and tortured! Jack slammed his fist on the steering wheel making the horn blare, and he vowed again that he would get her back safe and sound. First, though, he had to set things up with Jesse, and as he punched in the number, Jack made a mental note to himself. Jesse dies tonight.

"Talk to me, Jack"

"Jesse, I've got your money."

"Well, now, that's good, Jack, and with time to spare, too."

"Put my daughter on. I want to know that she's all right."

"She's fine, Jack. A little worse for wear, maybe, but she's fine. Trouble is, it's not my turn to babysit her right now, so you'll have to trust me this time. Don't worry. She's safe for now. I'm not gonna kill the golden goose that's gonna get me a big payday. I'll produce her when you show up with the money."

"No."

"No? Whad'ya mean no?"

"I mean I'm not showing up with the money and jewels unless Lisa is there. We're also gonna meet at a place of my choosing where I feel safe. I want someplace where I can see all of the players."

"And just where do you have in mind, Jack?"

"Sunset Park. I'll meet you where second base used to be on the American Legion field. I'll meet you where you and I used to be best friends."

"Huh. Sunset Park at second base on the big-league field. Okay, Jack. We'll play it your way for now. I'm an easygoing kind of guy. The park closes at eleven. I'll meet you there at midnight. And, Jack, you better have everything you said that you were bringing. Otherwise, I'll feed your daughter to the carp out at Lake Mead in pieces! You hear me, Jack?" Jesse said with menace in his voice.

"I hear you. Now you hear me. If I find out that one of your apes has molested my daughter, I'm gonna kill him, and then I'm gonna kill you. You hear *me*, Jesse?"

"Ha ha ha, yeah, I hear ya, Jack," Jesse said as he hung up.

Jack had just bought himself an extra three hours, and he decided to make the most of it. He needed to get something to eat and get some rest. It had been a long night, and it was sure to be another long one coming up.

Jack also needed to update Kiersten. He had talked to her a couple times since the kidnapping, but he hadn't told her anything. Now he figured it was time to come clean. She deserved to know the truth about him and her granddaughter, so Jack made the call.

"Hello?"

"Kiersten, it's Jack."

"Jack, what's going on? What have you heard?"

"Kiersten, I've got some things to tell you, and I haven't got much time, so let me finish before you ask any questions."

"What things, Jack? Lisa's all right, isn't she? God, Jack, please tell me she's okay."

"She's fine, for now, but time is short. I know the people that have her. In fact, I used to work for the man in charge, and ..."

"JACK! WHAT DO YOU MEAN YOU KNOW THEM? This is about *you,* isn't it, Jack?"

"Kiersten, PLEASE! Yes, it's about me, but it's also about Lisa. She witnessed certain things that she shouldn't have, and now she's caught in the cross-fire. The good news is that I have the money. I won it playing poker, and I'm going to use it to buy back Lisa."

"Jack, if these people are as ruthless as you say, then they can't be bought!"

"Kiersten let me finish. You're right. They are ruthless, but I know this man, and I believe that I can bargain with him. I will trade my life for Lisa's, if I have to, but I don't believe it will come to that. Either way, I WILL free Lisa. I just want you prepared to get her if needed. Keep your phone charged. Everything happens tonight."

"Oh my God, Jack. Oh … my … God. Jack you stay safe and bring her home. Bring her home, Jack. And bring yourself home, too."

"I will, Kiersten. I will. Say a prayer for both of us."

"You know I will, Jack."

By now, Jack was in Henderson, and he figured his best bet at staying alive long enough to make the meeting with Jesse was to get out of the valley. There was no telling how many other men or women were out there looking to score the bounty on his head. Plus, he didn't even want any involvement with Metro, right now, because he had no idea who might be the snitch that the Fixer had alluded to. Those being the circumstances, Jack decided to go someplace where anyone looking to do him harm would stick out like a sore thumb: Boulder City.

Boulder City is an anomaly in Nevada, because there is no gambling allowed within the city limits. The city was created to house all of the men that were working on Hoover

Dam back in the 1930's. The federal government wanted the thousands of workers to stay away from the casinos, bars, and whorehouses in Las Vegas, so they set up tents and small buildings near the construction site with no liquor or women allowed. Well, they went to Vegas anyway, but Boulder City was born, and it was still a dry town until 1969 when the alcohol prohibition was lifted.

Boulder City has remained a sleepy little town where every other weekend there is an art festival, where somebody driving thirty miles over the speed limit constitutes a crime wave, and where everybody knows everybody's business. Jack figured it would be the perfect place to hole up until it was time to get Lisa. It was somewhere he didn't figure to be recognized.

As he drove past the jagged face of Black Mountain, Jack heard Don Henley emote the last line of *Hotel California* on the radio. "You can check out any time you like, but you can never leave!" made a chill run up Jack's spine. He cranked up the volume when he heard Don Felder launch into his epic guitar solo. As Joe Walsh entered the fray and lashed back at Felder, Jack passed the last vestige of gambling before the Boulder City limits called Railroad Pass.

While Felder and Walsh faded out like a requiem to a venerable flamenco dancer, he eased into Boulder City and found a little motel with a diner next door nestled on U. S. Highway 93.

Jack went into the small lobby, and he popped the knob on the little silver bell on the counter with the palm of his hand creating a crystal-clear DING. A kindly looking old woman came to the desk from her living room in the back. Her hair was stark white, short, and combed back with a bit of a curl around her ears. She was wearing an old blue and white gingham skirt and a faded blue button up cotton blouse, and she looked like she had just stepped out of the 1950's. She gave Jack a big smile, and he noticed that most of her upper teeth were missing, but instead of being put off, that warm smile with all the space in it endeared her to him. He suddenly felt safer for some reason. She gave him a nod as if she knew what he was thinking and handed him the registration log.

"It's $35 a night. Are you staying more than one night, young man?"

"No, one night will do. I would like to ask a favor, though. If anyone calls or comes asking for me, I'm not here. I badly need some rest, and I don't want to be disturbed by anyone. Can you do that for me, ma'am?" Jack asked as he slid the unsigned log to her with two hundred-dollar bills laid out on top of it.

"Sure thing. You go on and get your rest. I'll see that no one knows you're here," she said with a wink as she stuffed the money into her bra under her blouse.

"One other thing," Jack said. "The diner next door. Do they deliver food here, by any chance?"

"They will if I ask them to," the old woman said with a nod.

Jack slid another hundred-dollar bill across the counter to the woman and asked, "Could you please have them make me the biggest cheeseburger they've got with grilled onions and french fries? Also, do they serve beer? I'd like a couple bottles of beer, if they do."

"No, they don't serve beer," she said as she took the money, "but I've got a couple of Buds in the fridge I'll bring you when they bring the food. Here. Go on down to room seven, and get yourself cleaned up. There's fresh towels in there, and you'll be comfortable and away from our other guests. I'll bring the food and beer down when it gets here. In the meantime, you relax. Miss Becky's got it all under control," she said with a big grin. Then she gave him an old-fashioned metal key with a palm-sized red plastic tag hanging from it emblazoned with a big white number seven. Jack turned it over in his hand admiring the antique from a bygone era as if it had emerged from a time warp.

It had been a long time since Jack had seen a room key like this, since nearly all hotels and motels had gone to magnetic key cards. In fact, Jack couldn't remember seeing one since his early locksmith days. It seemed like ten lifetimes ago. Where had the time gone?

Time. Jack needed some time. Time to eat, time to rest, and time to gird himself for the ordeal to come.

29

Jack woke up at eight o'clock to the gentle plinking of *Dixie*. "Hello, Abbie," Jack said with a sleepy smile.

"Hey, Jack, hun. How y'all doin', Sweetie?"

"Better. I got about five hours of sleep. I think I slept face first in the pillow. Ha! I'm looking at myself in the mirror, and I've got sheet marks all over my face!"

"I wish I was there to kiss those wrinkles away, Jack. I surely do."

"I would like that, but I'm too hot of a commodity right now. Somebody tried to cash my ticket this morning after the poker game."

"Yes. Lars told me."

"Lars?"

"Lars is the gentleman that I asked to keep an eye on you."

"Oh, you mean the Fixer? His name is Lars? That's funny. I always figured he'd have a name like Frank or something. Should I call him Lars or just Mr. Fixer?"

"Sweetie, I think it's best if you just call him Sir," Abbie said with a laugh.

"Ha! You're probably right! Hey listen, Abbie. I need to say something serious to you. I stopped at the bus station after I left the Nugget this morning. I put the extra money that I won this morning in a locker there. There's about $52,000 from my winnings plus I put another $10,000 in there. I also included a will of sorts that I had notarized at the bank. In the will, I left everything I own in your control. I stashed the key to the locker in the flower pot by your front door. If I don't make it through this tonight, would you please give the $52,000 to Lisa? That's assuming I can get her out. Also, I'd like you to keep the other $10,000. Of course, if neither one of us makes it, I want you to have it all."

"Oh, Jack, hun, don't talk like that! I don't want anything happenin' to you!"

"I don't either, but I'm just being real. I have a plan in my head that should work. I know Jesse, and I know how he thinks, but there are too many wild cards in this deck. I don't really know what's going to transpire, and if I have to sacrifice myself for my daughter, I will."

"Sweetie, let Metro handle this. They're trained to do this sort of thing. Let those SWAT boys do the dirty work."

"I wish I could just let them do it without me, but Jesse will never let my daughter go if I'm not there. He wants me, not her, but he'll kill her if I give him any reason, and I can't do that. Don't worry, though, I've got a trick or two up my sleeve, so to speak."

"What do you mean? Jack, hun, don't you do anything foolish, now! I surely don't want any of your money. I want you!"

"It's alright. I think I've got it wired, but I'm gonna do whatever I have to do. Promise me you'll take care of the money. Please?"

"Oh, Jack, you know I will, but I don't want any of it. I'll give it all to Lisa."

"No, please do as I ask. If I make it through this, I'm gonna wrap my arms around you and never let you go. I'm also gonna take you to Ireland like you always wanted. You've always dreamed of going, and I'd love to be there with you, but if I don't make it, I want you to go without me. Go for both of us. When you do, just know that I'll be there watching over you. When you're looking out over those lush green Irish fields that match your beautiful eyes, when you feel the cool breeze gently kiss your angelic face, and when your gorgeous Irish red hair tousles in that same breeze, just imagine it's my fingers softly sliding through your hair to hold your lovely face so I can kiss those sweet lips of yours one last time. Please? Promise me?"

"Okay, Jack, hun. I promise, but you have to promise me somethin', and I'm serious about this. You have to promise me that you won't give up tryin' to make it back to me. I don't care what it takes. Don't you give up! You hear me? I love you, Jack. I surely do, and I do NOT want to lose you, so you do whatever you have to do, but you come back to me, Jonathan James Diamante, you hear me?"

"I hear you, Abbie."

"Swear it to me, Jack. Swear to me that you will not give up until you are back in my arms," Abbie said as tears rolled down her cheeks.

Jack could tell she was crying even though he couldn't see her through the phone. "I swear it, and I love you, too. I truthfully didn't believe I would ever be able to love another woman after Melinda died. She meant the world to me, and I still love her so, so much, but God help me, I love you, too. I want to see if we can make a life together, but I won't have a life if I lose Lisa."

"I know, Jack, I know. I surely do wish I could kiss you right now."

"I wish I could kiss you, too. I wish I could hold you so tight that you couldn't tell where I left off and you began."

"Good God almighty, Jack! I can't take this! You better get your sorry ass back into my arms, or I swear to holy God that I will chase you down through Heaven or Hell!"

"And what'll you do if you catch me?"

"I will kiss you so long and so hard that the angels will sing and the demons will blush! And *then* I will tan your hide but good for leavin' me, you sorry excuse for a poker player!"

Jack laughed. "You sound pretty serious. Hey, I may be a sorry excuse for a poker player, but I did pretty well last night and this morning, didn't I?"

"You're damn straight I'm serious, and yes, you did, Sweetie, but of course you know it was because I was dealin' the cards," she said with a wry smile.

Jack grinned and said, "You may be right. Good things always happen to me when I'm around you, even if it's just being able to look into those lovely eyes of yours and see them looking back at me."

"And don't you forget it, Jack Diamante! I won't presume to say that I'm the best thing that's ever happened to you, but I'm the best thing that's ever gonna happen to you from here on out!"

"Yes, you are, Abbie Duncara. Yes, you are."

"I love you, Jack, hun, and you remember your promise to me."

"I love you, too, Abbie. I'll see you on the other side."

With that, Jack pushed the END button on his phone and prayed to God that it really wasn't.

THE SHOWDOWN

30

Jack sat up on the bed and pulled out some shoes that he hadn't worn in about fifteen years. They were running shoes with thick soles that he had used for a security job he'd done back in the day. He had carved out the padding in both shoes and put a hard-plastic box frame inside each sole. This gave him room to install a microphone in one shoe and a very small video camera in the other along with a transmitter for each.

The video camera and microphone both pointed out of the toe in each shoe, and while they could easily be detected up close, at night or far away they were effectively invisible. In addition, if searched for a wire, nobody ever seemed to check shoes. Jack had built these shoes for an undercover detective working a drug sting, and he had helped monitor the transmissions. When the job was finished, Jack had kept the shoes. They were his size, and he thought that one day they might come in handy.

The transmitters sent their signals out on a preset frequency that could be monitored or recorded up to 500 feet away if the signal wasn't blocked by two inches of lead or steel or three feet of concrete. They would work perfectly out on the open baseball field. He had a small car lock remote that he had modified to activate them when the time was right.

Jack was going to have an audio/video recorder in his car that would provide a clear testimony as to what transpired that night. If things went south, he wanted to make sure that Jesse paid dearly, even if Jack had to do it from the grave.

Lastly, Jack checked his weapons. He pulled the snub-nosed .38 from the ankle holster strapped to the inside of his left ankle. He thumbed the cylinder release, made sure it was loaded with +P hollow point cartridges, and with a flip of his wrist he snapped it back into place.

Reaching into the gym bag he pulled out the two derringers loaded with .410 shotgun shells, opened the breaches, and made sure they were ready.

Content that he had done all he could do to prepare, Jack heaved a heavy sigh and gathered all of his things. It was about 9:45, and he wanted to get to Sunset Park well ahead of Jesse, so he figured it was time to go meet Fate out on open ground.

On his way out of Boulder City, Jack stopped at a 7/11 to pick up a six-pack of beer and two energy drinks. As he climbed back into the car, he mused at the 7/11 name and how it once meant they were open from 7:00 a.m. to 11:00 p.m.—at the time that was considered extreme, but long ago they had all gone to 24/7. "Times change," he thought. "People, too."

When Jack fired up the car, the radio popped on, and the strains of Kiss' *Detroit Rock City* blasted through Jack's skull. He closed his eyes for a moment as the guitar solo wailed a mournful tune. Then he looked left and right and pulled out onto Highway 93 and began his trek to what he knew would be the Valley of the Shadow of Death.

The drive back into the valley gave Jack a chance to think about what he was about to undertake. In the heat of the discussion with Jesse and during the bustle of preparations, everything he had planned had made perfect sense. He was even optimistic about his chances. Now that he had time to think, all that came to mind was everything that could go wrong. What if Jesse didn't bring Lisa? What if she was already dead? Jesse might not even care enough about the money to worry about a trade. He might just decide to save himself the contract price and kill Jack himself or have one of his thugs do it.

Jack suddenly got an icy feeling in his bones. He thought he knew Jesse well enough to anticipate his moves, but did he really? Jack hadn't gotten any vibe that Jesse was bent so far that he would be involved in the High Society robberies and murders, so what made him think that he had a good handle on Jesse now? It was maddening to think that all of Jack's efforts and hopes could go for naught and that Lisa might die tonight or might be dead already. The thought made Jack instantly nauseous, and a surge of bile erupted into his mouth and singed his dry throat. He regretted not buying some antacids along with the drinks and did his best to swallow down the toxic swill along with his fears.

Jack decided the only way he could pull this off was to assume the best, but plan for the worst. If Lisa died tonight, Jack would make sure that Jesse would draw his last breath as well. Jack didn't know if that vow would require him to join the two of them in eternity, but he was willing to make that sacrifice. It suddenly occurred to Jack that he was ready to kill or be killed. He had never faced that thought before, but rather than run from it, he embraced it. No matter the circumstances, if he was going to go down, he was going to go down moving forward.

Just as he let that thought carom around in his head, he remembered the promise he had made to Abbie. He had told her that he would do everything in his power to come back to her, and he hoped that he could keep that promise, but he also reasoned that the only way to do the awful things he would probably be required to do was to put Abbie out of his consciousness.

There must be zero reservations in the tactics he must be willing to employ and absolutely no hesitation in their execution. He had to focus on the enemy in front of him rather than the oasis beyond.

As he steeled his resolve, Jack remembered a story he had heard about Cortez arriving in Mexico with his soldiers. When faced with an overwhelming number of Aztec warriors, Cortez ordered the ships to be burned. This left the soldiers with no option other than to fight like demons. Jack figured that stroke of genius was apropos to his particular predicament. He would need to think and fight like a demon to defeat a demon.

31

Jesse was sitting on the sofa in the den of his condo with a Corona in his hand when Roby walked in. Jesse said, "I talked with Jack earlier. Seems he's got the hundred grand together and is ready to swap it for his kid. We set a meet at the old American Legion baseball field out at Sunset Park at midnight. Of course, we'll get there a little early and see if we can get a jump on that son-of-a-bitch."

"Do you want me and Toby to go get rid of the girl now?"

"No, we're bringing her along. There'll be plenty of time to kill her after we kill Jack and take the money and jewels. If I know Jack, and I do know Jack, he'll just start shooting if his daughter isn't there. He'll figure he's got nuthin' left to live for, so he might as well take ol' Jesse down with him. Besides, she'll make a good shield in case he gets antsy.

"Go round up Toby with the van, and head over to the warehouse. Make sure you duct tape her mouth and zip tie her hands. Zip tie her ankles, too, but use four of them in a string. I want her to be able to walk, but I don't want her running. And no rough stuff with her until we get the goods. I want her looking nice for Jack. It'll keep his temper in check. After we've killed Jack, you can have all the fun with her you want. Just make sure you get rid of all the pieces afterward so nobody finds her. I don't want to hear on the news how they found her body behind some liquor store on Tropicana. I've got some business to attend to, so I'll meet you there at eleven. Make sure you bring the sawed-off, too. That shotgun at his daughter's head should slow Jack down if he gets any funny ideas. You got everything I told you?"

"I got it, Jesse. No problem."

"You'd better listen to me good about the girl. Keep your pecker in your pants, Roby."

"I hear ya, Jesse. We'll be on our best behavior and meet you at the warehouse at eleven."

Roby and Toby were a matched pair. They almost looked like twins, although Roby was the older of the two, and Jesse thought of them as human pit bulls. He had met them in prison out at Jean. He helped them both get their GED, and they provided the muscle that kept Jesse's back protected. It was a symbiotic relationship that continued outside of prison. Jesse had the brains, and they had the brawn. They also both had a mean streak a mile wide, and Jesse always had to keep track of them to make sure they didn't get themselves thrown back into prison for getting into some bar fight or worse. On certain occasions, however, Jesse had turned them loose on someone with devastating effects. One guy ended up in the hospital with no memory and eating from a tube in his stomach. Another had his severed head mailed back to his gang.

This sanctioned anarchy served two purposes. Word got around not to cross Jesse, and it sated the pair's need for mayhem. Without an outlet now and then, Jesse knew they would eventually find their own release, and it wouldn't suit his purposes to lose his prized pit bulls due to some extraneous bloodthirsty forays.

As he was musing about some of the more heinous antics committed by his brothers in crime, Jack heard the doorbell ring. He noiselessly approached the front door and peered through the peephole. Slowly a grin spread across his face.

He opened the door and looked the visitor up and down. Standing there holding a black clutch in black six-inch heels, a tight, black, pencil skirt, and a plunging, jade green silk sleeveless blouse, that exposed more of her breasts than it concealed, was Julie McKenna. Her blonde hair gleamed in the light shining from just above the door, and she had a wry smile on her face.

"Well, Jesse, you called me. Aren't you going to ask me in?"

With a gallant half bow and a sweep of his arm, he said, "Enter, fair maiden."

Once inside, Julie turned back around to face Jesse as he closed the door. "I never thought I'd hear from you given the recent chain of events."

"To what are you referring?" Jesse said with a coy grin.

"Jesse, I took Jack's statement, and it's all around Metro that they're searching high and low for you. You're not a big secret anymore, although, I don't think this place is on their radar. Why did you call me and ask me to come over?"

"I haven't seen you in three or four years, and I missed you. I thought we might have some fun together. You know, have a few drinks, tell a few gambling jokes, make up some lies, get naked and have something to eat. That sort of thing."

"Really? I didn't think I was your flavor anymore. I've heard you like to dine on unripened fruit these days. Once they can't say teen at the end of their age, you drop them like a hot potato."

"Well now, it's true that I've always said that if you're old enough to set the table, then you're old enough to eat, and the young ones are enthusiastic, but they lack a certain panache that only comes from experience and a true sense of style. I miss that sometimes. Julie, my dear, you drip panache, among other things, and I was longing for a taste of the good ol' days. What do you say? Are you hungry?"

Julie smiled at Jesse and unbuttoned her blouse.

32

After Julie gathered her clothes from various rooms and left, Jesse made a phone call before he left the condo. He wanted to make sure he knew as much about Jack as possible before he made the rendezvous.

"Hello?"

"Hello, Rabbit."

"Hey, Jesse. What's shakin'?"

"You are you little shit if you don't have some information for me. Otherwise, Doctor Roby is gonna make a house call."

"Jesse, all I know is that Jack's got the money. He cleaned up big time this morning down at the Nugget, but I have no idea where he went after that. I tried to follow him, but I lost him when he got into the parking deck elevator. I tried to catch up to him by taking the stairs, but I had to check every level. The next time I saw him, he was driving past me and heading out of the deck. I asked around, but no one saw him after that. I did hear that somebody got shot in the parking deck, but I couldn't find out who it was. Metro had it tied up pretty tight. That's it. That's all I know. I swear!"

"Okay, Rabbit. You call me if you hear anything. I mean it, or the next thing you hear will be your bones snapping," Jesse barked as he hung up the phone.

Jesse's next task was to meet a man at McMullan's Irish Pub across the street from the Orleans on West Tropicana. It was a rowdy Irish bar where you could slip in and slip out without drawing too much attention, since it was usually loud and busy. When Jesse walked in, he immediately saw the man he was looking for. Jesse sat down at the stool next to him at the bar and ordered a Corona.

The man never looked at him. He just took a sip from his Bushmill's and soda, lowered his head a bit, and said, "You're a hot property now, Jesse. I don't think I should be seen with you."

"Relax. I've got a present for you," Jesse said, and he passed the man an envelope under the ledge of the bar. "That's for the info on Jack at the Nugget."

The man kept his right hand on his drink, and with his left hand, he took the envelope and thumbed it open. He glanced at the money inside the envelope and took another drink. Then, as he raised his glass at the bartender indicating he wanted another one, he stealthily folded the envelope with his left hand and put it into the left rear pocket of his pants. With the envelope safely concealed, he said, "Homicide is on to you. They know who you are and that you're somehow involved. They don't know how deep you're in, but Diamante tied you to the necklace. They typed the blood on the necklace, and it matches the victims' types, but they're still waiting on DNA to come back. Meanwhile, Diamante's all they have to tie you to it. They didn't make any decent fingerprints that I know of."

"Sounds like I've got an even bigger issue with my ol' buddy Jack than missing jewels. Well, I've got a plan for that, too."

"Yeah, well, you might need another plan. We scraped your shooter up off the cement in the Nugget parking deck. I warned him not to make a run at Jack there. I told him to follow Jack out of the deck and take him when he got back to his apartment, but evidently, he got greedy and didn't listen."

"Did Jack kill him?"

"We don't know who killed him, but your man took two small caliber rounds to the head. It looked professional. Very slick. I doubt it was Diamante. You didn't put Jack's bounty up for competition, did you?"

"No, I didn't. A professional tap on my shooter, huh? Interesting. Jack, you never cease to amaze me. Alright, anything else I should know?"

"That's all I've got. They put me on another detail as of this morning."

"Then I'm out of here. I've got an appointment to keep. Keep up the good work, Detective McGreer. You're an asset to the community," Jesse said with a chuckle and a smirk.

33

When Lisa heard the van pull up outside the warehouse, she didn't know whether to be hopeful or not. She knew that the deadline was close, but she didn't know if her dad was going to be able to do anything to save her. When Roby and Toby had been there last to give her some water and check on her, she had overheard them talking about getting the money from Jack and then killing them both. She knew her dad was resourceful, but she had no idea how he would be able to stand up to the three of them and come out alive. And if *he* died, she knew she was going to die, as well.

Roby threw open the rolling door, and the van pulled in. The headlights threw a huge shadow of Lisa sitting in the chair on the far wall, and she had to close her eyes to shield them from the searing headlights. Lisa could feel the beams of light on her face, and they seemed warm compared to the cold, dark warehouse air.

With her eyes tightly squinted, she couldn't see what was happening, but she could hear Roby and Toby talking and laughing as Toby got out of the driver's seat. Then she heard the van door slide open and lock back. She figured that she was going for a ride, but she didn't know where she was going or how the ride would end. Simultaneous emotions of hope and despair rattle around inside her.

Roby came up and pulled the blanket off of her. His voice was terse as he said, "Time to go bitch. Let's not keep daddy waiting. We've got a family reunion to attend. Don't you just *love* family reunions, Toby?"

"I sure do. They're always so festive and heartwarming. All the loved ones are gathered together with great expectations. I love the looks on everyone's faces as they see each other and think they'll make it out alive. I especially love to see their expressions when the first one dies and the other ones realize that everything's just gone to shit!" Toby made a face imitating Edvard Munch's, *The Scream*, making Roby laugh. "That's a classic and such a touching end to their little tragedy. In fact, it brings a tear to my eye just thinking about it," Toby said stifling back a snicker.

"Oh, Toby, now you've got *me* all weepy, too," Roby said, and then both of them fell out in belly laughs.

"Where are you taking me?" Lisa stammered.

Roby said, "None of your damn business where we're taking you, but you can look forward to the party you're invited to after we do your father, because you're going to be the guest of honor. You might even say that you're going to be the life of the party. That is as long as you're alive!" Then Roby and Toby grinned and gave each other a high five.

Toby went behind the chair and cut all of the zip ties holding Lisa down. Roby then yanked her to her feet, but Lisa almost collapsed to the cement. He legs were like runny Jello from sitting for so long, and the pain from the cuts was still excruciating when she moved. It was like they tried to tear open with every step, and she squealed in pain with every step.

Roby grabbed her by the arm, shook her violently, and yelled, "Shut up!" Then he nodded to Toby, and Toby came over with duct tape. Roby grabbed Lisa by her long blonde hair to immobilize her head while Toby slapped a big piece of duct tape over her mouth. "That's better," said Roby as he smiled.

Lisa was loaded into the van just as Jesse pulled up in his Cadillac. He was carrying a roll of gauze, and he climbed into the van next to Lisa. "Lift up your legs, Lisa. I'm gonna bandage up these legs of yours, so Jack doesn't see our handiwork." Jesse wrapped her legs with the gauze, but the movement from the chair had opened the wounds, again, and the white gauze was soon showing blotches of red.

Jesse climbed out of the rusty, dark blue van and motioned Roby in next to Lisa. "Zip tie her ankles like I told you. Remember, I want her walking, but not running. Got it?" Roby nodded and zip tied each of her ankles tightly. Then he connected two more zip ties in between her ankles that allowed her feet to be about eighteen inches apart. Once completed, Jesse looked at Toby in the driver's seat, held up his right index finger, made a twirling motion, and said "Let's go. Follow me out, and stay close behind."

As the van backed out of the warehouse, Jesse pulled down the rolling door and secured it. Then he climbed into his Eldorado, started it with a roar, and turned on the headlights.

Pulling out in front of the van, he let an evil grin stretch across his face. He was looking forward to staring Jack in the eyes and seeing fear down in his soul when Jack realized that neither he nor his daughter was going to make it out alive. Jesse savored that thought as he drove out to what he knew would be their final confrontation in the shadows of some of their finest times together.

Jesse grinned bigger at the irony of it all. Tonight was going to be special.

34

Jack pulled into the parking lot by the old baseball field after about an hour of driving. It had been dark for about five hours, and all of the kids had gone home. Jack could see that there were a few cars over by the lit basketball courts where a pick-up game was still going, but things seemed to be winding down.

Sunset Park used to be the center of the amateur baseball universe in Las Vegas during the '60s, '70s, and '80s. It had started with four contiguous little league fields, and then a full-size field with major league dimensions was constructed in the '70s. Jack had played on all of them growing up, but the big league field, as it had been nicknamed, was where he had played American Legion baseball with Jesse. They had made quite a double-play combination and experienced many triumphs together on that hallowed piece of real estate.

Unlike the little league fields, the big-league field had real sunken, cement dugouts that echoed with cheers and curses, agony and ecstasy on every play. Las Vegans were always passionate about their baseball. Jack remembered one episode when one of his coaches ran to the top of the dugout steps and began screaming at the home plate umpire. Midway through his diatribe, the coach accidentally spit out his front false teeth. The coach never missed an insult as he continued to yell while he picked up his dentures. Meanwhile, everyone in the dugout began howling with laughter because no one could tell what the coach was saying anymore. It all became gibberish without his teeth in place. This was a world of dreams and adventure when they were kids. Now it was a forgotten void where human lives were going to be exchanged for money or blood.

At some point, the folks at the Clark County Parks and Recreation Department figured that they didn't want to keep up the field, so they tore down the outfield fence, the dugouts, the backstop, and the grandstand. All that was left were the stadium lights that had illuminated so many summer nights in Jack's youth. They stood cold and dark like sentinels looming over the ghostly field, the headlights of passing cars adding a faint pulse of light to the eerie half-light glow of Vegas. No matter where you went in Vegas, it was never totally dark.

Sunset Park was also the place where Jack had played his last baseball game. It was where he found out that Melinda was pregnant with Lisa, where he had proposed to her, and where she had said yes. He remembered back like it was yesterday and then felt like it had been a thousand years ago. His life had changed forever on that day, and the probability that his life would change or end forever tonight sent a chill through him. The wanton seeds that he had sown had commuted him full circle back to the origin of his little family. With a shake of his head, Jack muttered to himself, "You can check out any time you like, but you can never leave."

Jack looked around at the abandoned baseball field, and he could still recognize the grass infield from the dirt base paths that, while grown over, were still visible to the eye of someone that had spent years running on them. He walked out to where second base had been and recalled how he had controlled his destiny when he roamed this small patch of real estate. He knew that he would have to control his destiny once again, so he started to prepare his killing field.

First, he took the six-pack of beer, opened each can, and poured them on the ground around where he planned to stand. When he had finished, the place smelled like a brewery, and he tossed the empty cans on the ground as if he had consumed them all in an attempt to prop up his courage. He wanted Jesse to underestimate him as much as possible.

Next, he took the derringers out of the gym bag. He had seen a small depression about fifteen feet behind him, and he placed one of the derringers there and put some loose grass over it. This would be his fallback position: his last stand, as it were.

He took the other derringer and put it in the right pocket of the windbreaker he was wearing. He had decided he could only conceal one of them between his buttocks and still adequately maneuver. It would be uncomfortable, but not nearly as uncomfortable as being defenseless if they took his .38.

Lastly, he reached into the gym bag next to the money and pulled out the two energy drinks. He put one in his left windbreaker pocket, opened the other, and guzzled from the can. He wanted to be razor sharp when Jesse showed up.

The money in the bag was really there just to keep Jesse interested. In fact, he had only put $20,000 in the bag. The other $80,000 he had put under the passenger seat of his car. He figured if he showed up with all of the money, Jesse would just kill him and Lisa and walk away. This way Jack could string Jesse along and keep him talking while he figured out the best way to free Lisa. After that, it was time for "Night at the Improv," and he would make it up as he went.

Convinced that he was as ready as he would ever be, Jack took another large swig from the can in his hand. "How has everything come to this?" he thought as he looked up into the night sky. The dry December air had cooled down from 70 degrees during the day to a breezy fifty degrees in a matter of hours, and Jack shivered from a combination of the cool breeze, the cold drink, and jangled nerves. "How, indeed, has everything come to this?"

With a long pull on the can, Jack drained the last of the liquid adrenaline and threw the can away from the others. With a sense of helplessness, he looked back up into the sky hoping to see something that would reassure him. The beam emanating from the top of the Luxor caught Jack's eye and reminded him of a story that his mother had told him about how prayers went up into Heaven to God's ears at the speed of light. Jack thought, "What the hell," and closed his eyes.

"Lord," he said, "I haven't talked to you for a long time. Hell, it's been since I was a kid. Sorry about that, Lord. I've done some pretty questionable things lately. Actually, for quite some time. I'm not proud of myself, and I hope you can kinda overlook some of that stuff. I didn't mean most of it. It just kinda happened. Anyway, you probably know that I'm in some deep shit here. Oh, sorry. I mean a bad situation. Oh, what the hell, Lord, I'm in some deep shit! You made everything, including shit, and you know how deep it can get sometimes. Well, I'm in it up to my eyeballs! The really sad part is that Lisa's in it up to her eyeballs, too. In any case, my little girl doesn't deserve this. I do, but she doesn't, so please, I'm asking for a big favor, and I know you don't owe me anything, but if you maybe owe Melinda something, please look after our little girl. Keep her safe, Lord."

Jack opened his eyes, but he quickly closed them again as a thought occurred to him. "And, Lord, maybe if you owe Melinda a little something extra, maybe you could watch my back, too. I'd kinda like to get out of this mess in one piece. Oh, and tell Melinda I love her very much. I love Abbie now, too, but tell Melinda I don't love her any less, and tell her I really miss her. Of course, I suppose if I don't make it through this tonight I can tell myself later. If that's the case, Lord, then please watch out for Abbie. I'm sorry if I'm asking a lot, Lord. It's just that You are pretty much the only one that might be able to pull all of this off, and I might never get another chance to ask. Anyway, I guess what I'm saying is I'd really appreciate every bit of help You can give me tonight. Amen." Jack then nodded his head once to himself convinced that he had said his piece and covered his bases.

When Jack opened his eyes, he realized that he'd been crying. He wiped his eyes with the back of his sleeve, and a sudden gust of wind blew his hair into his eyes. As he pushed the hair back into place, he heard, "I love you, Jack. You kept your promise. I'm so proud of you, Jack."

Jack wheeled around to see where the voice had come from. All he saw was the empty parking lots, the acres of grass and trees, and the glow of the city. Jack pinched himself hard to make sure he hadn't fallen asleep and was dreaming everything. The pain made him realize that he was still at Sunset Park, still standing at second base, and more determined than ever to make Jesse pay.

Just then he saw two vehicles pull into the parking lot by his car. It looked like a dark van and, sure enough, a sparkling red Cadillac Eldorado. Jesse was here. Jack looked at his watch. It said 11:40, and he was glad that he had decided to come early.

Jack bent down and took the .38 out of its holster and put it in his left hand. With his right hand, he took the derringer from his pocket. He opened up the waistband of the jogging pants he was wearing, and he wedged the derringer in nice and tight. Then he switched the .38 back to his right hand and pressed the remote to turn on the camera and microphone.

Meanwhile, Jesse and two men got out of the vehicles with what looked like a female and started walking toward Jack.

When they got about forty feet away, a car's headlights flashed across the quartet. Jack could tell that the female was Lisa from her long blonde hair, and it appeared that she had something dark across her mouth. By the way she was walking, it looked like her hands were secured behind her back and that her feet were hobbled. He also saw what looked like bloody gauze wrapped around each of her thighs, and she was noticeably limping. Jack gripped his pistol tighter and said, "Jesse Brizetta, is that you?"

"Well, of course it is, Jack. Who the hell else do you think is gonna be coming out here at midnight with your daughter in tow, huh? Have you got what I came for?"

"Yeah, I've got it," and Jack touched the side of the gym bag with his foot.

"You mind if I take a look?"

"Not at all. Come on over."

"Looks like you've been having a party, Jack. I'm a little parched. You couldn't have saved a beer for your ol' buddy?" Jesse said as he closed the distance to about ten yards.

"Sorry, Jesse. I was pretty thirsty. I guess I got a little selfish, but I'm sure you'll forgive me just this once," Jack said sarcastically.

When Jesse got about five yards away, Jack raised his pistol and cocked the hammer back. The clicking of the mechanism startled Jesse, and Roby, who had been restraining Lisa, let go of her right arm, pulled out the sawed-off shotgun from under his coat, racked the slide, grabbed her arm again, and pointed the shotgun at Lisa's head.

"Boys! Boys! Relax! Everybody's got jumpy nerves tonight. No need to go off half-cocked," Jesse said laughing. "Get it, Jack? Half-cocked? Ha ha, man I crack myself up. Jack, why don't you throw that measly little .38 over to me," Jesse said as he reached into his waistband and pulled out a 9 mm Beretta semi-automatic pistol.

"You're a funny man, Jesse. I give you my gun, you shoot me and Lisa, and then you ride off into the sunset. I don't think so. The Second Amendment says I've got a right to keep and bear arms, so I think I'll continue to exercise my constitutional right. As long as we all act like adults, here, there's no reason I have to pull this trigger on you, right?"

"Sure, Jack. I see your point of view. Just remember Roby's point of view. He's viewing your daughter down the barrel of a sawed-off shotgun, and frankly, he'd rather pull the trigger than breathe. The only thing keeping her alive right now, Jack, is me. Do we understand each other now?"

"Perfectly. So tell me, how did you get hooked up with these animals? Why are you cleaning up their dirty laundry?"

"Their dirty laundry? No, you don't understand, Jack. This is *my* dirty laundry. I met these boys out at Jean, and we schemed this up together after we got out. Haven't you been reading the news reports on how they think there are *three* home invaders? Well, one, two, three. Surprise, Jack! The gang's all here! The High Society Gang, that is!" and Jesse laughed again. "I love that name, Jack, boy. I truly do! It would've been better if I'd thought of it, of course, but I like it anyway!"

"So, you're the one that's been robbing and killing these people. Innocent people like Toby and Elena Moscowitz, is that it?"

"Well now, Jack, I can't take all of the credit. I mean there are three of us, but I certainly did my part. Let's just say I own an equal share of the deeds and rewards."

"How did you become such a cold-blooded killer, Jesse?"

"Every man's a killer, Jack, if he's got the right motivation. I killed a man out at Jean. I'll bet you didn't know that, on account that you never came to see me. Guy thought I looked like his bitch, so he jumped me in the shower one day. When I wouldn't put out, he started cutting me up. The floor was slippery, and I got him down. I shoved that shiv in his neck and pulled out his throat. Another guy saw it, so it went down as self-defense, but I learned that day that I could kill another human being. A world of possibilities opens up to you once you cross that line. Truth is I got to liking it. I'll bet right now, Jack, that if Roby pulled that trigger, you'd become a killer and never think twice. Of course, then nobody gets what they want, do they Jack? Now put that gun down before Roby gets antsy and blows her little head clean off."

"I'll lower my gun when he does."

"Now, Jack, seriously. Do you really think you can stop Roby with that .38 before he pulls the trigger?"

"Nope, but I can sure as hell put a bullet between *your* eyes. If he so much as twitches, you die. Got it?"

"Yeah, I got it, Jack. Let's all act like civilized businessmen here, huh?" Jesse turned his head and yelled, "Roby, lower the shotgun. Jack here is just about to show me $100,000." As Roby lowered the shotgun to waist level, Jesse turned back to Jack. "Satisfied, Jack? Now toss the bag over to me."

Jack moved a little over to his side, reached down, picked up the bag, and with a swing of his left arm he tossed it at Jesse's feet. Jesse squatted down and unzipped the bag. Reaching in, he pulled out the $20,000.

"Uh, excuse me, Jack, but this bag is awfully light. Where's the rest of my money, and where's the rest of my jewels? You didn't make a deal with somebody else, did you, Jack? Or maybe you thought I'd give you the good ol' boy discount?"

"No, I've got the rest of the money and the jewels, but they're hanging from one of these trees out here. I'll tell you which one when I get my daughter."

"Sure, Jack. I give you your daughter and you leave me holding the bag. Ha ha ha! Get it, Jack? Holding the bag? Ha ha ha! I swear I ought to be doin' stand up! Seriously, Jack. Where's the rest of it?"

"So, Jesse, I'm curious. How did you get past their security system? I put that system in myself."

Wagging his left index finger at him Jesse said, "You're changing the subject, Jack, but okay. I'll tell you. It's simple. You remember Jon Kilgore from high school? He was always good with electronics, right? Well, he works for the monitoring company, and he would tell me how to bypass all of the systems before we went in."

"But why did you guys have to kill the Moscowitzs. They were good people. He was like a kindly uncle to me. I just don't get it."

"Simple. The old man wouldn't tell us where the safe was, so Roby, here, cut on his wife a little. Not much. Just enough to make her bleed real good. Then he wouldn't tell us the combination, so Roby and Toby cut on her a little more. Actually, they cut a lot. She was bleeding like a stuck pig by the time the old man finally told us the combination."

"That's a lie! Toby would've given you anything if it would've saved Elena."

"Ha! Okay, you caught me stretching the truth a bit, Jack. Truth is we just wanted to see her bleed. The old man gave us the safe and combination in no time flat. In fact, I couldn't get the guy to shut up."

"So why did they end up killing Toby? You got what you wanted!"

"Oh, they didn't kill him, Jack. I did. I slit the old man's throat because he wouldn't quit yapping and HE PISSED ME OFF! AND, JACK, YOU'RE PISSING ME OFF, TOO!"

"Sorry about that, Jesse," Jack said with a crooked smile. "By the way, smile. You're on candid camera!"

"What did you say?"

"Lieutenant DeLuca, I believe you've got all the information that you need. Could you please have one of your snipers put a laser on Mr. Brizetta, here?" Almost instantly a red dot appeared on Jesse's chest. "You're right, Jesse. The gang's all here and my gang has high powered rifles pointed at each one of you."

"Why you son of a BITCH!" Jesse yelled as he raised his pistol and fired at Jack. Jack's left side exploded, and he felt a deep burning in his abdomen as the bullet pierced his flesh. Jack pulled the trigger on his .38 as he was falling back, but the shot went wide and high. When he tumbled back onto the ground, his head snapped back hitting something hard, and his pistol bounced out of his hand and onto the grass out of his reach.

Roby started to bring the shotgun up towards Jack, but a red dot appeared on his chest, and he convulsed as the first bullet hit him where the dot had been. Dazed, he turned and looked at Lisa as if she had done something to him. That's when the second bullet hit him in the forehead. Red mist filled the air as his head exploded like a ripe watermelon and he toppled backward.

Toby started running toward the van in the parking lot. He pulled out a handgun and started shooting in all directions. As he got close to one of the light poles, he slowed up in order to pull out a spare magazine from his pocket to reload. When he came to a stop at the pole, two shots rang out, and Toby fell to the ground in a heap against the pole.

Lisa started screaming through the duct tape when the first shot was fired at Jack. She continued to scream as the bullets slammed into Roby. When Roby's head burst apart, she was covered in a light spray of red, and her screams went up an octave. However, she suddenly realized that no one was guarding her anymore, so she started hobbling toward the trees as fast as she was able. Halfway there, she was intercepted by a member of the SWAT team and taken down to get her out of the line of fire.

Jesse had flopped on his belly after he had fired the first shot at Jack that started the melee. Realizing the bullets were going elsewhere, he slowly started crawling toward Jack with a psychotic look in his eyes. He was screaming obscenities at Jack as he slithered on his belly closing the distance between him and his ex-best friend.

Jack was sprawled on his back with his legs spread when Jesse started screaming. Jack looked through watery eyes and could see him getting closer and closer. When he got to within eight feet of Jack, Jesse reared up on his knees and started to bring his pistol up to aim it at Jack. Just before Jesse was able to level his pistol at Jack's head, the bottom of Jack's pants exploded with a roar, and five 000 buck pellets rocketed at Jesse, pummeling him in the chest. Jesse was thrown backward like someone had jerked his leash, and his legs sprung into the air as he landed on his head and shoulders.

Foggy headed, Jack pulled his hand out of his pants still holding the derringer. As he sat up, Jack looked down at his windbreaker. It was soaked on the front and left side, and then he felt the burning all through his abdomen. Jack's eyes rolled back into his head, and he fell backward as his vision faded out. His last thoughts were, "Oh my god, he shot me good. I'm going to die here drenched in my own blood. Where's Val? Oh, Abbie ..."

35

Lisa came running over to where Jack lay on the ground. With the duct tape now removed, she was screaming at the top of her lungs. She was followed by five SWAT team members and Lieutenant DeLuca. Lisa threw her arms around the limp body of her fallen father. When she felt how wet he was, she screamed even more.

The paramedics arrived soon after and drove up beside the scene. Lisa had to be pried off of her father in order for the paramedics to get to Jack. They quickly checked Jack's eyes and pulse searching for signs of life. When they determined that he was still breathing, they started feverishly cutting away his drenched windbreaker, shirt, and pants looking for bullet wounds to staunch.

Within minutes they had Jack loaded into the ambulance. Lisa rode with him and kept repeating "Daddy" over and over again as she held his hand. Tears streamed down her face as it wrenched in agony. She couldn't bear the thought of losing her father after watching her mother die, as well.

Roby was pronounced dead at the scene. Jesse and Toby were still alive, but both had been shot multiple times. Jesse had five bullet holes in his upper chest and was bleeding profusely. Toby survived being shot in the chest and hip. The chest wound was superficial, but the shot to his hip had shattered his femur and prevented him from running any further. Both had to wait about five minutes for two more ambulances to arrive before they could follow Jack to the hospital. Toby wasn't in critical shape, but Jesse was losing a lot of blood. The paramedic that had stayed behind to tend to them was working feverishly on Jesse to mitigate his blood loss.

When Jack's ambulance arrived at University Medical Center, he was surrounded by doctors and nurses and whisked into an operating room. Lisa watched forlornly as they wheeled her father away, and she wondered if she'd ever see him alive again.

One of the nurses ushered Lisa into a nearby room and started examining her. She was absolutely covered with fine droplets of blood and brain tissue all over her face, hair, chest, and arms. The blood had gone from bright red to a dark crimson/brown color as it dried, and she looked almost alien with blood sprayed all over her face and her bright blue eyes peeking through the morass of matted, blood-stained hair.

A doctor came in and started asking Lisa questions about Jack and what had happened. Lisa was in such a state of shock that it all seemed like some surreal, horrific nightmare, and she was only able to stammer out a few incoherent answers. She still had nasty open cuts on her legs from the torture she had endured at the hands of Roby in the van. The doctor cleaned and sutured them, and that's when Lisa started to feel the pain. Agony and nausea came over her in a wave, and she fought for consciousness as her head swooned. She didn't want her father to die while she was passed out on a hospital gurney away from him. She felt he needed her, and she'd be damned if she was going to let him down, so she endeavored to stay lucid.

About thirty minutes later, two detectives came into Lisa's examining room and questioned her about the shoot-out. The nurse had given her a shot for the pain and had cleaned most of the blood off of her, so she looked better, but she was feeling pretty raw and loopy. She did her best to answer the detectives' questions, considering her physical and mental state. Understandably, though, her perspective was that everyone was shooting at her, but she recounted it as well as she could. She also gave them details about her kidnapping and torture.

Throughout her stay in the Emergency Room, Lisa kept asking over and over about the condition and whereabouts of her father, but no one could, or would, give her any information. The more she got stonewalled, the more frantic that she got. The nurses fought to restrain her, but finally, they had to heavily sedate her.

Hours later, Lisa woke up in a hospital room in restraints and started crying. She surmised that no one had told her about her father, because he was dead, and she couldn't bear it. As her sobbing became louder and louder, a nurse came in and injected something into the I. V. line attached to her arm. Lisa started to feel warm in her arm and then the rest of her body.

She lapsed back into sleep, but before she faded completely away, she thought she heard someone say, "Yes, that's her. No, we haven't told her, yet."

36

Jack felt like he was floating. He had no sense of time or weight. It caused him to remember back to when he was fourteen years old. His parents had taken him to Huntington Beach in Southern California. It was Spring Break. He had brought an old inner tube along, and he had paddled out away from the beach about a hundred yards.

Out on the Pacific Ocean, he bobbed lazily like a cork. His feet were hanging in the cool water, and the bright April sun was warm on his face. He felt so at peace out there. The seagulls floating overhead would squark and caw as they scanned the ocean for fish. They seemed to be saying, "Relax ... Relax ... Relax," and Jack did. He laid his head back rinsing his hair in the cool salt water. He didn't have a care in the world. With his eyes closed as he tilted his head back, the sun and gentle ocean waves seemed to drain away, not only his strength but his need for strength.

That's how he felt now. He was utterly without the strength to twitch a finger, but he also felt that there was no need to move or worry about his lack of control over his mobility. He was at peace.

He relaxed as he was bathed and soothed in bright light all around him, and he wondered if this was Heaven. He knew it couldn't be Hell. It was too peaceful. He had no fear or apprehension, only remorse. He didn't know if Lisa was dead or alive, and he was dismayed that he had probably failed her. He seemed to remember hearing her scream, but it all seemed so far away, now. He hoped that she was alright, but he suspected otherwise. He felt sad that he wouldn't get to walk her down the aisle on her wedding day or see her have kids of her own. He felt like crying, but the tears wouldn't flow for some reason. He felt a sense of loss, but there was no emotional pain associated with it.

He figured that if this was Heaven, he might be able to see Melinda soon. He wanted to see her so badly and hold her in his arms as he had on Earth. He longed to feel her arms around his neck and the silken tickle of her hair against his face. He also wanted to tell her how sorry he was that he hadn't been able to save Lisa. He hoped that she would forgive him, but he wasn't even sure if he could forgive himself. He imagined, though, that if Lisa had died as well, then all three of them would be together again as a family. The thought of having his family reunited warmed his heart and made him feel like crying again. But still, the tears wouldn't flow.

He was sure of one thing, though. If this was Heaven, he wouldn't be seeing Jesse anytime soon. He did remember shooting Jesse in the chest and seeing him fall back. He hoped that Jesse had died, and he took some measure of satisfaction from the fact that he had been the one to pull the trigger. Then he remembered Jesse's words, and in a flash, he realized that Jesse had been right. He had become a killer, too. "Well," he pondered, "if I'm in Heaven, I guess I was forgiven. Let's hope Jesse took the express elevator south."

Then he thought about Abbie. He was sad at the prospect of not being able to see her anymore. He had so wanted to be a part of her life, but now he knew that would never be. He hoped that she would have a good life without him, but he couldn't help the feeling of loss and despair at having missed out on the chance to know her and love her. It seemed as though he was destined to float in this purgatory longing for things that would never be, whispering prayers that wouldn't be answered, and wishing that he had been a better husband, father, and man. The sorrow he felt in that moment was overwhelming. But still, there were no tears. There was only the vacuum left from what might have been but wasn't.

Then he sensed something reassuring. It was something warm and inviting. It was just a faint murmur. It drifted in and out like a mother's lullaby heard from miles away. There seemed to be two or three notes of a beautiful song that he knew well, but couldn't place. They echoed all around him and teased him. His mind yearned to nurture the seeds of recognition, but the harder he tried, the more it wafted away as if a receding fog had claimed it. It was like trying to grasp steam from an old teapot with a pair of forks. Jack felt it was something important that he should know, but he couldn't put a finger on what it was. It was elusive, and he felt like he was trying to remember a dream after he'd awakened, only catching snippets, but he knew it was wonderful. It reminded his heart of better times when those that he loved were in his arms and safe. When his biggest worries were passing a test in history class, figuring out what pitch was coming on a 3 and 2 count, or trying to remember Melinda's birthday. It was seeping into his consciousness little by little. Then its fingers eased into the glove of his mind that welcomed it like the long-lost love that it was. Honeysuckle. He smelled honeysuckle. It was honeysuckle … bourbon … honey … and doves cooing.

"Jack, hun, are you waking up, Sweetie? Lisa, dear, he's opening his eyes."

"Daddy? Daddy? Oh, Daddy, I love you so much!" Lisa said as she hugged him.

Jack opened his eyes slowly and realized he was lying down. Lisa was hugging him, and he slowly tried to put his arms around her, but they felt like lead and were restrained by the I.V. tubes inserted in them. Frustrated at his inability to hug Lisa he then looked up into Abbie's grinning face with a look of anguish. Her auburn bangs fell slightly into her eyes picking up the shine from the overhead lights, and her long hair fell in gentle curls around her face and down over the bodice of her white cotton dealer's shirt. With a big smile on her face, her viridian eyes sparkled with the dew of happy tears that had been aching to flow. The hospital light shone from behind her head, and Jack swore she looked like an angel complete with a russet and gold halo. He wasn't exactly sure where he was, but it felt like home. The two people he loved most on earth were here with him, and he could see them and touch them. Then he realized that seeing Abbie meant that he and Lisa had survived. Jack and Lisa were both alive!

"Well, I see our sleepy-headed hero is waking up from his nap," the doctor said as she entered the room. "How are you feeling, Mr. Diamante?"

"A little groggy. Who are you?"

"I'm Doctor Haskell. I'm the surgeon that stitched you up."

"How many days have I been unconscious?"

"Days? Oh no, sir. You only came in here about five hours ago. We gave you a pretty strong sedative and some pain medication. That's why you're groggy."

"But I was shot. I was dying. I don't even remember how I got here."

"You came with me in the ambulance, Daddy," Lisa piped in.

"Yes, you did, and yes, you were shot, but you were never dying," Doctor Haskell said with a bit of a grin.

"But I was covered in blood from the bullet wound. I was soaked in it!"

"Oh, you were soaked, all right, but you weren't soaked in blood. You were soaked in Red Bull."

"Red Bull?"

"Yes, the paramedics that brought you in said there must've been a can of it in your jacket pocket. The bullet hit the can before it entered the side of your abdomen. My guess is that the can exploded and covered you in Red Bull. The bullet wound itself was fairly minor, as bullet wounds go. It entered the left side of your abdomen and traveled about three inches before exiting out the back. We were actually more concerned about your head."

"My head? I was shot in the head, too?"

"Ha! No, you weren't shot there. As I understand it, you fell backward and hit the back of your head on a large, exposed sprinkler head there on the field. It gave you quite a bump and split the scalp. You probably lost more blood from your head than you did your side."

"How come my side hurts so much, then?"

"Well, I had to cut you open from the entrance to the exit to make sure we removed any fragments or foreign material from the wound. You'll have a nice little three-inch scar there. Here, I brought you a souvenir. I pulled this out of the wound."

Doctor Haskell reached into her pocket and pulled out a scrap of aluminum about the size of a half dollar. She handed it to Jack, and he saw two red bulls about to butt heads. Jack started to laugh. It reminded him of him and Jesse, and the more he thought about it, the more he laughed.

"OWWW!" Jack screeched.

"Hey, take it easy! I don't want you pulling out those stitches! That's some of my finest knitting," Doctor Haskell said with a grin. "You've also suffered a pretty good concussion, so let's try to hold the laughing and bouncing around to a minimum, shall we?"

"Alright, Doc. I'll be good."

"That's more like it. Abbie, you make sure he's on his best behavior."

"I will, Kim. Thanks," Abbie said as the doctor left.

"You know the doctor, too?"

"I know a lot of people you don't know, Jack, so you'd best watch yourself!"

"Hey Dad, I met your friend, Abbie, here. She's pretty cool. She brought me down from my room to be with you. Nobody would tell me where you were or even if you were dead or alive, but Abbie came and straightened them out."

"What do you mean no one would tell you about me?"

"I guess there was a slight mix-up with the hospital staff, Jack, hun. Lisa, here, had a police guard on her room to protect her, but the staff thought that maybe she was one of the bad guys. They brought Jesse and some other guy in here, too, only they were handcuffed to their gurneys."

"So, Jesse's alive?"

"I'm told that he was when he came in. I know they had both of those guys in surgery when you were in there, but I don't know how they made out. Anyway, I got Vinnie to fix things for Lisa."

"Vinnie?"

"Lieutenant DeLuca. You know his first name is Vincent, but his friends call him Vinnie."

"Vinnie, huh?" Jack said raising both eyebrows.

"Hey, Jack, I told you, one foot on both sides of the line, remember?"

"I remember. Lars and Vinnie, is it? Okay, I've gotta keep a closer eye on you!"

"I sure wish you would, Jack!"

"So, Val, you say you met Abbie where?"

"In my hospital room. They put me in there after they stitched up my cuts and stuff. They wouldn't let me out until Abbie came. I was just waking up, and I started crying, again. I thought for sure you were dead because they wouldn't tell me anything about you. That is until Abbie came. She told them off good! Then she came in and held me and told me you were alive and going to be alright. Then she talked the doctor into letting me come down here. We've been talking here in your room waiting for you to wake up." Lisa leaned to Jack's ear and said, "You know what, Dad? She smells just like Mom did. I think that's so cool!"

"I know, Val, honey. So do I. So do I."

"Jack, hun, pardon me for asking, but why do you call her Val? I thought her name was Lisa?"

"It is. We named her Lisa after a friend that Melinda and I knew in high school, but from the day she was born, on Valentine's Day, she was our personal valentine to each other. She was our perfect expression of love, so Valentine became Val. To everyone else she's Lisa, but to us, she has always beenVal."

"It means I'm special to them," Lisa said. "I remember when I was little, people would call me Lisa, and I wondered why they did that, but I got used to having two names. Abbie, you can call me Val, if you like. It's okay."

"Well, Val, Sugar, I would be honored."

"So, why did Doctor Haskell call me a hero?"

Lisa piped up, "That's because I've been telling everybody how you saved my life and stood up to those assholes! I mean jerks. Sorry, Abbie."

"You go right ahead, Val, hun. You call 'em assholes if you like. You *earned* it! As for you, Jack Diamante, I don't know whether to kiss you or kick you in the ass, you boneheaded hunka man, you. What made you think that gettin' into a gunfight with Jesse wasn't breakin' your promise to me, hmmm?"

"I promised to do everything in my power to make it back to you, and somehow that's what I did. Whatever happened, I just couldn't let them hurt Val anymore. I couldn't. But I had made arrangements with Vinnie," Jack said as he rolled his eyes, "to watch my back and bring in the cavalry at the right time. I wasn't alone out there, but I sure thought I'd screwed up royally when Jesse shot me."

"Well, alright, then. For now, you get a kiss, and I'll save the ass kickin' for some other time," she said with a grin as she leaned down and gave Jack a tender kiss on the lips.

Jack blushed as he saw out of the corner of his eye that Lisa was watching him. "It's okay, Dad. Go ahead and kiss her. She deserves it!" And Jack did just that. He reached up with his right hand into Abbie's silky red curls until it reached the nape of her neck. Then he pulled her mouth to his and gave her a deep, soulful kiss. When he opened his eyes, it was Lisa who was blushing and rolling her blue eyes to the heavens.

"Dad!"

"Hey! You said she deserved it! I'm gonna give her the best I've got!"

"Whew! Jack, hun, I do declare I have *got* to have some more of that! Right now, though, Val dear, let's let your daddy get some rest. He's had quite a night, what with dyin' and comin' back to life and all," Abbie said with a grin. "Whatcha' say us girls go get somethin' to eat and get to know each other a little better?"

"Sounds like a plan, Abbie. See ya, Dad. I'm sure glad you're alive." She leaned over, hugged him, and said, "I love you so much, Dad. You *are* my hero."

"I love you too Val, so very much. Now you girls stay out of trouble!"

Abbie and Lisa laughed as they left the room, and Jack smiled as tears began to roll down his cheeks. Then he closed his tear-swollen eyes and thought, "Thank you, Lord, for saving my baby and me. And thank Melinda for me, too. I know she must've been pulling some major strings with You to allow us to make it back alive."

37

Lieutenant DeLuca entered Jack's hospital room with a sly smile on his face. He was carrying what looked like a small Easter basket that was filled with Forget-Me-Not flowers. He set the basket down on Jack's rolling table and said, "How ya doing, Jack?"

"Pretty good, Lieutenant. Doc Haskell says that I can probably go home in a couple of days or maybe sooner." Looking at the basket, Jack said with a wry grin, "That was awful nice of you to bring me flowers."

"They're not from me, wise guy. Julie McKenna sent them. I guess you two knew each other in high school?"

"Yeah, you could say that we knew each other in the biblical sense," Jack said with a chuckle.

"I figured as much. She is a friendly one, that Julie. She and I used to be an item back when I was still in Patrol. Man, we tore up some back seats," Deluca said laughing while shaking his head.

Jack nodded in agreement. "We tore up a few back seats, front seats, couches, and sleeping bags, too."

DeLuca looked up at the ceiling wistfully. "There was even a buddy's bed that we borrowed that he refused to sleep in afterward," DeLuca said laughing again. "Wow. That's a wild trip down memory lane!"

Jack laughed and said, "That's Julie, alright." Shifting in the bed, Jack tried to straighten out his hospital gown underneath him. "Man, I'm looking forward to wearing real clothes. These peek-a-boo pajamas just don't cut it."

"I know. I've worn those a time or two," DeLuca said nodding. "Say listen, I want to thank you, again, for calling us in on the festivities last night. You really went above and beyond the call of duty. It took a pair of steel cajones to stand out there and get all of that information like you did. Ingenious idea with those shoes, by the way. I'll have to remember that. Something bothers me, though. I've had a chance to really review all of the audio tapes, and there was a reference to 'other jewels' several times. We never did recover most of the jewelry that was stolen. You mind explaining that to me?"

"I was wondering when you'd catch that," Jack said with a wide grin. "All along I knew that I was going to need an ace-in-the-hole. Until I called you in, that was my ace. Once you were on board, I no longer needed them, so I sent them by Fed Ex to your office. If Fed Ex is on time, you should have them sometime this afternoon."

"Okay, well, I'm curious, then. Why didn't you have a courier bring them over or bring them in yourself?"

"I couldn't risk being seen with you or going to your office, and I didn't want the jewels showing up too soon. Loose lips sink ships. There had been too many coincidences lately, and it was *strongly* suggested to me by a credible source that someone on the inside was leaking out vital information about me. No offense, but I couldn't trust that it wasn't one of your guys. I had to suspect everyone. I didn't even tell Abbie where I was. Not that I suspected her, but someone might've overheard our conversation or something. I couldn't chance it, and I wanted every edge I could get. I guess it's just the poker player in me."

"I see. Hey speaking of poker, I heard about that epic hand you played the other night at the Nugget. Man, I'd have given a week's pay to see the Duke's face when that last seven hit the board. You must've been sweatin' bullets, though, when you first saw his hand."

"Naw, piece of cake. I knew I was getting the last seven in the deck." Jack said with a laugh and then winced in pain.

Lieutenant DeLuca laughed and said, "Yeah, and they're gonna put my face on Mount Rushmore, too!"

"Say, listen," Jack said with concern, "I hear Jesse made it through the shootout and was brought in here, too. What's his status?"

"He came out of surgery a couple of hours ago. They plugged up the five holes you put in him. He's sleeping it off two floors down."

"Do I need to be concerned for my safety or Lisa's safety? Knowing Jesse, he'd give his eye teeth for another crack at me."

"No need to worry. When he comes to, he'll find he's handcuffed to his bed, and there's a twenty-four-hour police guard outside his room. Nobody gets in or out except doctors, nurses, and Metro."

"How about wrapping him in his bed with barbed wire and putting a couple tanks outside his room? No offense, but Jesse can be slippery, and I don't want him ever breathing the same air as my daughter ever again. In fact, I was kinda hoping that he'd be sleeping on a tray in the morgue."

"Jack, you make him out to be a cross between Houdini and Beelzebub."

"More like Vlad the Impaler. You didn't see the blood-thirsty look in his eyes when he was crawling toward me. After surviving the blast of 000 buck shot I gave him, I'm thinking nothing short of a wooden stake through his heart will stop him!"

"Well, in spite of your concerns, I think we can adequately secure one damaged bad guy," DeLuca said with his arms folded across his chest.

Abbie and Lisa came back into the room while Jack and DeLuca were talking, and Abbie stopped, put her hands on her hips, and put a stern look on her face. "Vinnie! Are you pestering my Jack?"

"No, no, we were just going over some details about last night and talking about his big poker game. Besides, when did he become 'your Jack', hmm?"

"Oh, I put my claim in on him a long time ago. He's been my Jack for some time now. He just didn't know it until recently, but you men wouldn't know anything about that." Abbie then noticed the basket of flowers, and she walked over to look at them. "Where did these flowers come from? I don't remember them being here when I left."

DeLuca raised his hand and said, "I brought them in. A friend of Jack's works with the court, and she asked me to bring them over to him when she found out that he'd been hurt. News travels fast around the department and courts."

Abbie pulled the card out and read it aloud. "Jack, I'm sorry to hear that you got injured. I hope everything still functions. Call me. I can't wait to give you some very personal therapy! Julie M."

Abbie looked at the card with disgust and said, "Well, I know just the place to put these lovely flowers," she said as she picked up the basket, carried it over to the trash can, and dropped them inside. Then she walked over to Jack's bed and gave him a big kiss. With her face still two inches from Jack's, she whispered, "I am *all* the personal therapy you're ever gonna need, Mr. Jack Diamante." When she rose up from kissing Jack, Lieutenant DeLuca raised both eyebrows and let his jaw drop in faux shock. Jack looked at him, shrugged his shoulders, and then broke out in a big grin.

"Dad, you are so full of yourself, right now!" Lisa said shaking her head.

Jack started to laugh and then winced, again. "Ow! Hey, cut me some slack, here! I've been shot, cracked in the head, attacked by an exploding can of Red Bull, and now I'm being verbally accosted! Where's the nurse? Where's Security? I'm being maliciously abused, here! Help!"

Now it was Lisa's turn to roll her eyes. She went over to Jack just as the nurse came into the room.

"Mr. Diamante is everything alright?" the nurse said with a worried look.

"No, nurse," Lisa said putting her hand on Jack's forehead. "I think he's got a terrible case of Woe-Is-Me, and he's suddenly become utterly delirious. I think he needs a triple dose of Get-Real."

Jack laughed and winced, again. "Owww! Do you see the abuse I'm taking here? Nurse, I need some really strong pain medication. It needs to be strong enough that I'll start liking these people, again!"

Abbie acted shocked and said, "Well, I never!"

"Oh, I didn't mean you, Abbie!"

"Damn straight, you don't mean me, Sparky!"

At that, everyone laughed, and it occurred to Jack that he hadn't laughed this much for a very long time. He thought of who he had lost and who he could've lost. Jack's eyes started to mist, and he took Lisa's hand first and then Abbie's kissing each of them in turn. Lisa then gave him a big hug, and Abbie gave him a kiss.

"Alright, Jack. I'll leave you in the capable hands of these three fine ladies. I'm sure District Attorney Allen will want to talk to you some more, but I think I've got all that I need. You get well. Ladies, take care of him."

"Oh, we will, Vinnie. Thank you."

"I'll get you some pain medication, Mr. Diamante."

"Thank you, nurse."

"Daddy, I need to go. Grandma Rose is picking me up downstairs. She said she wants to see you, but she has to get to work. She said she'll see you tonight when she gets off. I'll be back to see you tomorrow, though." She leaned in, gave him another hug, and whispered, "I love you, Daddy. You'll always be my hero."

Jack squeezed her tight. He wished that he could bottle this moment, but for the first time in ages he knew that there would be more moments like this, and so he let her go with a kiss to the forehead and whispered, "I love you so very much, Val, and I'm so proud of you. I know your mother is proud of you, too."

Lisa then gave Abbie a hug before leaving. "Thanks, Abbie, for everything."

"My pleasure, sugar. Now remember Val, I'm picking you up at ten tomorrow morning. We've got work to do!"

"I know. I'm looking forward to it. I'll see ya tomorrow!" With a spin on her heels and a couple of skips, Lisa left the room, and Jack had the biggest grin on his face as she exited.

"What are you smiling about, Jack? You look like the cat that ate the canary."

"I'm just smiling at you two. Val hasn't had anyone really to confide in since Melinda died. Her grandmother has always tried to be there for her, but it's been hard on both of them. Up until now, she really hasn't responded that well to me, and frankly, I screwed things up pretty good after Melinda passed. That's why I couldn't fail her this time. I just couldn't!" Jack's eyes welled up with tears, again, but he began to smile as the tears rolled down his cheeks. "And, Abbie, I didn't. I came through this time. I really did! When she called me her hero just now, I felt like a father, again. A real father. I felt like I haven't felt since she was little. I don't really know how to describe it, but it's good. It's so good."

"Jack, hun, you've always been her father. She's looked up to you all her life, even when she blamed you for everything. We had a long talk, she and I. We got to know each other better, and she's loved you and missed you this whole time. When her momma died, she felt betrayed. Not by you, but by life. Of course, how do you blame life when you're just a kid? So, she blamed the only person that she felt capable of fixin' everything. Only you couldn't. You and Melinda were one, and when she died, a big piece of you died, but how's a child supposed to understand that? What she understands now, though, is you willingly laid your life on the line for her. Only a true father that loved her would do that. She understands that you love her very much, and she loves you right back. She's a special girl, Jack, and you're a special man."

As the tears continued to flow down Jack's cheeks, he started to shake his head. "Abbie Duncara, I have had the unbridled honor to know two of the most special women in the world. My sweet Melinda was one, and you are the other. How does a man like me ever deserve such fortune?"

"Don't speak too soon, now. You remember I still owe you an ass kickin' for puttin' yourself in harm's way like that! If you *ever* do that again, I swear your life won't be worth spit!"

Jack grinned through the tears and stammered out, "Yeah, well, I hope I never have to, but if I do, it'll only be because my little Val needs me to do it ... or because you do."

"And that, Jack, hun, is why I can truly say that I am blessed to know you because a *real* man stands up and says 'here I am' when a sacrifice is needed for his loved ones. There are too few real men these days. Lord knows I don't think that you're perfect, but I'll take an imperfect real man over a wannabe every day of the week and twice on Sunday!"

Doctor Haskell walked in and said, "I hope I'm not interrupting anything. You two seemed to be having a pretty serious discussion."

"Nothing we can't pick up at a later date, Doc," Jack said with a wink to Abbie.

"Kim, you heard him. You're my witness, so I'm holding him to it!" Abbie said with a big smile.

"Well, good, I'll swear to it, but you're going to have to pick it up somewhere else. All of your tests have come back, and it looks like you are good to go! The CT scan was negative, and it looks like your incision is stitched nice and tight, because I *am* the best O.R. stitcheroo in the entire valley, thank you very much," she said with a smile and a flourish as she gave a half bow. "I want you to stay here one more night just to be on the safe side, but barring any unusual setbacks, you should be able to go home tomorrow. We'll send you home with some antibiotics and pain medication, but other than that, you don't need me anymore. I would like to shake your hand, though. I didn't realize the whole story behind why you were here when you ended up on my operating table. I heard what you did for your daughter, and you are tops in my book!" she said with a smile and a wink as she clasped his right hand with both of her hands. Jack smiled at her, and then she walked out.

Jack looked up at Abbie, and she raised her right eyebrow at him, "Now, don't you get any ideas, you old hound, you. You're mine, remember?"

"What? All I did was smile at her."

"That's right, but too many women will take a smile too far. Remember, I know how to hurt you, Jack," and she started to tickle his right side. Jack moved away from her dancing fingers, started laughing, and then howled in pain.

38

Jesse lay in his hospital bed pretending to be asleep. He had been served dinner, and the rolling support cart with his tray of food was next to his bed on the right side away from the door. Outside the door was Officer Korther who had been assigned to make sure nobody went in or out of Jesse's room unless they were authorized.

Jesse hadn't eaten much of his dinner. He wasn't very hungry. The pain medication they were giving him had somewhat stifled his hunger impulse. What the medication hadn't stifled was his desire for revenge. He had heard some of the nurses talking outside his room about a man that was on the fifth floor of the hospital that had saved his daughter from a gunfight. They were all captivated by the story, and Jesse knew they had to be talking about Jack.

Jack had put five lead balls into Jesse shattering his left collarbone and partially collapsing his left lung. The surgeons had patched him up with screws, pins, and sutures, and they had re-inflated his lung. He was attached to monitors, and I.V. tubes in both arms were pumping in a variety of antibiotics in addition to the three units of blood he had received to replace all of the blood that he had lost. The other thing attached to him was a pair of handcuffs on his left wrist. They kept him shackled to the hospital bed. He couldn't even get up to go to the restroom. When he complained, the nurse gave him a bedpan, and Officer Korther told him to be glad that he was alive.

Jesse *was* glad that he was alive. He was also glad that the nurse hadn't taken the food tray away, because on that tray was a fork and a spoon. They didn't trust him with a knife, but the fork and spoon would do. He had hidden them in the covers until the time was right. He knew that he had shot Jack out at the park, but he didn't know how badly Jack was hurt. However, Jesse vowed that if it was the last thing he did, he was going to get to Jack and finish the job.

At seven o'clock, the shift of night nurses came on and began getting reports on the patients from the day shift nurses. Since the nurse's station was about twenty feet down the hall from Jesse's open door, he could hear conversations, but he couldn't make out exactly what was being said. What he did know was that his day nurse, a pretty blonde named Bonnie, would be going off shift, and Officer Korther was hot to trot for her. Officer Korther always chatted her up when she came in to take care of Jesse, and he had found out that she was single with no boyfriend. Korther had even told her to call him Danny. Any time nurse Bonnie had her back turned to Korther, he was eyeing her up and down with a leer. It didn't take a genius to know that Korther had already undressed her in his mind and was making some lewd moves.

At almost seven-thirty, Officer Korther got up from his chair outside Jesse's room and headed to the nurse's station. Jesse knew that Korther considered himself quite the ladies man based on his conversations with all of the nurses, and he figured that Korther was making his move to arrange a little post-shift rendezvous with nurse Bonnie, and as long as she didn't shoot him down too fast, Jesse would have the time that he needed.

He quickly grabbed the fork and spoon from under his covers. He took the spoon and wedged the handle in between the third and fourth tines of the fork. Then he wrenched the handle around until the outside tine was perpendicular to the rest of them. He quickly used that protruding tine to pick the lock on his handcuffs. It took him all of about five seconds. Next, he pulled out the I.V. tubes, and lastly, he disconnected the electronic leads that were stuck to his chest. As soon as he did that, the warning beeps started sounding, but he quickly shut them off using the button that he had seen the nurses use. With that, Jesse was free.

Jesse's chest and left shoulder shot jolts of pain when his left arm hung down as he made his way to the door, but there was no time to worry about something as trivial as pain. He carefully peered around the door frame to the left and looked down the hall. Sure enough, there was Officer Korther talking to his favorite nurse. Jesse recognized the tufts of her blonde curls on the top her head showing above the high desk counter, and Korther was leaning on the counter facing away from Jesse's room while he tried to coax nurse Bonnie into being his next conquest.

Looking to the right, Jesse spied the door for the stairs about four rooms down. With a little luck, he could make it to the stairs without being detected. Carefully he slipped down the hall and opened the stairwell door without a sound. It made a small click as it shut behind him, but he calculated that everyone would be too busy to hear it.

He then climbed up the flights of stairs leading to the fifth floor. He opened the door and peered out. There were several people walking in the hallway, but he didn't see any cops, so he made his way out as if he belonged there and was making his way back to his room. Dressed in a hospital gown he was just another patient wandering the halls.

With all of the exertion, his breathing and pulse had elevated significantly. His chest was throbbing like someone was pounding a stake into it, and the pain medication seemed as though it had suddenly disappeared. Sharp fiery darts of pain were radiating from Jesse's neck to the left side of his chest. In spite of the searing discomfort, Jesse made his way down the hallway glancing in each room to find Jack.

After about ten rooms, Jesse finally saw Jack in his bed asleep. There appeared to be no one else in the room, so Jesse glanced both ways to make sure no one was watching him. With the coast clear, he silently slipped into Jack's room and shut the door behind him.

39

The room was deathly quiet with no monitors or breathing apparatus operating. Jesse could hear Jack's steady breathing and see his chest rise and fall. Jack was attached to only one I. V. tube with his head slightly elevated above the rest of his body. To Jack's right and away from the door, the evening food tray sat next to the bed on its rolling stand. It was littered with abandoned scraps of food, empty containers, and empty cups. It looked to Jesse like Jack had had a good appetite and had eaten his fill. In all, he looked quite peaceful. Jesse was determined to make sure he stayed peaceful forever.

As he approached the near side of the bed, Jesse tried to be as quiet as possible. The pain in his neck and chest had become excruciating, and every movement sent a wicked bolt of pain slicing through him. He briefly looked at his own chest and noticed that he had bled through the bandages and his gown where the lead balls had been removed. Raising his left arm had become an exercise in masochism, but since he had decided to strangle Jack while he slept to keep things as quiet as possible, he would just have to grin and bear it. To keep Jack silent while he exacted his vengeance would require both of his hands, so Jesse braced himself for the personal torture to come. To Jesse, it would all be worth it to watch the life seep away from Jack's terrified eyes.

As he stood poised next to Jack, he summoned every bit of rage in his body and lunged for his neck with both hands.

When he raised his left hand, he uttered a half grunt, half groan through gritted teeth. It wasn't extremely loud, but it was enough that Jack opened his eyes just as Jesse fell toward him.

Jack had no time to raise his arms in defense. Jesse's hands were both around his neck before he could react, and panic raced through Jack's eyes as Jesse began to squeeze in earnest. He tried to pull Jesse's hands from his neck, but Jesse had leaned in and was using his body weight to brace himself and add extra force to the pressure on Jack's throat, thus completely cutting off the precious air flow.

As Jack struggled for air, he knew he had to somehow get Jesse to loosen his grip. He could feel Jesse's thumbs on his windpipe, and it felt like his airway was collapsing. Jack's only weapons were his hands. They were free, but useless in trying to dislodge Jesse's ever-tightening grip on his throat. Somehow, he had to get Jesse to want to let go. Jack almost dismissed that errant thought as soon as it popped into his head until he saw all of the blood now soaking the front of Jesse's gown. Remembering his own bullet wound and the pain that it had caused him, Jack balled up his right fist and hit Jesse as hard as he could on the left side of his ribs. Jesse grunted but didn't loosen his grip. Then Jack took both of his hands and balled them together into a giant fist. Then he began pounding Jesse on his clavicle area where he saw the most blood. After three strikes, Jesse screamed and let go of Jack with his left hand.

Jesse's left arm was now hanging by his side, but he continued to squeeze on Jack's neck with his right hand, and he was still cutting off the blood flow to Jack's brain. Jack began to get dizzy and his vision started to tunnel. He knew he couldn't hold out much longer, so with a wild swing of his arm, Jack slammed his right hand palm down onto the food tray. It landed on the edge of his plate that had leftover gravy and mashed potatoes on it. The plate flipped and splattered the food all over the tray and onto the floor. He had grabbed Jesse's blood soiled gown with his left hand, balled it into a fist, and twisted the wet material to hold Jesse in place.

Meanwhile, he kept slapping his right hand down onto the tray over and over until it landed on something cold and metal. Jack's hand finally closed over the knife that had been waiting on the tray all this time, and he swung his arm in an arc past Jesse's now useless left arm and plunged the knife into Jesse's neck. While holding Jesse's neck immobile with a death grip on his gown, Jack then pulled the knife back out about two feet and plunged it into his neck again with all of his strength.

With the first penetration, Jack had severed Jesse's carotid artery, and blood was now spraying the bed, food tray, and both men. Jack pulled the knife out once more and plunged it in a third time as deep as he could. Then he shoved Jesse back with his left fist in a punching motion. He simultaneously unclenched both fists, thus releasing the gown and leaving the knife embedded in Jesse's neck. Jesse released his hold on Jack as he fell back, and he scrabbled at his own throat while twisting to the floor in a torrent of blood. Jesse continued to claw at his throat until he was able to finally extricate the knife, but his life was spewing out onto the floor like a river through a ruptured dam. He kept trying to staunch the flow, but each surge between his fingers brought him closer and closer to his final breath. He thrashed around in his pooled blood for about ten seconds, and then he went completely still after one final twitch.

Jack was surprised that no one had heard the commotion in his room until he saw that the door was closed. He immediately searched for the emergency call button and pushed it. About five seconds later, a nurse answered, "This is the nurse's station. Can I help you with something?"

Jack tried to speak, but his larynx felt like it was crushed, and all he could groan out was a raspy, "Help!"

He heard footsteps rushing down the hall to his room, and a nurse opened the door and stepped in. When she saw Jesse on the floor in a lake of blood she screamed. Then she left the room and screamed down the hall, "CODE BLUE ROOM 532! GET A CRASH CART STAT! AND CALL SECURITY!"

The overhead intercom immediately started calling out the code blue and requesting security to Jack's room. Two more nurses and a doctor careened into the grisly scene with a crash cart. One of the nurses slipped roughly to the floor as her shoes lost purchase on the blood-slicked linoleum tiles. She was slathered in blood from head to toe on her right side, but she scrambled to get back to Jesse and clamped both hands on his punctured neck. The blood flow now was down to a trickle as they all tried to assess Jesse's wounds and establish a pulse. They started CPR and worked feverishly, but it was too late. Jesse was gone.

Another doctor and nurse hurried into the room and began to inspect Jack for wounds. His face, clothes, and bed were drenched in Jesse's blood, and they thought it was Jack's. When they couldn't find the source of his blood loss, they frantically asked Jack where he was bleeding. Jack tried to speak, but his throat was almost swollen shut. All he could do was shake his head no.

By now security had arrived. They viewed the scene and assumed that Jack was the bad guy and started to cuff him, but Officer Korther was right behind them. He had discovered that Jesse was missing, and he answered the call to Jack's room when he heard the call for security along with the code blue. He figured that would be the best place to start looking given the circumstances. He told the security guards that the criminal was the one bleeding on the floor.

After about fifteen minutes, more police arrived, and they started taking a statement from Jack. By then, the nurses had cleaned up his hands and face searching for wounds. His I.V. had been ripped out of his arm in the struggle, and blood had been slung around on his arm.

The room looked like an abattoir given all the blood splattered and sprayed across the linens, walls, and floors. Jack was starting to get his voice back, but he was still very hoarse and could barely talk above a whisper.

When Lieutenant DeLuca arrived, the statements had been taken, but Jesse's body was still lying on the floor as the CSI techs worked to gather as much evidence as possible. Jack was moved to a different room with his belongings, and he was allowed to shower and put on a fresh gown. A nurse reestablished the I.V. in his other arm and gave him more pain medicine. The police were still taking pictures and collecting evidence, but after talking to everyone, DeLuca came to Jack's new room.

"Hey, Jack, how do you feel?"

"Rough," was all Jack could whisper.

"I'll bet. I wanted to let you know that we've talked to everybody, including our CSI people, and everything they've found supports your story about what happened. I am truly sorry for the lapse in security. Heads are gonna roll on this one. Man, that's a helluva way to spend a quiet evening. You just don't do anything half-assed do you?"

Jack managed a weak smile and shrugged his shoulders. Then he motioned for DeLuca to come closer. "Could you do me a favor?" Jack whispered. "Can you call Abbie for me?

I can barely talk," Jack said as he handed his phone to DeLuca with Abbie's number already punched up.

DeLuca took the phone and said, "Sure." He hit the send button and switched on the speaker.

"Hello, Jack?"

"Abbie, this is Vinnie. Jack's here on speaker listening."

"What's going on, Vinnie? How come you're talking on Jack's phone?"

"There's been an incident here at the hospital, and Jack wanted me to call you."

"What do you mean an incident? What's going on? How come Jack's not talking? Oh my god, Vinnie, is he hurt? What's happened to Jack?"

"The long and short of it is Jesse got loose and attacked Jack. Jack's injuries are minor, but his throat took a beating, and he's having trouble talking. That's why he asked me to call, but he's right here listening, and he got a big smile on his face when he heard your voice," DeLuca said with a smile.

"Well, I'm comin' right down there. I'll be there in about twenty minutes, Jack, hun, and I'll give you more to smile about than just my voice. Vinnie, how did Jesse get to Jack? I thought y'all had him locked down?"

"I don't know exactly what the circumstances were, but somehow he got out of his room and up to Jack's room."

"My God, Vinnie! How can y'all screw up your security like that? Well, you better have Jesse under lock and key now, or I swear on the bible I will make your life unbearable!"

"Well, I'm safe then. Jack saw to that. He killed Jesse in the struggle. Jesse Brizetta is toes up on a slab as we speak."

"Thank you, holy Jesus! Alright, then. I'm fixin' to leave now, Jack. Thanks, Vinnie." With that, she clicked off.

DeLuca handed the phone back to Jack, and Jack whispered, "Thank you."

"My pleasure, Jack. I'll let you get some rest. You've had one helluva forty-eight hours, compadre! Take care," DeLuca said as he waved and left the room.

40

By the time Abbie arrived in Jack's room, he had been given more pain medicine, and he had a cold pack wrapped around his throat. His voice was starting to come back, but he was still quite hoarse. "Abbie," he struggled to get out.

"Oh my *gawd*, Jack, hun. I'm so glad to see you alive. What on earth happened?"

Jack swallowed hard and said, "Most of it's a blur. Jesse jumped me in my bed. He tried to strangle me, and he had me good, too. I thought I was dead. I thought he'd finally gotten me, but then I saw he was bleeding pretty bad, so I hit him where he was bleeding. I kept hitting him until I got one of his hands off my throat. Then somehow, I got my hands on a knife, and I stabbed him in the neck. I kept stabbing him over and over until he quit strangling me. I seriously don't know how I made it. I guess my time's not up, yet"

When Jack had finished, he closed his eyes, exhaled heavily, and started shaking his head as if he couldn't believe that it was real. Jack opened his eyes and opened his mouth to say something to Abbie, but his eyes suddenly rolled up into his head. He started breathing very shallow and very rapid, broke into a cold sweat, and his whole body began to tremble. In a panic, Abbie screamed out the door for help. Jack's nurse burst into the room, took one look at Jack, and called for a crash cart. Jack looked like was having a heart attack. Two more nurses came running in with the crash cart followed by a doctor. One nurse pulled Abbie out of the way while the another one took blood pressure readings. The third nurse attached Jack to a twelve-lead electrocardiogram. As the nurses shouted out Jack's vital signs and ECG readings, the doctor issued orders. Immediately, they started forcing I.V. fluids into him. Within a few minutes, Jack's pulse and respiration began to drop, and he stopped shaking. Abbie could only watch as a nurse kept wiping his forehead until he quit sweating. It was all she could do to keep herself from climbing onto the bed with Jack and holding him. Meanwhile, another nurse kept checking his blood pressure, pulse, and respiration to make sure that Jack returned to normal.

Jack was soaked to the skin with sweat as he became aware of his surroundings. The doctor was standing over him shining a penlight into Jack's eyes, and Jack started to fight against the blinding light. Clearly disoriented, Jack asked, "Doc, what happened to me? One moment I was talking to Abbie, and the next thing I knew the room started spinning."

"Mr. Diamante, you had what's called an adrenaline crash. When someone has had an extremely traumatic episode as you did, your body goes into fight or flight mode and dumps a huge amount of adrenaline into your system. It's not uncommon for there to be a resultant crash afterward where the body basically collapses some time after the threat or danger has passed, especially when the adrenaline dump is sustained for an extended period of time. The symptoms can actually mimic those of cardiac arrest or a stroke, so they're very serious. You're okay now, and there shouldn't be any more problems. As a precaution, though, we're going to closely monitor your vital signs for the next hour or so, but I don't anticipate any more trouble. If all of the vitals are within reason, I'll have the nurse give you a sedative so you can get some rest."

"Thanks, Doc. I could really use something to smooth out my nerves. I'm pretty jangled."

"No problem."

In about an hour, a nurse came in and injected something into Jack's I.V. Within about three minutes, he was sound asleep. Abbie sat by his bed and watched over him, but even with the sedative, Jack was sleeping fitfully. After being asleep for less than an hour, Jack bolted upright in the bed and screamed with a terror-stricken look on his face. He was drenched in sweat, and when he saw Abbie, he didn't recognize her at first. Then he remembered where he was and the fact that he was alive.

Abbie hurried to the side of the bed and put her hands on either side of his face. "Jack! Are you all right, hun? What happened?"

"Oh, Abbie. I saw Jesse right in front of me. He raised his gun and shot me point blank. I mean I heard the gunshot, and then I woke up. Everything's okay, right?"

"Yes, Jack, hun. Everyone's safe. You're safe, and Val's safe."

Jack's nurse came running in when she heard the scream, and Abbie asked her to get Jack some more medicine to help him sleep and a dry gown. She knew that without the medicine, Jack might not get any sleep at all. Even with the medicine, Jack still woke up several more times screaming that he'd been shot or shouting, "Val! Val!" with his gown soaked in sweat. He told Abbie that each time he saw Jesse closing in on him and shooting either him or Lisa and each time, Abbie would hold Jack's hand or stroke his head and talk softly to him. He would apologize for being such a pain, but she just kissed him back to sleep. It was the first in a long series of nights that would be interrupted by horrific nightmares for Jack, and each seemed as real as the events that caused them. But each time, Jack thanked God that they were just dreams and that he and Lisa were alive.

THE PAYOFF

41

"Honestly, nurse, I don't need a wheelchair. I'll do fine, and I would rather walk out of here than be wheeled out like a slab of meat. It kinda creeps me out, actually."

"Hospital rules, Mr. Diamante. You may be discharged, but until you leave the premises, you're my responsibility."

Jack finally relented and sat down. His stay in the hospital had been extended an extra two days as a result of Jesse's attack on him. His stitches had pulled apart and his side had to be resewn. The doctors also wanted him observed to make sure that he didn't have any more acute stress reactions before they would release him, but as much as he appreciated all of their concern and care, he just wanted to go home. It seemed like years since he had been anything except a patient. The constant routine of being stabbed with needles and having bloody bandages removed and reapplied had lost its initial entertainment value for him. In a word, Jack was antsy. He wanted out of the hospital and back to normal life as soon as possible.

As he was wheeled out of the hospital room to the elevator, Jack felt like he was on display. A few people even stopped what they were doing to shake his hand and wish him well. Abbie had brought him some comfortable clothes the previous day to wear, since the clothes he had worn the night of the shootout had all but been shredded by the paramedics and hospital staff. He was also wearing a baseball hat with "SWAT" embroidered on it that Lieutenant DeLuca had given to him, so at least he felt presentable.

The television news crews had been intolerable when they came through previously while he was still in his hospital gown and tried to interview him in his hospital room. Jack had no desire to be put in any spotlight, but he knew that they were back in full force today, and they would want his account regarding the gruesome details of Jesse's bloody death. Jack had seen the television news trucks outside the hospital from his window, but he wanted no part in any of the limelight that they offered. He just wanted to be left alone, and he wondered how they had found out when he was being released.

Jack felt very awkward getting all of this attention for killing a man. Everyone made such a big deal as if he had single-handedly brought down the High Society Gang. In a statement that had been released in lieu of any interviews, he had made sure to praise Metro, the SWAT team, and all of the doctors and nurses, but today he knew the focus would just be on him, and it made him very uncomfortable.

"Is there a back elevator or something, nurse?"

"Sorry, Mr. Diamante, we only have the one set of elevators. I guess this is your fifteen minutes of fame."

"Yeah, well, I wish it would stop, already. I feel foolish like everyone expects me to start jumping over buildings or something. I'm just an ordinary guy."

"You may think you're ordinary, but you did a very extraordinary thing. People have been living scared all through-out the valley over those home invasions. It had everyone on edge, and now people can relax a little. If nothing else, you showed that an ordinary person *can* do extraordinary things, and it gives us all hope."

As the nurse wheeled Jack into the warm sunshine outside, he was inundated by reporters shoving microphones and recorders in his face. Everyone seemed to be shouting at once. "Mr. Diamante! How do you feel about going home after being attacked in the hospital and having to kill a man?"

"Mr. Diamante! Do you hold Metro responsible for the attack on you?"

"Mr. Diamante! Do you feel safer now that Jesse Brizetta is dead?"

Jack felt trapped and obligated to say something. "Everyone, I'm very blessed to be alive and doubly blessed that my daughter's alive. I know you folks are just doing your jobs, but right now I'd just like to go home and be with my family. Please."

Through the bedlam, Jack spied Abbie. She had been waiting to pick him up. Feeling like he had been set upon by a pack of hyenas looking to feast on his carcass, he waved to her and mouthed, "Help me!" She swooped in with her car like a white knight and rescued him.

When Jack had told her that he was being discharged, Abbie had offered to pick him up from the hospital. His car had been towed from Sunset Park to his apartment courtesy of Metro, and he didn't want to take a taxi. Besides, he welcomed every opportunity to smell the honeysuckle, sip the bourbon, taste the honey, and hear her say his name over and over. Given his recent experiences, he wasn't taking anything for granted anymore.

In spite of all of the kindness shown to him by the hospital staff and absolute strangers during his stay, Jack was looking forward to getting back to his apartment and his own routine. He also itched to get back to the poker table. He longed for the thrill of the competition, although it would probably seem pretty tame compared to the events that had enveloped him over the past week. Jack was looking forward to tame, though.

Jack also wondered what lay ahead between him and Abbie. She had made it abundantly clear that she wanted to be a big part of his life from now on, and Jack welcomed that, but he had never even been out on a date with her. His life had been such a blur for the past week that he wasn't really sure now what to do or how to behave. Everything had been so intense lately, including emotions, that he wasn't even sure what was real and what was surreal.

One thing he knew, though. When he thought he was dead, as much as he hoped that he would be with Melinda, he also knew that he loved and would miss Lisa and Abbie. He really hoped that she felt the same way about him and wasn't just swept up in the emotional hurricane that had invaded their lives.

When Jack had settled into the car seat and Abbie closed her door, Jack looked over at her with a sigh and said, "Thank you, Abbie. You're a life saver."

"My pleasure, Jack, hun. Do you want to go anywhere special?"

"No. Just get me outta here. I want to go home, please."

Abbie smiled and said, "Your wish is my command!"

They had been driving for about twenty minutes through traffic without saying a word when Abbie looked over at Jack and asked, "You're pretty quiet, Jack, hun. You feelin' all right? You need some pain medication or somethin'?"

"No, I'm fine. I've just been thinking, is all. So much has happened in the last week that I just have to take a step back sometimes and take it all in. It has literally been such a physical, emotional, and psychological roller coaster ride with so many ups and downs that I feel like I'm looking up at the ground and down at the sky. It started with the realization that Jesse was somehow involved with the deaths of my good friends. Then Lisa was kidnapped, and I had no idea how I was going to get her back. Then I thought I would have enough to buy her freedom by selling Melinda's ring only to find out I was $50,000 short. Then the poker game absolutely wrenched me into knots, and suddenly I had the money I needed, but I was almost killed in the parking deck. Then I have the shootout with Jesse. I end up shot, and I think I'm dying, but I wake up alive in the hospital. Jesse attacks me, again, and I'm almost killed there in the hospital, but he dies a vicious death at my hands instead, and it all ends up with everything settled as it should be. Frankly, I don't know if I'm coming or going!"

With a smile, Abbie said, "You're doing both, Jack, hun. You're going away from the hospital, and you're comin' home with me, and I couldn't be more pleased."

Jack smiled back at her and shook his head saying, "That blows my mind, as well. This whole you and me thing is still sinking in. Meanwhile, I'm trying to wrap my head around the fact that I killed a man that had been my best friend for over half of my life."

"He wasn't your friend anymore, Sweetie. He wasn't the friend you knew."

"I know, but I still took a man's life, and maybe the most awful thing is that I'm glad that I did it! I'm glad he's dead! He tried to take Val from me, and I wanted to kill him myself. I was truly disappointed and worried when I heard that he was still alive. I didn't want him going to jail. As he lay on the floor bleeding to death, I sat there on the bed almost beside myself with glee. I felt like I had just wrestled with Satan himself, and I gloried in the fact that I had killed him, but he was still a human being!" Jack pounded his fist several times on the dash of the car before settling back in his seat and blowing out a huge sigh. "Jesse told me when we were out on that baseball field that we all had it in us to be killers. He was right. What kind of a monster does that make me, Abbie?"

"Jack, hun, that doesn't make you a monster in my eyes. That makes you a father and a man protecting himself and his loved ones. The good guys prevailed that night, thank the good Lord! As for the 'you and me thing,' as you put it, we're gonna work that out as we go. We'll just navigate by feel," she said with a wink and a nod. "I'm just tickled and grateful that you're comin' home in one piece from that hospital. You've been through a hellacious experience, and you deserve to have things be easy for a while."

At that moment Jack realized that they hadn't been driving to his apartment. He swiveled his head around from side to side trying to get his bearings. They were in a neighborhood of Spanish-style stucco homes instead of his rundown apartment complex. At first, he thought they had made a wrong turn, but then he recognized that they were pulling into the driveway of Abbie's single-story house. He had only been here once before to stash the locker key, and he looked at Abbie confused.

"I thought you said you were taking me to my apartment."

"I never said any such thing. I just said that I was picking you up, and you asked me to take you home. This is home. At least it is for the time being. Val helped me pick up some of your things from your apartment a couple of days ago. I have a spare bedroom that we fixed up for you. You're gonna need some help here in the next week or so, and I intend to be there when you do. I met Val's grandmother, Kiersten, and they said they'd stop by in a couple of hours to see you."

"Why you little schemer. That's what you and Val were talking about at the hospital the other day. By the way, I hope you know what a huge compliment she has paid you by her telling you to call her Val. She has never, and I mean *never*, told anyone else that. Not even her grandmother. Melinda and I have been the only ones to call her that until now."

"Well, she's a very special young lady. We got to know each other pretty well since y'all landed in the hospital. If I had a daughter, I would want her to be just like Val. Now let's get you inside."

Once inside, Abbie gave Jack the grand tour of her home. They made their way through the great room and into the kitchen. "Jack, the fridge is stocked, so you let me know if you want anything. And by the way, you officially are now out of rain checks for breakfast at Abbie's. You will be required to cash in all of them, pronto!" Abbie said with a grin.

"I wouldn't even think of eating breakfast anywhere else. Or lunch or dinner, for that matter," Jack replied with an even bigger smile. "In fact, I'm quite looking forward to the home-cooked meal you've been teasing me with ever since I've known you. You'd think by now that you'd have come across with the goods!"

"Teasing you? If anybody's been teasing, it's been you! I swear, since you gave me that hug at the Bootlegger, you've done nuthin' but set me on fire and then turn the hose on me! You know, I still may open up a can of whupass on you, Jack Diamante. Don't you tempt your fate with me!" Abbie pointed her finger at Jack and then poked him in the chest with it. She put the sternest look on her face that she could muster, but Jack couldn't help laughing. Then Abbie's face softened into a big grin.

After showing him the rest of the formal part of the house and back yard, Abbie led Jack down the hall to the bedrooms. "Jack, for now, this is gonna be your bedroom. Val and I put all of your things in here. I hope you'll be comfortable," she said as she opened the door. There on the bed in Jack's room was an old, familiar black gym bag. He walked over to the bag and opened it. Inside was bundle upon bundle of hundred-dollar bills. Jack just looked at it and shook his head.

"It's all there, Jack," Abbie said with a proud smile. "That's a little over $160,000. Vinnie said they didn't need the bag or the money in it since they had the video and audio of that night. Then Val and I got the money from the locker and your car and put it all together. You should've seen her eyes when she saw all of that money in one place! Then I told her in detail the story of how you won it at the Nugget in that epic poker hand so you could save her. I wish you coulda been there. She just sat there with her mouth open listening to how her papa slayed the poker giant!" Abbie's eyes sparkled when Jack looked over at her with a sheepish grin. "Ya know, Jack, hun, that is the stuff of legend. Poker players here in Vegas will be talkin' about you and that hand for a long, long time. In fact, I bet in a couple of years there'll be at least fifty people who'll swear they were at that table playin' against ya!" Abbie said with a laugh.

Jack laughed with her at that thought and then shook his head. "I wish I had been a fly on the wall to see Val's face when you told her the story. That would've been priceless," he said with a wistful look in his eyes.

"Oh, you can tell her your own self the next time y'all are together. I know she wants to hear it from the horse's mouth."

"There are times that I'm not sure if I was at that table myself," he exclaimed. "It all seems so unreal, like some crazy movie or something."

"Oh, you were there, Sugar, and so was I. It was all I could do to keep from screamin' when I turned that seven over. My Lord that was a glorious moment for me. I almost cried right there at the table. I wanted to kiss you so bad I ached!"

"You mean kiss me like this?" and Jack took Abbie in his arms. He placed his lips on her lips and plunged his tongue into her mouth as deep as it would go. While his mouth and tongue were occupied, he breathed in deeply the heady scent of honeysuckle. His arms pulled her in as tight as she would go, and his right hand slid down to the small of her back and gently pulled her toward him. His left hand cradled her head feeling the silkiness of her hair sliding between his fingers as she cocked it slightly to her right. Then his right hand slid six inches lower down until he found the curve that fit his hand, and he squeezed subtly but firmly. Meanwhile, her arms and hands roamed across his back until she settled both of her hands into the back pockets of his jeans. Then she pulled in hard and squeezed. Belly to belly they rocked back and forth in an embrace that simultaneously relaxed their souls and agitated their libidos.

After what seemed like days, Jack broke the kiss but didn't let her go. Abbie stood there with her eyes half closed and gasped slightly, while Jack held her tight against his body and examined every facet of her eyes, lips, nose, cheeks, and hair. He loved how her shiny auburn bangs fell loosely into her emerald green eyes, and he suddenly thought of Christmas coming up. There were strands of her hair resting against her flushed cheeks and the rest cascaded in a silken tapestry down her back. He noticed how her eyelashes seemed like butterfly wings moving slowly up and down. Her pert little nose turned up right at the end, and he kissed it ever so gently.

Abbie gasped a breath of air and whispered, "My Lord, yes. Exactly like that."

"Abbie, I've been dreaming about kissing you like that ever since I hugged you tight at the Bootlegger the morning that all of this chaos started. I felt a little foolish at the time, and I knew I needed to let you go, but a big part of me didn't want to let go at all!"

Abbie grinned mischievously and said, "Yeah, I felt that big part of you."

Jack blushed beet red and stammered, "That's not what I meant. I knew I'd gotten myself in a fix back then."

Abbie just started laughing. "Jack, hun, you had us both in a fix! I wasn't sure you were ever gonna think of me that way instead of just another person to share a conversation, but that football hug sealed it for me! I couldn't wait to get you in my arms again, and I wasn't gonna settle for just a hug." She gave another laugh and said, "That's why I ambushed you in the casino before the poker game. I was gonna make it hurt if you ever tried to live without me." Abbie grinned from ear to ear, and her face beamed.

"Well, you succeeded. I've had visions about this kiss, but they pale in comparison to the real thing."

"You ain't seen nuthin yet, cowboy," she said as she winked her left eye and then her right.

"Listen, Abbie, I'm not perfect. I've had my demons, and I don't know if they've all been exorcized, yet. God knows this whole ordeal with Jesse's got my head screwed up good."

"I know, Jack, my love. I don't need perfect, and I know you loved your Melinda very deeply. I can see that in your eyes whenever you talk about her. I just want your eyes to sparkle like they do right now whenever you talk about me.

Not every man knows how to love a woman deeply. You do, and if I ever get you to love me that way, I'll be the happiest woman on the planet. As far as Jesse is concerned, you faced the real demon alone in that hospital room, but we'll face whatever comes afterward together."

Abbie gave Jack a squeeze with both hands in his back pockets and said, "There's one room I haven't shown you, yet, Jack. It's *my* bedroom. It's across the hall. When you're ready, I'd like to give you a very personal and extended tour of it. In fact, at some point, I hope it becomes your bedroom. You just let me know when you're ready, Sugar."

"Abbie, I think I'd really like to see your bedroom. Do you think you could possibly show it to me now?"

"Oh Jack, hun, I thought you'd never ask," she said with a misty gleam in her deep green eyes.

Abbie bowed her head slightly as she took Jack by the hand and led him out of his room, across the hall, and through the doorway to her bedroom. As they passed through the doorway, Jack paused and pulled Abbie back into his arms and began to kiss her. Then he reached back and closed the door.

42

It had been about a month since "the Hand," and Jack was sitting in seat seven at table 22 in the back of the poker room at the Golden Nugget. It was the same table where he had claimed the climactic pot in that legendary game, but he always sat in the seventh seat now. He figured he had used up every ounce of luck in seat three.

He was also a month removed from killing his once best friend and saving his daughter's life. He still had nightmares about twice a week, but they no longer ended with him waking up in a sweat-soaked panic searching for bullet holes.

The preparations for Toby's trial were progressing on schedule according to the District Attorney's office. He had been charged with multiple counts of murder, attempted murder of a police officer, kidnapping, burglary, and dozens of other charges, and if convicted, Toby would have to spend four or five lifetimes in prison. That is if they didn't fry him first. Jack figured no punishment was enough after what they had done to Lisa and all of the others, and if he had his way, Toby would end up extra crispy.

They had also arrested Jon Kilgore as an accessory to all of the murders in addition to all of the felonies committed for giving out the security information. However, Richard Allen had cut a deal with him to testify against Toby. He would have the murder charges dropped if he cooperated fully, which meant he might not spend the rest of his life in prison. Jack didn't care as much about Kilgore's punishment just as long as Toby quit breathing sooner rather than later.

Las Vegas had returned to normal—which is abnormal compared to anywhere else. Jack was no longer a celebrity with the tourists, although, every once in a while, someone would go out of his way to shake his hand and say something like, "Hell of a draw, man!" Jack would thank them and smile. He assumed they meant drawing the seven of diamonds at the poker table on that fateful day, but every time they said draw, he thought of drawing the derringer from between his legs. If only they knew!

The locals, however, would always remember "the Hand" and the man that brought down the High Society Gang. That would always be a part of Vegas lore until the desert winds swept away the last casino. And Jack found that he didn't mind that. He knew that too often people lived and died without ever leaving so much as a whisper of an impact on their community, and when they did, it was often for having done something abominable. He was proud to have left a positive mark, even if it wasn't world-changing. He knew it had changed his family and his life for the better. There was no doubt about that. All he had to do was look at his beautiful daughter to confirm that.

Lisa was going to graduate from high school this year and planned to attend UNLV in the fall to study nursing. She wanted to make a difference the same way the nurses had for her mother and father. Plus, she knew that Melinda had wanted to be a nurse, and it seemed like the idea had a certain symmetry. She and Jack often talked at length about her future plans and dreams, and they had become very close again.

Returning to the present, Jack looked down at his hole cards and saw a pair of aces. He capped his hole cards with a curious card protector. It was a smooth, rounded piece of clear Lucite with a scrap of aluminum embedded in it. On the scrap were two red bulls about to butt heads. He raised five times the big blind, and everybody folded except for the two tourists at the table. A few minutes later, Jack was able to drag a big pot while the tourists shook their heads.

It was about then that Jack noticed a new dealer walking towards his table preparing to tap in. She had long auburn locks that fell in waves around her cherub-like face and tumbled half-way down her back. Her eyes were so green that they almost looked like they glowed. She was built like an hourglass, and she exuded a feline elegance as she strode over to table 22.

The woman spied Jack out of her peripheral vision, as well. She turned her head and looked at him longingly. She fixed her eyes on him as though she was seeing him for the first time. She saw his light brown curly hair that was slightly tinged with flecks of gray. When he turned his head, she saw the scar above his left eye, and she remembered back to when he had first told her how he came to obtain it. She saw the impish grin on his face, and it made her smile. She always liked the way his grin stirred feelings of mischief and mystery.

As she looked at Jack sitting there at the poker table, she couldn't help but remember the first time that they had made love. The lusty memory caused every erogenous zone on her body to tingle with expectation. It was as if she and Jack were skin-to-skin all over again.

Goosebumps raced up both arms and down both legs as her face flushed slightly. A small breath of air caught in her throat as she remembered sailing into ecstasy with him.

Abbie settled her shapely body into the dealer's chair with the grace of a ballet dancer. As she picked up the deck and began to wash the cards, Jack noticed Abbie was wearing a huge diamond engagement ring. When she moved her hands back and forth, the ring caught the light from above the table and sparkled like it was bursting.

Jack looked up into Abbie's eyes and saw that she was smiling at him. As he looked at her and realized her attention was on him, his eyes twinkled ever so slightly and he blushed through a smile. In return, he saw her smile broaden and tears begin to form in her eyes. He looked back down at the ring that he had put on her finger and then back up into her misty emerald eyes and he wondered to himself ... How has everything come to this?

Meanwhile, the woman wondered how everything had come to this, as well. All of the loss and gain, heartache and love, and death and life caused her emotions to roil inside. It finally became too much for her, and she stood up from the poker table.

As she was rising, she brushed her left hand down the front of her white blouse, and it lingered at her taut belly. She wondered how long she would be able to keep her shape as the unborn child in her womb continued to grow.

She had only discovered that very day that she was officially pregnant, but she had seemed to know the instant that the child was conceived. It was to be her first, and it was as if the child had been speaking to her from the very beginning. The Voice inside her said different things to her. They had been loving things, and she sang softly to her baby when she was alone.

However, tonight the Voice inside her was saying something different. Tonight the Voice screamed for blood. The Voice wanted Jack's blood because this was Jesse's child.

As she stood staring at Jack, she reached into her purse that was still perched on her seat at the poker table. She slowly withdrew a locking blade stiletto knife and pushed the release button. The pearl in-laid handle was five inches long, as was the shiny steel blade now locked into place.

From her place at seat eight on table 21, Julie McKenna rounded the table on her left and began her approach toward Jack as she focused on the back of his head. She looked almost regal as she moved slowly forward between the other poker tables. Her white blouse and black skirt were tight against her skin. Her make-up was perfect from her smokey eyes to her ruby red lips, and every silken blonde hair on her head was in its perfect place. It was all meant to be perfect for the perfect occasion.

She knew Jack had started to play poker again, and she knew he'd be in his favorite poker room at his favorite table in his favorite seat. She had managed to obtain a seat at a table next to his and behind his field of vision. She planned to thrust the needle-nosed stiletto deep into Jack's back and pierce the heart of the man that had killed her child's father. As she approached closer, her vision began to drift down to his back and tunnel into a six-inch circle.

The Voice drove her savagely toward her target. It spurred her on with a demonic ferocity to drive the stiletto deep into his back with as much force as she could muster. "You must avenge me!" the Voice implored. The Voice was unrelenting, and as she moved to within three feet of him, she raised the glistening knife above her head and screamed with a banshee cry, "JACK! JESSE SAYS HELLO, YOU SON-OF-A-BITCH!"

As Julie began to swing her right arm down, the player in seat three on table 21 abruptly pushed his chair back in disgust and stood up when he saw his pocket aces get cracked. The chair slammed into Julie and jostled her, altering the arc of the stiletto. Instead of striking Jack in the middle of the back, Julie punched the knife into his right shoulder causing him to throw his head back in agony. Made for puncturing rather than cutting, the stiletto made a small incision and thudded into the hard-flat bone of Jack's right scapula. Julie pulled down with the knife expecting it to slice through his shoulder, but it only scraped along the bone for about an inch.

Enraged that her first attempt had been thwarted by fate, she snapped her head back and withdrew the knife from Jack's shoulder. Her formerly perfectly coifed hair was now swept across her face covering one eye and sticking to her lips. Disheveled, but unperturbed, she raised the stiletto again above her head and prepared to bury it into Jack's heart. But before she could end Jack's life and still the Voice, a loud crack deafened the room. Julie paused her right hand, and it drifted slowly downward about six inches as she looked down at her right breast. There she saw a red spot of blood quickly growing on her chest like a red rose opening its petals, and she shook her head once in disgust as if she couldn't believe what had just happened.

Julie raised her head abruptly, and she shook her head again trying to dislodge the blonde strands of hair clinging to her face, but they were now plastered there with sweat and lipstick and wouldn't budge. With a brisk sniff of the now pungent, bitter sulfur smell in the air, Julie stiffened her back and widened her now bloodshot, watery eyes intent on finishing her mission, but the metallic double click clack of a derringer hammer being locked into its firing position was heard right before another deafening crack. Julie immediately collapsed on the floor, and all eyes immediately focused just past the seated Abbie to see the Duke standing next to her at seat one with a smoking .38 derringer extended at arm's length in his right hand and poised over her head.

As the whole room sat utterly muted in shock, the Duke said, "I'm sorry I hesitated with my first shot, Jack." With a sly grin he said, "I was musing about a game we played together about a month ago. As I recall, you bested me on a very big hand. No matter. You should have someone take a look at that shoulder of yours. By the way, nice catch."

Jack clutched at his right shoulder and looked at the Duke with shock and disbelief. "You just shot someone, and you're still focused on the seven of diamonds I caught?"

"Oh, I wasn't referring to the seven of diamonds, Jack. I was referring to this fetching, scarlet-haired damsel seated to my right. Nice catch, indeed!"

T. R. LUNA

T. R. was born in Michigan, but moved to Las Vegas with his parents as a one-year-old child. He grew up in Vegas during its mob heyday in the 1960's and 70's, so headlines about the mafia and mob culture were not unusual. Neither was the presence of celebrities in mundane surroundings like the grocery store or little league games, since many of them kept residences in ordinary neighborhoods—Redd Foxx lived in his. Overall, he has spent forty years of his life living in Vegas.

Growing up, he loved all sports, but baseball was T. R.'s game. After high school he played college baseball with fullride scholarships to Arizona Western College and the University of Nevada, Las Vegas (UNLV). He played in semi-pro leagues until he was twenty-nine.

T. R. has received three college degrees including an MBA from UNLV, and has worked in numerous industries and a multitude of positions in management, sales, and education. He also made a living for five years as a professional poker player and poker dealer. Currently he is a Math Professor at a college in Georgia.

At church while a senior at UNLV, T. R. met his wife. They've been married for thirty-seven adventure filled years, and they have three children and three grandchildren.

READER'S GUIDE

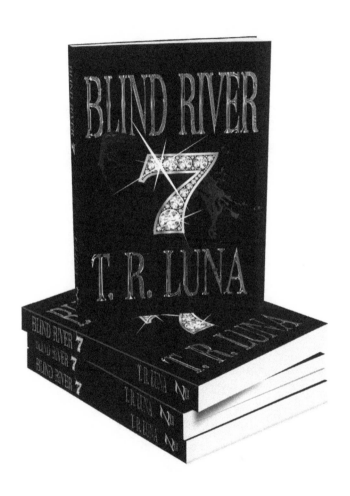

1. Considering the end of the book, did you find it satisfying/earned? Were you surprised by the ending?

2. What are the qualities that Melinda and Abbie shared that made them both good for Jack?

3. Given the circumstances and the characteristics of the men involved, what do you think of the way Jack handled getting Lisa back? What could have, or should have, been done differently to ensure her safety?

4. What character did you identify most with and why?

5. If Melinda hadn't become pregnant and Jack kept his scholarship to play baseball, do you think he would have eventually been swayed by Jesse to join him and his "gang"?

6. Why do you feel Lisa allowed Abbie to call her Val?

7. Do you feel Jack deserves absolution from his past from Kiersten or Lisa? Why or why not?

8. How do you feel Abbie will influence Lisa as she gets older?

9. What theme stands out to you and why did you connect with it?

10. If not set in Las Vegas, Nevada, what might be a good alternative city that something like this could have taken place? Could he have made the money some other way in another city?

A Note from the Publisher

Dear Reader,

Thank you for reading T. R. Luna's debut novel, *Blind River Seven.*

We feel the best way to show appreciation for an author is by leaving a review. You may do so on any of the following sites:

www.ZimbellHousePublishing.com
Goodreads.com
or your favorite retailer

❧

Join our mailing list to receive updates on new releases, discounts, bonus content, and other great books from T. R. Luna and:

Or visit us online to sign up at:
http://www.ZimbellHousePublishing.com